I0613502

RECEIVE THE LATEST NEWS

Find out about my follow-up books and other news.

**Sign up for my newsletter at
www.gerardoneillbooks.com**

THE GIRL WITH TWO NAMES

GERARD O'NEILL

Cover design by Adrijus G. at RockingBookCovers.com

2nd edition

ISBN-13: 978-0-9943654-2-2

To

Atsuko and Maaia

PROLOGUE

CATHARSIS

The snorts, grunts, and squeals grow louder. It will burst from the bush line above me, but I dare not look back.

The slope is steep and thick with thin, burned saplings. All about me are the same stunted bushes.

I run.

My feet are hitting the uneven surface ahead of the rest of my body. Sharp thorns and stiff brush tear at me as I push through the undergrowth.

"It's right behind you!" I hear Paul shout. "Find a tall tree!"

I dare not look back lest I stumble and fall.

I hear sharp hooves tearing the ground behind me. The stench of the beast's fetid breath envelops me.

Where's Bill?

I face a rock wall. It's a dead end. I turn to face the thing that has risen on its back legs to tower over me. Curved tusks protrude top and bottom from a wide-open maw. Front legs chop the air and strike me to the ground.

I am unable to move beneath its weight.

Coarse black hairs sprout from the mottled pink skin. The face so close to mine, I can count each bristle. I see the whites of small hating eyes insane with rage.

Finally, I see Bill. He's closing the gap. He holds a large hunting knife above the pig's neck, but instead of plunging the knife into my attacker, he turns his gaze to the sky.

I scream for him to see me.

The pig does. It stabs and tears. It chomps into the softest parts of me first.

But wait!

I am getting ahead of myself.

1

My name is Yayoi Shimano and I hate Yaya!
I hate her so much I want her to die.
If she dies, I live. It's her, or it's me.
I might be a bitch, but Yaya is a nightmare.
I see her staring back at me in the mirror, painted, wild-haired, and sequined-suited.
She's the one they have come to see.
You are wondering if I am crazy. Of course you are.
I might be. I should be.
You see, I'm an idol.

The band and my two backup singers stand in a circle in the center of the room. They call to her. "Yaya, come on!"

When she joins them they all link arms, and standing shoulder to shoulder they bow their heads and close their eyes. At her call, they break, pumping the air with their fists, and shouting in unison. "Let's go!"

The band run up the stairs to the stage first. When she reaches the top of the stairs, she lingers in the darkened corner, just out of the spotlight. It's all part of the act. The audience loves the drama.

She runs on the spot, pumping her legs like a sprinter before a race. Even now, at the last minute, she is fast-forwarding through her routine, visualizing each set piece she will perform. There can be no mistakes.

Her performance is polished to perfection. The concert will be a seamless blending of elements. Everything has been planned. Right down to the what she will say between her songs. There is no room allowed for error.

My fans never hear the songs the way I wrote them.

They are my songs! And yet they are not any longer.

A committee of company experts reshapes each of my children. Once they give them back to me, reformed into something slicker but with less soul, there's not a single pause, beat, or note, much less a line of a lyric that I can change. They even choose the song list I sing from.

Performing on stage is a rush.

For several years, I have craved the hit like a cokehead craves their drug of choice. Lately, though, the euphoria I felt at the beginning of my career has disappeared.

I remember Mother telling me the day would come when I

would no longer want to continue. She laughed when she saw my horrified face. Then she told me what happened to her.

She said there would be no sudden flash of realization. Only a gradual slowdown.

I remember laughing at the suggestion I would lose interest in my music.

"Never, Mother! I can't burn-out doing something I love. That's impossible!"

Lately, I have been staying in my bedroom, alone with my guitar and keyboard. Yet, I've only been touring for four years. Surely, the day Mother warned me about couldn't have arrived?

"*Ike*, Yaya. *Ike*, Yaya."

She lets their voices pull her out of the shadows.

"*Ike*, Yaya. *Ike*, Yaya."

The chant from the audience is a wave breaking over her as she sprints up the steps and runs into the whirling bright light. Above the swaying arms and clutching hands, Yaya skips, marches, kicks, and struts. She owns the stage.

The spotlight follows her in a zigzagging arc as she runs from one end to the other. Yaya is a comet, and she careens across her universe.

She waves, she blows kisses, and she pumps her fists in the air. She screams greetings into the tiny microphone held in a bracket to the side of her cheek. Her amplified screech cast across the stadium. Sometimes she catches someone's adoring gaze, and when they realize she has seen them, they jump and scream her name, but she's already looking at someone else.

In front of her is a surging mass of bodies. A single great pulsating solar storm. On the stage above their heads, Yaya feels the energy. It's rocket fuel.

She hollers to her audience. "Come on, Yamanashi. Louder!"

They love it and reply as one.

It's not enough for her. She urges them to higher and higher levels of excitement. "Are you going to rock tonight?"

There's an explosion of sound from all around her.

The keyboardist strikes the first chords. The snare and bass combination kick in, and Yaya lets them have what they have come for.

2

While Yaya performs in front of the microphone, receiving the adulation, it's me, Yayoi, who endures the countless interviews with vacant television hosts and the ubiquitous product placements. Yaya wears Prada. Yaya drives Lexus. Yaya shops at Isetan. The interminable questions about eating habits and favorite foods. All directed at the idol.

But what questions for me, Yayoi? I am real. She is not.

Why should it be news that celebrities desperate for a way to escape the big lie turn to alcohol, coke, and heroin? Why wouldn't they? It's an understandable retreat from the total unreality that surrounds them.

Yaya is the nickname invented for me by J-Big Corporation. It's a brand. An image. The name is attached to my recordings. The name interviewers, variety show hosts, and fans recognize.

Cyber-singers like Yaya don't ponder anything more serious than clothes, hairstyling, and food fads.

I can't pretend wild enthusiasm for the mindless questions from *the likes of TV game show hosts and fan magazines columnists. It's easier to let Yaya take over, and these days she is taking over more often.*

My contract demands I subject myself to the simple and inane several times a week. Whenever the company requires it. I guess they created her just for that reason.

It all makes me feel much older than my twenty-three years.

I used to enjoy being her. Overnight success convinced me I was a female fortress. I was Yaya the unstoppable, the undefeatable. The J-Pop equal of a swordsman who never lost a duel. I should have known better. Samurai rarely lived long lives. Yaya the Miyamoto Musashi of J-Pop will not have a long life.

In just a few short years, I became an arrogant diva, but when catastrophe swept through my hometown, it forced me to face how much I had changed. Somewhere along the way, I had turned into a neon-colored, plastic-coated, spiky-haired, jumping Popsicle who expected the world to fall at her feet.

It is plastic Yaya from la-la land who makes all the money for Yayoi to give to her father and the family members who somehow managed to survive the flood.

With each passing day, I am losing more of Yayoi, and there seems to be no way out.

When the tsunami struck, my world collapsed into a gray place that was filled with ghosts. Even before the catastrophe changed Japan forever, my marriage to the famous actor, Shimano Noritake, had turned rotten. Life with Nori was unbearable. We pretended in public to be a couple, but it was only to preserve the illusion our industry demanded.

The entire top level of the apartment block belonged to Nori and me, and along with it came a 360-degree panoramic view. On a cloudless day, we could see clear across Tokyo: the sprouting gray aerials, satellite dishes, electrical wires. The endless concrete blocks. I always wanted to live in the mountains. Nori told me that wasn't a practical idea. He preferred to live in the stomach of a concrete monster.

In our apartment, tinted paper curtains hid the city. I had a curtain for every season: Pinks, blues, and yellows for spring, cool blues and greens for summer, the colors of maples for autumn, and warm wine-reds, and chocolate for winter. The diffuse light was always soothing, and I pretended we lived somewhere beautiful.

One evening, I walked out of the elevator and paused outside the door and did something I didn't usually do. I gazed up at the night sky, and I guess I had something of an epiphany.

It all started with an invitation to go out for drinks and a meal together from my old school friends. My first thought was to politely refuse. I chose not to reply. As the day of the party drew closer, I changed my mind. Any excuse to get out of the apartment and away from my husband was a good one. It was fun. I hadn't had a fun time for quite a while.

It was well after midnight when I bid them farewell. The taxi had dropped me in front of the lobby and the doorman had let me inside. I walked out of the elevator on the top floor and crossed the balcony to our front door. I fumbled in my coat pocket and found my keys.

That's when I turned to gaze up at the sky. I thought about the millions of glittering stars hidden by the haze. They were there, I just couldn't see them. It was one of those moments when I noticed something of the world outside of me that resonated deep within, exactly like a melody or a particular lyric can do. Standing there outside my front door, and not wanting to walk inside, it just seemed to me awfully ironic how the idea of a glittering star lost in the haze so perfectly described me.

When I opened the door, the sensor in the alcove clicked on, and a soft glow lit up the dark hall. I kicked off my shoes and stepped onto the glossy timber floor. I looked back at my shoes, lying where I left them. That wouldn't do. He would be first up in the morning, and he would trip over them. That would make him angry.

I slid open the door to the walk-in shoe room. His shoes were arranged in straight lines on the racks like good little soldiers. I placed my shoes on my side and in my bare feet I walked softly the living room, stopping outside the sliding wood panel door. I was listening for the sound of snoring coming from his bedroom and I was disappointed to hear none.

I opened the door to find Nori in his oversize American leather chair sitting in front of the television. A half-empty bottle of whiskey and a tumbler on the coffee table. He twisted around to glare at me. He was drunk. When he drinks, he's not nice to be around.

"It's three o'clock in the morning!" He informed me.

"I thought you'd be asleep, Nori."

"Who were you with?"

"My friends."

"And what about the second party you went to?" He sneered. "Who did you end up with?"

"Don't be disgusting!" I told him, and I dropped my coat over the back of a chair. At that moment, I wished I smoked tobacco. The ritual of lighting a cigarette allows time to find the appropriate answer to a difficult question without having to worry about appearing stupid or guilty. "I was with my old school friends." I thought then to give him a little more information. "The last party was at a karaoke."

"I left a message on your *keitai*!" He said. He stood up and staggered toward me.

"Really?" I replied, taking a step back. I dug around in the pocket of my coat and pulled out my phone.

"Oh—you did too. I didn't even think to look. I guess I thought you would be asleep."

"You think I believe every bullshit story you give me?"

"I'm going to bed," I told him.

"No, you're not!"

"We can talk in the daytime."

"I have to be at the studio at ten in the morning!" He said, speaking like he was the only one who worked.

"Then why did you wait up for me?"

"Because I wanted to see what time you got back."

"Nori! I can see my friends, can't I?"

"Who…? No, don't bother. You will lie anyway."

I wanted to be angry with him, but I couldn't find it inside, so my voice came out kind of tired. "Like the lies, you tell me, you mean?" I stared into his face, realizing too late he had given himself over to his anger.

He struck me with an open hand, knocking me to the ground. I got to my feet to face him. I don't know why I did that. It would have been better to stay on the floor. The next blow struck me in the chest. He punched me again and kept punching until he was standing over me with a triumphant sneer across his face.

I turned away from his hideous mask. I told myself it wasn't him. It couldn't be. That was when he told me his new rule.

"From now on, whenever you know that I'm going to be home in the evening, you come straight back from the studio! When I'm not home, you can do as you please. When I'm here, so are you!"

I waited until I heard him close the door to his bedroom. Only then did I allow the tears to flow. I raised my hand to my mouth to stifle the sound. I didn't want to give him the satisfaction.

In the days that followed he tried kind words and gifts, but it was too late for him to repair the damage. I decided that night I had to be free of him. Our marriage was poisoning everything good in my life.

I didn't have to wait long before he went on one of his golfing weekends. I gathered everything I needed from the apartment, and left my keys on top of a goodbye note. It took just a few lines to write down all I had to say. When I closed the door on the home we had shared since we married, I knew it was for the last time.

3

My manager, Koga, is an accountant to the core. He never bothers to disguise the fact. He's never happier than when he's totaling figures in columns. I know the man has a good heart, but he's also a company employee through and through. To Koga almost everything is about fulfilling obligations. To him my responsibilities should have been clear to me from the moment I stamped my *inkan* on my contract with J-Big.

He has asked for a meeting to discuss a video shoot that will promote my new single. He tells me the shooting location is in New Zealand. We will be outside Japan for twelve days in a group of small islands just a few hundred miles north of the Antarctic. The company likes the idea of attaching my new release to the image of a clean environment. That could only mean a boring film shoot against a background of cute penguins. I'm not looking forward to it.

J-Big has grown tighter and tighter with their budgets. They've removed most of the fun that once made-up for the inconvenience and pressure of location shoots. There were no more free tickets to exclusive clubs, extravagant restaurants, and fun adventure tours. I just hope they haven't scrimped on the hotel or the limousine that takes me to and from the sets.

Koga has noticed I am not happy about the idea. He tries to make it up to me by taking us to a fashionable new burger bar in Shinjuku. I sit with him and my personal assistant at a thick polished wood counter and study the menu. I could continue to sulk just to rub the salt in, but actually this place isn't too bad, and I'm here with Shizue.

Shizue's been my PA for two years. She's far more than just that. She's a veritable human dynamo with energy to spare, and she's so smart I decided to make her my confidant. When we are alone together, I even bother to call her Shi-chan. *Chan* is a word we Japanese will add to the name of a child, or to the name of someone who we want to show we care for very much. Even though she's a year older than me, she calls me Ya-chan. We treat each other as equals, even though the company doesn't compensate us in the same way. Of course not.

While we order our food, she tells us that earlier in the week, Jamie, the cute Brit TV chef, was here with a group of celebs earlier in the week. They included the gay Tokyo TV host Shizue and I both find so annoying. She's the one with pink, blue, and green fluorescent hair whose name I never remember.

I am really interested though when she tells me Watanabe Ken ate here the previous week. Although Nori is much younger than Ken, my husband resembles the older actor. Watanabe is sexy at sixty, and he's mature and sophisticated as well. I wish my husband was more like him. It's so disappointing to discover your partner isn't the person you thought they were, and really disappointing to discover as much after you marry them.

I look up as Takeshi Kitano and his entourage pass the front desk and see him glance back at me. He gives a goofy smile. He's real casual though, just as if it was only an accident he looked in my direction. He always feigns surprise when we bump into each other. I've seen that twitch under his eye. It gives him away every time. So, I giggle and give him a discreet chest-high finger wave.

Two years ago, we were guests together on a TV variety show. Since then, I always greet him as Beat-o with an exaggerated 'oh' sound at the end. He calls me Yaya in return, even though he knows I hate it. It's tit-for-tat between us. We've carried on like that for ages. I am pleased to see him. He's a fun guy.

Jazz-funk music fills the restaurant. It's the delicious flute from Plum Blossom. The wind instrumentalist Yusef Lateef's Eastern Sounds album was one of my first discoveries among Nori's collection of vinyl records. He does have good taste in music. Whenever he was out of the house I foraged through his records. That was one pleasure I enjoyed courtesy of my husband.

"Rinko-san is sitting by the wall," Shizue hisses in my ear.

I slide the sleeves of my Versace leather jacket further up my forearms and take a quick peek in a discreet manner over my shoulder. Kikuchi Rinko is sitting with a friend just two tables away from us. She's so hot. I wish I could be like her. If I was allowed to be myself I would be. I pretend not to notice her because, actually, we've never been introduced.

My manager gives a polite cough and taps the filming schedule. He's so keen to run through the list of things-to-do that he's already finished his meal.

I lift my sunglasses to read the papers he pushes along the counter. I don't spend more than a minute glancing at them. I do my best to pretend I am paying attention to whatever he's saying, but I'm barely absorbing the details. That's what Shizue's paid to do.

I try to smile politely, and I make sounds that show my interest when it's appropriate. I do whatever the company tells me to do anyway. So what does it matter? I hate routines. Why can't we just enjoy hanging out in this place? Koga knows I am short on patience, yet he persists with his full recital of dates, times, and place names.

I am surprised at just how delicious the sushi burgers taste. I will eat several then go to the washroom to vomit them up. It must be the bite of the horseradish sauce—I always have too much—because suddenly, I have this great idea!

It's all very vague at first, but then—bam! It hits me. I know what I need to do. Well, not exactly. There are details I must sort out, but tall bamboo grows from the smallest of shoots or something like that.

The film shoot will take me out of Nori's reach. Good! It would be even better if the break were longer. Too bad our time in New Zealand will be so short. But— wait! It doesn't matter, because I will do a runner. I will lose myself in New Zealand, and I will do it so well that they will never find me. Not until I'm ready to be found. Yes, this is indeed a great plan!

In Japan, I am a prisoner of doubt, guilt, and regret. A different environment will help me see with fresh eyes again. I am breathing deeper than I have for a long time.

I am not sure why the thought of escape excites me, but I find myself anticipating an adventure. The thrill of decisions made on my own without either Nori or J-Big telling me what I must do.

I feel alive.

As each day passes, I grow more impatient for our departure. It never enters my head to discuss my idea with Shizue, since it's only partially formed. I do speak to Mother though. Sure, it's a one-way discussion, but it leaves me feeling more determined. Yes, I think it's a good plan!

4

The flight crew warns us we are about to go through a storm as we descend into Wellington City. The weather is nothing unusual for the time of year they tell us gleefully as the plane is buffeted violently from side-to-side. The wheels screech as they hit the wet tarmac and the passengers clap their hands happily.

Rain slashes a plastic window as we walk through the aerobridge to the terminal. It doesn't dampen my spirit. I feel invigorated by my new environment and the excitement of our landing.

Koga is glued to his *keitai*. He keeps himself occupied by busily scrolling through his messages. The corners of his mouth are turned down in the typically exaggerated manner of a company executive. His face resembles the painted mask of a kabuki actor. He is tired, and he doesn't mind showing it. My manager does not like being outside of Japan.

The terminal building has a small-town feel that's in stark contrast to the large size of the foreigners who move about inside. I've forgotten how big they can be. I can't help sneaking a stare at them from under my floppy green hat and oversize sunglasses.

The first time I lay eyes on him, he is in the terminal building enthusiastically greeting a couple of passengers. Two Japanese men who are older than him. I can tell the two men are Japanese just from the way they respond to each other. Their body movements are efficient and coordinated. They also share typical small physical features, wear dark suits, and long woolen coats tailored to fit narrow bodies. They are salarymen. Japanese executives on a corporate business trip. I can guess from the nervous smiles this is their first trip outside of Japan.

He has brown hair that curls under his ears, and a nose that almost dominates his face. I like a refined and big nose on guys. His is a nose that says this is a strong and smart person.

He walks like a big clumsy cat, and he has a cute face, never mind the nose. He isn't cute in the way we Japanese mean, when we associate it with small soft features. He is cute in a rough boyish way, with a face that's all freckles and smiles.

How would he react if I was to walk up to him, and… Mm, but what would I do next? I have no idea. I could write the name of my hotel and my room number on the back of a business card and slip it into his hand.

I would need to get to know him first, and that would take days! Anyway, I'd need at least two drinks before I could give him my room number. Thinking about it is fun.

He gazes over the heads of the milling passengers and notices me. Even from this distance, I can see his eyes are clear like the surface of a moonlit lake. His gaze is quite intense. It feels as though even his glance looks deep into me. I lift my glasses onto my forehead and glare right back then casually shift my attention to the space between us as if I hadn't noticed him.

How the heck did he know I was staring at him anyway? Despite myself, I can't help glancing back at him once more. A stupid reflex action I regret as soon as I do because now he's grinning at me like a damn monkey. He doesn't even know me!

I feel my face glowing and I curse under my breath. I turn around and walk a little too quickly over to Shizue.

"Hey, what's up?" She asks me.

"That guy standing over there with the salarymen. Do you see him?"

She raises up on her toes and scans the airport like a meerkat standing on a rock.

"Oh, don't make it so obvious!" I plead. I blow my hair out of my eyes, pretending to fuss with my suitcases, making sure to keep my back to the smiling man in his oversize suit.

Koga looks up from his *keitai* with a frown. Nothing could be worse for his schedule than a complication.

"*Kakkoii, ne?*" Shizue says as she stares at the guy with a look of admiration. "It's unfortunate that he looks a little stupid."

"You say similar about nearly every gaijin."

"No, I don't!" She snaps, and she gives me the duck face pout she equates with mild indignation. "He's standing there staring at you. Oh, wait. Now he's turned away. What a relief! I thought he was coming over to ask for your autograph."

"Come on," Koga calls, with an impatient frown. He pushes his trolley into the fat rumps of an elderly couple. "*Ah, gomenasai,*" he says, giving them both a quick bow of apology.

He circles the startled pair and hurries off ahead of us.

"We better catch up with him," Shizue says with a groan.

I glance over my shoulder, but the foreigner and the salarymen have melted into the crowd.

Rain slides down the blue glass windows of the terminal creating tiny rivers that flatten under the gusts of wind until they are webs that blur our view of the outside world. I push my baggage trolley through the exit doors and brace for the cool, wet lash of the storm, but instead, I find the air moist and warm. I might still be in Tokyo in the rainy season, only I am in a different hemisphere, far from home. It feels good.

Feeling fish-eyed and slack-jawed with tiredness, we watch the driver load our bags into the trunk of a black Mercedes. Inside the car, Shizue sits beside Koga in the back, scanning her phone for messages. I pull down the sun visor and check my face in the mirror. I can see blue, swollen rings under Shizue's eyes. She must have been tapping away on Koga's tablet for the entire flight, checking every detail of our schedule. She looks up to see me watching. "One of your bags is missing," she tells me. "We'll find it soon."

She's using her personal assistant voice just like she does whenever Koga is present. I suppose, in a way, we are friends. Yes, I know it's pathetic turning to a professional relationship to find a friend. That's what happens when you spend too much time wrapped up in a safe cocoon, protected by minders.

I listen to my tired reply in the customary fashion required by our roles. It sounds a lot like a recorded message on an answering machine. The same reply to everyone. "Thank you, I appreciate your help."

Oh, what a company-clone I am.

5

I twist another thick towel around my head, letting the end fall over my shoulder as I gaze down at the street below my window. Where are all the people walking along the pavements? Where is the bumper-to-bumper traffic? What is it with this beautiful, empty city?

The phone rings, and I pick it up, expecting to hear Shizue letting me know they have found my suitcase.

"Ms. Shimano, you have a call from Tokyo. A Mr. Shimano Noritake. Would you like me to transfer it to your phone?" The woman stumbles over the unfamiliar vowel and consonant combination in my husband's name.

It doesn't matter. I hesitate, trying to think of a way I can avoid talking to Nori. "Please tell Shimano-san, I am not available at this time."

I put down the receiver without waiting to hear the reply from reception. I'm a world away from him, yet still, he attempts to control my life. He can try whatever he likes, he will not find his way back into my heart. Gossip magazines can say what want because I don't care that they know anymore.

The thought of Nori ringing the hotel desk makes me laugh. What an idiot. He could have reached me directly through my *keitai*. What is the point of ringing the front desk? He knows I wouldn't answer once I saw his name. He knows me too well.

The phone call has made me uneasy. He wants me to know he can find me wherever I am. That's his game. A knock at the door snaps me out of my thoughts.

It's Shizue looking bright and cheerful. Not a trace of tiredness on her face. She walks past me into my room without waiting for an invitation, berating me when she sees I haven't dressed. This is typical of her, and I usually find it amusing. Her personality always annoyed Nori, and he never missed the chance to tell me every time their paths cross. Yayoi, why must you have an assistant with no manners? He would ask.

Shizue looks at me in mock anger. "Ya-chan, why do you always get up so late?"

I laugh at her attempt at an angry face. "Give me a moment to throw on some clothes, and I'll be with you."

Shizue sits down with a heavy thud, letting her Hermes shoulder bag drop from her arm onto the table-top. She arches her back, and stretches her arms over her head, yawning loudly.

I choose a bright silk scarf and hesitate in front of the

mirror. No, I don't need a scarf, I think, and I toss it back into the open suitcase, and wander back into the bathroom to fix my hair.

"We are going to miss breakfast," Shizue calls out.

Ignoring her is never a good idea. She only gets more persistent.

When I look around the bathroom door she waves to me from her chair and taps the face of her gold watch. Shizue must be the only woman I know under forty who still wears one.

"Give me a break, I call out."

I know what she's doing. She will be gazing out the window, pulling at her earrings in her distracted manner, and pursing her lips or frowning her disapproval.

But, I see that I'm wrong when she appears in the doorway behind me. She has finished the routine and run out of patience. "You can always go down to the restaurant by yourself," I tell her, tossing away the headband. I'll wear it loose after all.

"You are skipping breakfast again," she tells me. "How many times did my mother tell me how important that is. I can't remember. Surely your..." Her voice faded.

Behind me, she stares at me wide-eyed, and she bites her lip. "I'm sorry I said that," she whispers.

I pull the comb through my hair a couple more times, then I turn to give her a bright smile. "I'm ready. Let's go."

6

I find Koga waiting in one of two chairs in a quiet corner of the set. He's glummer than usual, and I can see he's nervous. There are only two reasons for him to be here. Either he brings bad news, or he has a favor to ask. He gets to his feet and returns my polite bow.

One of the young runners on the set sets a pot of green tea and two cups on the table. She stands to one side as the tea steeps, turning the pot to help hurry the process.

When Koga coughs impatiently, she bows and pours the tea, and with a cute bow, she makes a quick departure.

I scratch at the hemline of my slacks, cursing under my breath when my nail catches in the fabric. It's a nervous habit I have developed waiting to be interviewed.

Koga sips at his tea and considers his words. When he puts the empty cup down, he sits back in his chair, looking as composed as he can. But he doesn't fool me. Beads of sweat are forming on his forehead again. "Yayoi-san—this morning your husband called me from his hotel. He arrived in Wellington last night. He asks that you join him for dinner this evening."

"Nori couldn't ask me himself?"

"He's found it difficult to reach you," he replies. He waits for me to answer, and when I don't he adjusts his tie and leans closer in his chair.

"This is a difficult situation." Koga is wringing his hands. "Please do your best."

I think he might as well have added the words 'for all of us'.

I straightening my jacket and sit up like I am in command because at this moment the decision is mine to make. "What are you asking me to do?" I know exactly what he is asking me to do, but pretend I don't. That way I can give him some room to accept my refusal.

He pulls out a handkerchief and dabs at his forehead, taking the time to fold and straighten the fabric before returning it to his pocket. It is a matter of accomplishing the small things he can, even while he sees the moment falling to pieces. "Please, Yayoi-san. This is crucial to the success of your new album. No matter what happens between you both—you must complete the video. I am sorry to make such a difficult request. But you understand why don't you?"

"I understand," I reply. I feel sorry for the man, but I can't give him the answer he wants to hear.

He groans as he gets to his feet, and tells me he will see me back at the hotel. I watch him picks up his brief-case and walk off the set. I actually feel impressed that he made such an effort in the first place. Then again, he really did have little choice. It's his job that's on the line.

On our way back to the hotel, Shizue suggests I leave a message with the reception at his hotel that I agree to have a coffee with him. Then I could later I could simply ring them with some excuse. I suddenly came down with food poisoning or a bad headache. Any excuse would do.

I remind her that last-minute delay tactics have never worked with Nori. He will persist until he gets whatever it is he wants. I tell her that Nori, by making his approach through Koga, intends for me to feel the full weight of my decision. He's growing more obsessive and more control-ling by the day.

Later, when I am back in my room, the receptionist rings to tell me my husband is waiting in the lobby. I let the receiver fall from my hand. What am I supposed to do? The nightmare just continues. I consider downing a mini bottle from my bar to give myself a boost, but I know he would only smell it on my breath, and see it as an invita-tion to have a drink with me.

I could ring Shizue and ask her to meet me in the lobby, but I know this is something I must sort on my own. It is going to be less complicated that way. Perhaps we can work things out in a way that's agreeable to us both.

I glance at my appearance in the mirror and straighten my blouse. When I'm satisfied, I close the door of my room and walk to the elevator.

7

By the time the bell rings and the doors slide open, I've composed my face into an expression of cool politeness. It's more for my benefit than for his. It's the mask that helps me steel my resolve.

We run through the awkward formalities demanded by etiquette. The quick bows of mutual respect that even familiar acquaintances will return to each other in greeting.

He glances around the lobby for an ashtray. "They don't like smoking in public places," I tell him. I keep my tone as a matter-of-fact as I can under the circumstances.

He chooses a coffee table and gestures for me to join him.

"This is supposed to be a hotel, isn't it?" He says with a slight frown, taking a small ash holder pouch from inside his jacket. Even in Japan, he is beginning to find it difficult to smoke a cigarette in a public place. He clicks it open and places it on the table. Then he takes out a flat silver case, selects a cigarette from under the white silk band, and snaps the lid shut. They are the only cigarettes he smokes. Hand-rolled from his favorite Tokyo tobacco bar. "You've been keeping well?"

"Yes, thanks. And you?"

"The same, thank you," he replies with a perfunctory nod, tapping down the end of the cigarette on the glass tabletop to compact the tobacco.

My grandfather was a heavy smoker, and in the mornings before school, I would roll him enough rounds to last him the day. Although he never asked me to do it, most mornings I would tap the ends and stack them neatly in his cigarette case for him.

Nori was at the peak of his acting career when I first met him. That was before his long slide downhill. I see he has developed an unhealthy skin pallor, and there's a glaze over the dark eyes that were once bright. His overindulgence in tobacco and alcohol is taking its toll. But, yes, once he was a man who had energy and wit to spare.

As an impressionable eighteen-year-old, I found myself so very attracted to him. It seems a lifetime ago. My family were always against our union, but that made me all the more determined. I was convinced the marriage would work. Nori was handsome, charming, and yes, he was energetic, although almost twenty years my senior. He was also the son of a family that owned one of Japan's largest recording studios.

It didn't matter to me that he already had two children. Somehow, the fact that Nori was older and experienced made his interest in me seem much more exciting. Despite all he had to lose, he was going to give it all up for me. Back then, I was so young and careless.

Now, I simply don't care. I despise him for what he has become. I despise him for not living up to my expectations.

Even when his wife discovered his affair with me, a young wannabe pop idol, he still continued to see me. One year after we met, he had divorced her. We were married only months later. It wasn't long after that I discovered he would do exactly the same to me, and not once, but many times, and with many women. Perhaps we were made for each other. We are two of a kind, both of us, selfish to the core.

His eyes never leave me as he performs his tobacco ritual. When he exhales, he closes his eyes to heighten the calming effect of the nicotine.

I grow impatient. "I was surprised when Koga-san told me you had arrived in Wellington."

I can tell Nori feels uncomfortable. He's out of his element. Unwilling to accept change. It is quite difficult to hate someone who is so obviously miserable. I glance away, pretending to blink a hair out of my eye. My stupid emotions!

Mr. Thin Mustache at the front desk has cleared his

throat several times since Nori lit up. After getting no response, he has decided to take the direct approach. He walks out from behind the white oak counter and taps a small white acrylic sign on our table. It has the familiar symbol of a red circle cut through by the diagonal line. "Sir, smoking isn't allowed in the hotel lobby."

Nori sighs and grinds the cigarette into the ash pouch.

The man, relieved at the quick capitulation, returns to his station behind the counter.

"Can we go up to your room?" Nori asks me.

I am dismayed by the prospect of being alone with him, but I am also resigned to listening to him tell me whatever it is he has on his mind. He's a stubborn bull of a man.

I should have refused his request. "Let's go then," I tell him. "I do have a dinner appointment I must keep. Thirty minutes at most. Okay?"

He nods his head in silence.

As soon as he walks into my room, he heads straight to the table under the window and sits down.

I grit my teeth. It's a bad habit of mine. By the time I am forty, my enamel is sure to have hairline cracks.

He lights up a cigarette and pulls and nods his head when I give him a saucer to drop his ash. "I called your office before I left Tokyo," he tells me. "They told me the shoot is to end in five days, isn't that so?"

I watch the smoke unfurl like a caption containing his words. I decide then and there not to tell him we're well ahead of our schedule with only two more days of filming remaining.

"So—how about I stay in this city until you finish and you and I go home together?" He asks. "We can sort everything out in Tokyo. The company and your fans will be happy to see us return to the country as a couple."

He looks up at me and nods his head again. "Everything is going to work out fine, you'll see."

I stare at him in silence, until he slaps his thighs, and with a resolute nod of his head, stands up to address me as if I'm a senior officer. Finally. So that is it. The reason why he came all this way. I should have realized of course. He's really so entirely predictable. For Nori, the world is made to revolve around him. So of course, he would not imagine I was ever going to say no once he saw me and made the situation clear.

"While we've been apart, I have considered how I behaved during our marriage. And—I would like to apologize—*Moushiwake arimasen.*"

Shocked at hearing his surprisingly formal apology that I am dumbstruck when he snaps into a low bow and holds it for the duration of his words. However, I am unmoved by his performance. He's not only been cheating. He's hit me and piled abuse on me for a long while. His fine apology as good as it is, and it is very good, could just as well have been pulled from any one of his yakuza movies. I've lived with this actor, and I've seen the scripts!

"Okay. I accept your apology, but why do you think this will change anything?" I ask him. I grit my teeth and take a deep breath. "Nori, I am not going back to Japan with you."

And I hold my breath, waiting for the temper that must surely flare. But, he remains calm.

He walks across to the refrigerator and examines the contents of the bar. "You know, if you don't go back to Japan together with me, I will finish your career." He says all of it as if he's running through a shopping bill. "You will no longer have a contract with J-Big." He gazes over his shoulder at me. "Who is going to distribute your music then?"

It's too much. First, he is apologizing, then he's threatening. But, this is Nori.

"It is possible to distribute online, direct to my fans, you know?" I tell him, folding my arms across my chest. "I don't need your family label any longer!"

He takes three miniature bottles of whiskey from the refrigerator and places them on the polished wood counter. "Let's drink to your success then. Let's celebrate your new independence."

Nori takes ice from the freezer and drops several cubes into a tumbler. He twists the tops off of the bottles, gathers them up in his hand, and tosses the liquor on top of the ice. I watch him as walks slowly around the room, swirling the ice and the alcohol. He peers into the bathroom then turns to look at the bed, staring at it for what seems an interminably long time.

He misses the intimacy, of course. No doubt he feels remorse too. It hardly matters. It's way too late for any regrets. If he's weighing up his options, I could tell him he only has one. Drink up and leave.

Through the large window, we see the lights of restaurants wink on, reflecting on the harbor water. The evening sky is a pale blue as darkness hangs like a shroud that's about to descend on the city.

He takes several gulps and sits down. "You really think you can make it on your own?"

I stare at him for a few seconds before I turn away in disgust.

He takes several more gulps. "I mean, sure, you're a performer. But what do you know about marketing or managing your own career?"

"How come, Nori—how come you've never bothered to ask me what kind of career I want!"

He rattles the ice around in his glass. "You seem to forget it's because of J-Big that you have any career at all."

"No one hears the music I write," I reply.

He laughs without any warmth. "It's like talking to a child! Why are you so naive?"

I can feel my cheeks redden. "I knew this would be a bad idea," I tell him. "I would like you to leave now."

I reach into my bag, and pull out my phone, pressing the speed dial number for Shizue. When she answers, I press the hang-up icon. Nori watches me quietly. There is something in his expression I didn't notice earlier. Regret perhaps.

He puts down his glass and holds his hands up in the air. "I'm going," he says, and he walks to the door and pauses. "I will stay in Wellington until the shoot finishes."

I wait until the door closes behind him, then I ring Shizue.

8

"I don't believe it!" I hiss to Shizue at the entrance doors to our hotel. I want nothing more than to walk right past him, but I know that won't decide anything.

What does he want?

"*Kuso!*" Shizue exclaims as she peered again through the open door into the lobby. Nori sits in a corner table beside a potted tree. "It looks like he hasn't been waiting long."

She glances back at the Mercedes. Our driver leans against the vehicle, engrossed in a phone conversation.

"We could get back in the car," she suggests. "Tell the driver to take us to a cafe. We could ring reception every so often to check if he's still here, and come back when he's gone. We could even call the police!"

"It's too late," I tell her over my shoulder. "He's seen us."

"I don't want to be alone with him. He has that smug,

self-confidence written all over his face. Whatever he's up to, he thinks he's winning."

"Okay then, Ya-chan," she says and she squeezes my hand. "Let's do this together."

At least. I can't see any paparazzi lurking in the lobby or outside the hotel. They would love to get a photo of the once-famous movie star, Shimano Noritake, and his estranged J-Pop idol wife as they fight over their future.

"Nori-san, you are back so soon?" I ask as we both take the chairs on the other side of the table.

I catch the scent of his cologne. It's too astringent for my taste, but still not strong enough to cover the smell of stale tobacco. His constant smoking must be killing off his olfactory sense.

He points to the briefcase beside him. "I've brought company papers for you to stamp with your *inkan.*"

"Why didn't you bring them with you the other day?" I ask.

"I thought it best we met first for a friendly conversation. To break the ice and set the mood."

"My mood has been great until the moment I saw you again."

"I only meant to ensure the continuation of our business venture," he replies with unnecessary formality.

"What business venture are you talking about now? Are you talking about our marriage?"

"You gave me no chance to raise the subject." He waits for my ask the question.

Shizue leans forward in her chair. "Any change to the

contractual agreement must be discussed when all parties are present. Including management!"

Nori glanced at her and laughs. It was a harsh sound.

"When you say management, you mean my family," he says. "Your employers! Isn't that so?"

The color drains from Shizue's face. She opens her mouth to speak, but she thinks better of it.

I catch her eye. "Shi-chan, it's okay." I have already resigned to the fact I won't be able to avoid stamping my *inkan* on the damn papers he has with him. I wonder what they are about.

She stands up, turning her back on him. I see the angry tears in her eyes. "Ya-chan, I'm sorry," she says to me, and she bows her head. I watch her walk off to the elevators.

A large tourist bus has pulled up at the front of the hotel. The passengers spill out of the vehicle. They mill about outside the coach like a flock of pigeons outside the entrance of a train station. A line of complaining middle-aged couples breaks away from the group to labor up the side ramp to the entrance doors. Behind them, a bellhop, his head down as he labors single-handedly under the weight, pushes the large chromed trolley piled high with luggage from the bus up the ramp.

A short man in a tight-fitting checked sports jacket weaves his way between the ladies hurries to the reception. When he gets there, he waits for all the tourists to shuffle into the lobby. Once they are all in he strains to get an extra inch of height and begins counting their heads.

Nori scowls and turns back to me. "You have your *inkan* with you now?"

"No."

"Well, we need it."

"What papers do you want me to look at?"

"You want a divorce, right?"

I nod my head in response.

"The documents must have your name stamp on them before we can terminate our marriage, and that also means our business contract," he says in an unsettlingly calm and even measured manner.

My heart is beating in my ears. It's one thing to end my marriage with Nori, but to step away from my recording deal is not so easy. J-Big promotes and distributes my music throughout Japan, an arrangement I've depended on for years. Never mind, I know this, and I've gone over it in my mind many times.

He returns from the water dispenser with a half-filled plastic cup. I sip the water and watch the tourists, wishing I were elsewhere. An old man with tufts of dyed bright orange hair appears beside us. He waves a hairy hand at our chairs and asks us in a thick European accent if the seats are free. I tell him we are leaving, and he calls out to a large woman in a blonde wig, and they begin to argue in earnest.

Nori tosses his empty cup into the bin. "We should go up to your room to sort this out. It shouldn't take long at all. How long does it take to stamp each page?"

"That depends on how many pages you have for me to stamp," I tell him.

"Not many at all," he says.

I want nothing more than to stamp the damn papers with my *inkan* and be done with him and J-Big. I nod my head.

"Let's go, then," he tells me.

9

Nori places his briefcase on the table in front of the window. He doesn't waste time and glancing at me to see if I mind, he opens the door of the refrigerator.

There are a lot of sailboats moored in the harbor today. There must be a regatta. I wish I was on one of those boats. I would set sail straight away.

He rattles through the bottles. "No *shochu* or *sake*? That's too bad. Well, a beer might be a good idea. Or a whiskey?"

"I wish you wouldn't." Even as I say the words, I know discouraging him from taking a drink is a waste of energy. Nothing has changed.

He takes two chilled tumblers from the top rack. "Is a whiskey and Coke okay?" He asks without turning around.

"That will be fine," I tell him without caring in the least.

He finds the ice cubes in the freezer and fixes the drinks on the counter. When he's finished he holds up the glasses for me to see, raising his eyebrows, as if seeking my approval. Of course. He wants me to be a willing participant in this weird charade. As if he ever needed or wanted my advice. He's play-acting. He's also delusional.

"A celebration drink," he tells me.

I take the glass and I sit at the small round table between us. We can see the sea shining like molten glass through the window. "So what exactly are we celebrating?" I ask.

Nori raises his glass. "To your new life, of course —*Kanpai!*"

The whiskey stings my lips, and I put the glass back down without swallowing.

Nori goes back to the refrigerator and returns with two more whiskey bottles. He offers me one, but I refuse. He drinks quickly. Then he drinks a second, and a third.

Each time he downs the liquor he crunches the cubes between his teeth slowly and methodically. It's a sound I've grown to hate. He gazes at me with a smirk of satisfaction, his jaws working, as he grinds down the remaining granules.

I stand up and stare out the window. I'm not looking at the view, though, I'm trying to work out how I can escape him. I grit my teeth and fight the overwhelming desire to use him as a punching bag. The thought lightens my mood a little.

He talks about the bad publicity that surrounds our

split-up, and how concerned management at J-Big has become for my well-being. His voice is a disinterested drone in the background.

I notice the briefest moment of silence as he hesitates. It's as if he's suddenly stricken with doubt over what the action he's decided to take, but he acts anyway. There's a dull clink as his tumbler meets the tabletop, and then he's knocked my chair over. He throws me against the end of the bed, and before I regain my balance, he has my legs pinned, and his fingers around my throat.

I panic, trying to pry myself free, but his grip only tightens. "Nori, I can't breathe!"

"Then stop struggling." His face is next to my air, and suddenly I can smell his breath. The dense mix of whiskey, tobacco, and halitosis hits me like another punch. For some insane reason, I am struck by how much just he's deteriorated since I have left him. He's stopped caring for himself.

He grabs a handful of hair and pulls me back. His other hand is over my face and when I taste the sourness of his thumb in my mouth, I bite down hard, driving my teeth into a knuckle. He cries out in pain and pulls back. That gives me the opportunity I was looking for. I strike him with an elbow to the right side, and as he crumbles, twist around and slam my other elbow into his left side. He curses, but he tightens his arms around my chest in a crushing bear hug and pulls me closer.

I wriggle and twist, but his grip is strong. I remind myself I am the one with the stamina, and my best chance of escape will come when he is exhausted. I know his smoking habit has gotten the better of him. Already he's panting from the effort he makes to overpower me. He is using his body weight to hold me down, and grasping for a wrist while reaching for the other.

I twist to stay out of his reach and pull myself free of his grasp, but he manages to grab my forearm and shove it up my back. I feel a sharp pain in my shoulder and cry out. He steps back and spins me sideways so that he has me pinned again against the foot of the bed.

I struggle like a wild animal, bringing my head back fast I strike his jaw, and I am rewarded by the sound of the solid smack. It isn't enough to escape him. He has turned his head just in time, and it feels like I have just head butted a bronze bust.

"You bitch!" He cries, spitting out the words, and striking my face with the heel of his hand. The blow makes my ear ring and I stagger. My legs give out and I fall across the bed, the coppery taste of blood in my mouth.

"You are still my wife!" He cries out, leaping astride me. He tears at my blouse, the buttons popping off as he rips the material aside. He's squeezing and twisting me, and he wants to hurt me. Nori has never been as violent as this before, and suddenly I feel very afraid of him. My husband has clearly lost his mind.

My head clears. and I bite at his ear, his cheek, anything I can reach to snap him out of it. He anticipates me, snatching a handful of my hair. Jerking my head to the side. I thrash about, until he pummels me into submission.

I glimpse the harbor through the window. The boats on the water look like fallen leaves. I try to project myself onto one of them. He is encouraged when I stop struggling and tears off the remainder of my clothes.

I close my eyes, clench my fists, and concentrate simply on hating him.

I lift my head from the toilet bowl and wipe the sick from my chin with the back of my hand. Pulling the remains of my clothes around me, I crouch and wait for Shizue. It seems like another eternity passes before I hear her knocking on the door. I let her in then run back to the bathroom.

"Ya-chan, I'm so sorry," she says, hurrying after me.

I turn the faucet as far as it will go, and close my eyes, letting my head drop as the sharp needles of hot water sting my neck and back. I can see only a boundless nothingness before me, and I want to stay there forever.

My knees press into the hard tiles of the shower floor. I reach for the tap above me to find her hands already there, shutting off the water. I try to stand, but I slump back to the floor. I'm babbling like a child about how I stupidly went with him to my room to stamp the damn documents.

She takes a towel from the wall rack and wraps it around me. Then she crouches beside me to gently rub my back. "Ya-chan, forget the stupid papers! What were you thinking, letting him into your room a second time?"

I shake my head, unable to find a sensible answer. All I want is for her to make things better again. She can't, and I let out a sob before I can stifle it.

She presses her forehead against mine and gazes into my eyes. "To hell with him and his family! There are other labels to sign with. I can help you—that's if you still want me as your assistant."

I draw the towel tight around me and walk through the suite to the bed. I flick the duvet over the blood-stained sheet. Too late. She's seen enough to know what happened. "Of course I do."

Then, the moment of extreme clarity hits me. I see the plan from beginning to end. It is almost perfect. "Shi-chan, you won't like the favor I'm going to ask."

"Ya-chan. Just tell me what it is."

She's worried about my state of mind. When she hears my plan she will realize it makes good sense.

"I need to disappear. I must find a place he won't find me."

"What are you saying?" She asks with a frown.

I take her hands and hold them tightly. "Ya-chan, I will stay out of Japan—at least for the time being. I want to pull myself together before I return. New Zealand is a country Nori is not familiar with. I'm already here—so it's perfect."

She set's the chair lying on the floor upright and sits down.

"I want you to make up a story to give Koga-san," I tell her. "One that satisfies the company long enough for them to stay off my back for at least two weeks. I'm going to need New Zealand dollars."

"Just remember you only have one month on your visa," she tells me.

"One month is all I need."

"You want the whole month?" She stares at me in astonishment. "To do what? Do you want to turn your private issue with Nori into a media event? What would doing that accomplish?"

I must not let her question me too closely. She will easily discover I've been making everything up as I go along.

"It's only for a short while. Please, Shi-chan. I need this!"

"It would be the same no matter which entertainer I worked with," she replies and looks away unhappily. "To be an idol, you have to be selfish."

"I am so sick of being her! You've no idea what it's like being Yaya. I don't want to do it anymore."

I've said too much, but I don't care anymore."

She has never heard me scream in anger before. Not like that. She stares at me in surprise and gathers her thoughts in silence. Then to my utter relief, she looks up smiling. She picks up the tablet from the table and runs her hands down the electronic pages of her calendar. "Right. I will need to think of something believable to keep the company off our backs."

Her words lift a great weight from me. I feel I can

breathe again after being stifled for what seems like forever. "I'll tell them you are taking a month to finish writing two more songs to include in the new recording."

"Everything will be fine—I promise," I tell her.

"I hope you're right, Ya-chan. I do hope so."

10

On the final day of the shoot, I arrive late on the set. Under the hot lights, the perspiration beads on my scalp and trickles down the back of my neck. I feel cold.

Director Morita Toshihiro is from Kagoshima City in Western Japan. The city that's famous around the world for its island volcano and samurai history. It is also very well-known inside Japan for the conservative values held by the male population.

Morita's not happy that I arrive late. I can tell from the way he looks at me when I walk onto the set. He watches me in silence for several minutes, before launching himself out of his chair.

"Are you okay?" He asks.

"*Hai*," I reply. The kind of answer that doesn't commit me to a straight yes or no.

Morita scrutinizes my face as though he were a

painter checking his subject before putting brush to canvas. He waves and the makeup assistant hurries over with her tiny box of work tools.

She dabs my face with a soft brush, apologizing as she rearranges the strands of my hair. Just as quickly she disappears again behind the lights.

He stands back to appraise the result, then gently touches the side of my face. The makeup I put on early that morning has hidden most of the swelling, but he can see through my protection. "Is there something you want to tell me?" His voice is gruff but low so he won't be overheard.

I shake my head. "No, I'm fine."

He brings his face closer and stares into his eyes.

If I say anything to him about Nori's visit, I might break down in front of everyone. Then I would ruin the final day of our shoot. "I'm fine," I tell him. "Really!"

His sharp eyes flick over my face, checking for any clues. He nods his head slowly and gives me a reassuring smile. "We want this one in the can today."

"I'm good," I mumble. "*Arigatou*."

It's impossible to keep anything like a secret on these shoots, let alone try to hide the marks served out by a violent husband. The drinking parties can start on the first day. That means so too, begin the stories. A nudge. An excited titter behind a cupped hand. Tonight we will celebrate the end of our shoot, but I won't be there.

Morita walks back to his chair. He picks up the water bottle from the armrest and falls into the seat. "Okay, everyone. Let's do it right!" He hollers. He runs his hand through his long hair and looks at expectantly.

I exhale and let Yaya take over.

The first assistant director glances at Morita for confirmation and turns to the waiting crew on the set.

"Scene twenty-two, take one. Action!"

The last thing I want to do today is walk to the small guardhouse at the front gate of the production studio to check through a suitcase someone brought in. The company would always send me a replacement for whatever was lost. They tell me to go and check what was in the suitcase, and, I find undergarments, extra shirts, and blouses in neat packages wrapped in clear wrap. Shizue's work. I nod my head at the security guard.

The man slides a paper in a clipboard over the counter for me to sign.

Behind the guard, I notice a red Nissan station wagon parked across the entrance road. The car must be at least twelve years old. The driver stands outside talking on his phone. A young guy wearing wrap-around sunglasses. He is doing his best to ignore the guard's stare.

"Was he the one who handed you my suitcase?" I ask the guard.

He peers out the opposite window. "Yeah, that's him."

I walk around the side of the guardhouse.

"Thank you for returning my suitcase," I tell him as I walk up to the car.

He looks up in surprise and ends the call. "I know you, don't I?" he says. "You were wearing a big hat and shades last time I saw you. That was you, wasn't it?"

Suddenly, I recognize the freckles and the nose. "Oh, it's you," I say and I laugh.

"I would have returned it much sooner," he tells me. "Sorry."

He's going to get into his car and drive off if I don't stop him.

"Oh, there's no need to apologize. That should be me for putting you to all this trouble." The words tumble from my mouth in my haste to keep him from leaving. "Are you going to the city?" I ask hopefully.

"No, I'm off home."

The guard pokes his head out of the booth. "Sir, you're blocking the entranceway."

The young guy waves a hand in acknowledgment and jumps into the car. He nods a friendly goodbye to me as he starts the engine.

I rap my knuckles on the glass of the passenger door.

He turns the engine off and lowers the window.

"I need you to drive me out of here."

"You want me to drive you where?" He asks, staring at me in surprise.

This isn't going as planned, but I can't turn back.

"Please," I smile as sweetly as I can. This must be the best acting I've done the entire week.

"Don't you have a chauffeur or a taxi?" He asks.

"Yes, but I'd like you to drive me," I reply.

"Drive you where? You should take a taxi."

"Please!"

He gives me a nervous grin and shakes his head. "Sorry, but I shouldn't be doing that."

"Please!" I ask again, with more urgency this time, my hand already turning the door handle. Then I open the door.

"Oh, what the hell!" He says with a stunned expression. "Knock yourself out."

I throw my suitcase into the back and jump in beside him "Thank you!" I tell him as I close the door.

The security guard crosses the road and peers down into the cab with a look of concern.

"Ma'am? Do I need to call anyone to let them know you're leaving the lot?"

"No," I reply.

The guard looks unconvinced.

I turn to my new driver. "Thank you. I appreciate this so much."

A sports car turns off the busy city street into the entrance and creeps toward the front gate.

The security guard straightens up as the car inches closer.

"Where is it you want me to take you?" My driver asks as the sports car comes to a stop opposite us.

I watch the side window of the sports car slide down. A plump faced middle-aged man sits behind the steering wheel. He stares at me. Then I see the camera in his hands.

"*Kuso!*" I exclaim.

"Do you know that guy?" My new driver asks.

"No, but I know what he wants!" I reply. "That's a photographer looking for a story." I turn away from the window. "Please—go," I hiss.

He starts the engine and plants his foot on the accelerator, swinging the car around in a wide turn, his front bumper narrowly missing the side of the sports car.

"I can't believe the week I'm having," he mutters, and he makes a hard turn into the busy street. We hear the shriek of brakes, the angry shouts of drivers, and the blare of their horns.

He flings his sunglasses on the dash. They clatter against the windscreen slide across to my end and I catch them as they fall. I glance through the back window and see the driver of the sports car trying to turn out of the studio entrance. By the look of the long lines of cars blocking his way, he has no chance of catching up with us.

"What did you ask me before?" I ask my driver.

He draws his hand down his face and glances across at me. His eyes are deep blue.

"I asked, do you know that guy?"

"I mean after you asked me that."

"Where do you want me to drop you off?"

"Would it be okay if you take me to your home?" I ask.

He looks startled.

"What?—No. That's not okay!"

"Please—I will explain," I tell him, panicking as we

stop at a red traffic light.

He must have hurried his shave this morning because I can see a pepper of stubble around his chin lips. "I think you need to tell me what's going on. Otherwise, I'm turning around and taking you back where I found you."

"I'm being harassed," I say. *It is not entirely untrue. The paparazzi are all over me. They probably already know that Nori was also in the country.*

"The dude with the dreadlocks in that sports car?"

"He was paparazzi," I say, nodding my head vigorously should he still doubt me.

"I could drop you off outside the police station. How would that do?"

"Right now, I need to be somewhere the authorities won't find me."

"But you don't know me!" He points out.

"I can see you are a nice guy," I tell him.

He falls silent. After several minutes of thought, he replies. "Well, don't expect too much."

"Excuse me?"

"I mean that I don't live anywhere grand. My home is not a big place."

"Oh, I see. No, I don't expect too much."

"Okay..." He says. He glances at me again with a bewildered look on his face. "You are a little bizarre. Do you know that?"

"Yes," I reply.

He turns back to the road ahead. "Why do I have the feeling this is not a good idea?"

11

The terraced hills are lined with old two-story weatherboard houses in hues of white. Soon we are winding our way up a steep incline, the road narrowing as we get closer to the top of the rise. The slope is splashed with a myriad of gray, green, blue, and red corrugated metal rooftops.

He doesn't say much, but I don't mind. I can tell his mind is racing through a zillion scenarios. In at least one of those I am sure to be crazy and dangerous.

"I'm Yayoi," I tell him finally after several minutes of silence.

He lifts his hand from the steering wheel to shake mine. "Bill," he tells me.

"Pleased to meet you, Bill-san."

"Are you Japanese?"

"Yes, is it so obvious?"

"A little," he replies.

. . .

He walks ahead of me down a path along the side of a neat gray painted weatherboard house. A muted mix of vehicle horns and engine noise drifts up to us from the suburbs below. From the house next door I hear the clink of kitchenware.

At the end of the small yard at the back, beyond the fence line, the houses drop away abruptly. Only the roof of the house behind his is visible. In the distance, I see the sparkle of the ocean between a cleft in the hill. I make a quick calculation. The house is about twenty feet above sea level. It wasn't enough for my liking, but at least the house was on a hill.

A big striped ginger cat stretches out on the welcome mat at a back door that needs a coat of paint. When the cat gets up and curls its body between Bill's legs, he runs his hand along its arched back.

While he fumbles the key in the lock, the cat looks up to meow pitifully at me. I am not good with cats. I stare down at the creature, hoping the message gets through.

The key turns in the lock, and he opens the door into the kitchen. A fly traces a slow circle above a sticky stack of plates in a stainless steel sink. "Breakfast dishes," he says, dropping his keys in his pocket. "I told you not to expect much." He disappears down a dim hallway.

"Do you live here alone?" I call out after him. The place looks cozy, but he's right. It isn't much.

"No!" He hollers from the other end of the house. "I share with my housemates, Jemma and Matt."

I hear the sound of a window sliding open.

"Take a seat," he says when he walks back into the kitchen. He points to the only furniture in the room. An old Formica-topped table with four chrome rimmed chairs around it.

"I'm going out to the gate to see if we have any mail."

I poke my head around the corner and see a living room with an old TV in the corner and a gas heater set in a brick fireplace. The leather settee and two huge chairs look old and worn. The ginger cat bounds into the room, and leaps up onto the settee as if to establish its territory. It watches me without blinking.

I return to the kitchen and find him pouring from a teapot into two cups.

"I was being nosy and looked at the living room."

"Make yourself at home," he says.

I feel a little embarrassed to be caught snooping about. It might not have been a great idea to invite myself to this stranger's home. Still, I can always call a taxi to take me back to my hotel. He isn't asking me a lot of questions. Surely he wants to know what I'm doing in Wellington. "So you're not married?" I ask him.

"No. I'm single."

"You must be wealthy."

He laughs. "What makes you say that?"

"You don't have children, but you live in a house," I say.

"That's right," he replies as he sits down at the table. "I share it."

"So, you must be able to save money," I tell him.

"Heck no!"

He may not be wealthy, but money's a subject people always like to talk about, and yet he doesn't. I sip at my tea. I haven't a clue what to talk about. I might as well tell him about me. "I'm with a film crew from Tokyo," I say. "We've been making a video promotion for one of my songs."

"You're a singer?"

"I write songs and I sing them."

"Yeah?" He scratches his chin. "So—are you famous?"

"In Japan," I reply.

He pushes the handle of his cup, turning it around slowly. He's filling in time. Waiting for me to call a taxi. He's showing a lot less interest in me than I thought he would. I guess he's shy.

"The filming finished today," I tell him.

He nods his head and looks uncomfortable.

"We have a short holiday before we return to Japan. Just a few days. But I want to spend more time in New Zealand."

"Yeah? As it happens I'm on holiday too," he says, and he stares down at his empty cup. "As of today."

Don't quit now, Yayoi! You have to convince him otherwise you are going back to the hotel.

"Do you have plans to go anywhere?" I ask.

"I'm visiting my family and friends up north."

"Up north?"

"The Bay of Plenty. It's on the East Coast."

"Will you be doing something special while you're there?"

"All depends on what you call special?" He says.

"I mean will you be doing something fun."

"I'm going bush," he says. He looks at my face and laughs. "That's what we call the forest."

"You are going bush? What do you mean? "

"Some people tramp the trails. Others fish the rivers. Others go hunting."

"Which group are you in?"

"The one hunting pigs."

"Isn't that dangerous?"

He shrugs. "It's all good fun."

I hesitate for just a moment. "Take me with you."

12

"Oh, hello," the tall woman says with an embarrassed smile. She pulls her ponytail tight through a green stretchy band, pushing the damp strands of her hair behind her ears. "Well, Bill. Are you going to introduce us? Oh, never mind. I'm Jemma."

"I am Yayoi Shimano."

"Hope I don't smell too much," she says as she joins us at the table. "I've just finished a workout." She drops a backpack onto the floor with a loud thump. "Oops, I forgot about the laptop again." She peers down at the bag at her feet. "Do think it's alright?" She asks Bill.

"Jeez, Jemma," he replies, rolling his eyes. "Start it up and find out."

"I don't really want to—why do I always forget it's in my bag?"

Bill suddenly pushes back his chair. "I got a phone call to make," he announces.

Jemma watches him pick his mobile off the bench and walk outside. She turns to me and smiles. "Are you two—like, together?"

"No way!" I tell her.

"Okay," she says with a laugh at my reaction. "You two are just working together, right? Say, are you going out with us in the evening?"

I shake my head.

"Let me rephrase that question," she says. "Do you wanna go out for a few drinks with us? Our regular Friday night thing the three of us do."

"I've got nothing planned. So, sure. That's if it's okay with your other housemate, and with Bill."

"Matt's got a farewell party dinner tonight—someone from his office has a birthday. He's promised to join us later." She plays with the glass in front of her, glancing at the open kitchen door.

"How has Bill seemed to you lately?" She asks me.

"Ah..." I shrug. "I'm not sure."

"Oh."

She studies my face for a moment, and she's about to pursue her question but my phone rings and the moment's gone. I reach into my jacket pocket. Speaking Japanese, I tell Shizue about my adventures, and, just as I knew she would, she completely loses it.

"You can't get into the car of someone you don't know!" She screams. "You might be kidnapped! Where are you now?"

"Don't be ridiculous!" I tell her. "Anyway, you've seen

him. Remember the tall, good looking guy I pointed out to you when we were at the airport?"

"The gaijin you were staring at? She asks. Her voice incredulous, as if I had just told her I was in the company of a psychopath. That was very possibly what she was thinking. "We don't know a thing about him. Do you have the name of the company he works for? He's given you his business card, right?"

"I'm in his home. I've met his housemate. They seem very safe."

"Please tell me what is a housemate?" Shizue wails.

It takes me several minutes to calm her down. I don't give her the names of my new friends or their address. She would like to think I would trust her enough to tell her such details, but it isn't about her. If Koga thought she knew where I was staying, he would demand she tell him everything.

I don't want to put her in a situation where she either has to betray my confidence or lose her job. I do my best to reassure her I'm safe. I laugh, and I promise her we will be eating breakfast in the restaurant together in the morning. I know it's a lie.

When Matt joins us he tries to talk Bill into going clubbing, but Jemma reminds Bill he's getting up at five in the morning, and he's looking at a day on the road.

They compromise by stopping at the Texas Bar for a last drink before heading home where they teach me the finer points of shooting pool and I'm soon relaxed enough to confide in Jemma I don't want to return to my hotel room. I explain to her that I've only recently ended a bad relationship, and I tell her how he followed me to New Zealand. Last I tell her that I will take a taxi back to my hotel.

"Don't be silly," she replies. "That creepy stalker ex-boyfriend of yours might be there. Why not stay with us tonight? That is if you don't mind crashing on our sofa."

"Crashing?"

"It means you get to enjoy the luxury of sleeping in our living room," she says with a giggle.

The yellow light of a street lamp shines through the Venetian blinds, painting stripes across the opposite wall. The door of the lounge is open, but I don't mind. I listen to the discordant sounds of snoring in the house. Somehow the noise of the others comforts me.

There's a rumbling sound from below the sofa. I peer down to see two enormous wide-open irises staring back at me. The cat gives a plaintive meow and lands in front of me with a soft heavy thump. Its wet nose bumps my face as it sniffs my scent. Satisfied I am no one else, it turns a tight circle, swishing its tail in my face and curls itself up in a furry ball. I think about throwing it to the floor, but the warm body snuggled close to my chest is not unpleasant and soon I fall asleep.

When I wake the cat is nowhere to be seen. I watch

Bill stumble down the hall to the kitchen, grunting under the weight of the full backpack he carries in his arms. I snuggle deeper into the warmth of the blanket, but it doesn't work. The sofa is lumpy and cold under me. It's time to get up.

13

I find him in the kitchen, poking the glowing elements of the toaster with a fork. Through the windows, I can see the pale light of dawn as it seeps between rolls of dark clouds. It reflects off the sea in a triangle of glistening silver between the hills. The linoleum is ice-cold under my bare feet, and to warm them, I hop from one foot to the other, rubbing the soles against my legs.

He looks over his shoulder to see me. "Oh, you're up."

His fingers the brush hot metal, and cursing with pain, he rushes to the sink and plunges them under cold water.

"Sorry about laughing, but that was funny," I tell him, pressing my hand to my mouth.

He turns off the tap and dries his hands on a crumpled tea towel that hangs over the oven door. He decides to ignore me for the moment, and places a frypan onto a ring and lights the gas.

"Do you think it will rain today?" I ask.

"Could be in for a shower," he replies as he stares at the pan. "Do you want eggs for your breakfast?"

"Yes, please."

I sit at the table and watch him prepare the food.

"How did you sleep?" He asks, turning around to look at me for the first time.

"Good. The cat jumped onto the settee. It was good company."

"That's Fred," he says and he laughs. "He was looking for a warm bed after I tossed him off mine."

"I didn't mind, I like cats," I tell him. I'm not sure why I'm lying.

He slides a plate of fried eggs and buttery toast in front of me.

"Are you leaving today?" I ask.

"Uh-huh," he replies. "I should have been on the road ages ago. Now I'm going to run into the morning traffic." He forks a piece of eggy toast into his mouth, chewing it quickly, and watches me poke the brown plateful of food he served up.

"You don't have to eat it, you know?" He says with his mouth full of egg and toast.

I guess Jemma told him pretty much everything I said to her at the bar.

He gathers up the last crumbs of toast with his fork.

"You better hurry if you want a shower. Jemma is up soon, and she'll take ages in there."

The text message on my phone is from Shizue. It's a typical book chapter from her.

> **Ya-chan, Koga wants you to meet with him tomorrow afternoon. Please ring him in the morning to confirm.**
>
> **Your husband visited him and demands you sign the documents releasing you from your contract with J-Big.**
>
> **There! Now I have passed on the message.**
>
> **I told Koga you are not available for several days. He bleats like a baby goat, but don't worry I don't think you need to sign anything. At least, not yet.**
>
> **You will let me know your plans, won't you?**
>
> **See you at the party.**
>
> **BTW I did ring Zach :)**

There's a follow-up text she sent at two in the morning. It asks why I'm not answering my phone. I see she has tried to call me several times.

Bill is on the back doorstep, bent over a bulky backpack. He pulls on the straps to compact it down to a manageable size. When he's happy with the result, he stands up and hefts the pack outside.

My phone beeps and flashes. It's too early in the morning for Shizue. I stare at the display.

This morning on TV I saw a photo of you and your boyfriend together in a car. They said you are running away. Is that what you are doing?

I sit on the top step dangling my phone by the strap, gazing across the backyard with a bent clothesline and weeds along the fence. I concentrate on breathing in the chill morning air through my nose and blowing it slow and steady out through my mouth. Nori should have been back in Tokyo by now.

This is bad shit!

I should get rid of my phone. I should walk out the front gate, grind it into the pavement under the heel of my shoe, and drop what's left into the rubbish bin.

14

I feel Jemma's hand on my shoulder and I don't mind that she gives me a gentle shake. It feels comforting. When her hair brushes my cheek though, I instinctively pull away from her, and I look up to see the concern in her face.

How long has she been standing there?

"Is there anything I can do?" She asks.

"It's that guy I was telling you about," I say. I am unable to cover the anger I know she hears in the tone of my voice.

"Is he stalking you? Because if he's bothering you, go to the police," she tells me. She cocks her head and frowns. "Is he your boss?"

I shake my head.

"That's a good thing," Bill says as he appraising a pair of boots he has pulled from the bottom of the hot water cylinder cupboard. He turns them over and gives an approving nod of his head. "I almost forgot I had these." He puts them down and looks up at me. "I mean he can't do anything to you if he's not your boss, can he?"

"It's a little more complicated, Bill-san. Anyway, I don't want to cause trouble."

"We can pick up the rest of your baggage from your hotel and take you to the airport," Jemma suggests. "That way you can avoid him at the hotel."

"Thank you. You are kind, but my bags are no problem. The company will take care of them for me."

They look disappointed with my answer and fall silent.

This is my opportunity.

"You know, I would like to stay in New Zealand a little longer. Do you know of a quiet place I could stay for about two weeks?"

Jemma slaps Bill on the back. "Take her up north with you. You could do with the company on a six-hour drive."

He places his boots in a carry bag and pulls the zip closed. "Yeah—maybe," he mutters.

Jemma sighs. "Stop feeling sorry for yourself, Bill! It's just life. You can easily get another job..."

She fell silent when he fixes her with an angry stare.

"I'm just saying," Jemma replies quietly.

Matt strolls into the kitchen bare-chested in his shorts and runners. He takes the toothbrush from his mouth and waves it in front of Bill.

"Come on, dude! How many beautiful women do you have offering to keep you company on a trip into the wilderness? I mean take a look at her, will you? Yayoi's a babe!"

I feel myself blush, and I don't like it. His remark reminds me how J-Big presents Yaya to the world. How my fans cry out 'cute' and 'beautiful'.

"I'm too big to be a baby," I tell him.

"Oh, definitely," Matt tells me with a grin.

"It's a small town," Bill tells him. "And really, what do you think Yayoi is going to do there? She wouldn't be happy stuck at a local motel."

"You could ask your friends if they would mind her staying with them, couldn't you?" Matt asks. "You know. Like a homestay. I don't think Yayoi is short on cash." He turns to me. "Am I out of line saying that?"

"No. You are right. I can pay my own way," I tell them.

Bill picks up his boots and stands up. "There are locals in the town who would jump at the chance to offer you bed-and-breakfast. There aren't that many ways to make money in Opuhunaki these days."

"Oh, come on guys!" Jemma snorts. "You're talking about just dropping Yayoi on someone's doorstep. That's not a good idea!"

"Your relations live there, right?" Matt persists.

Bill nods his head.

"Do you think any of them would put Yayoi up in their home for a couple of weeks," Matt suggests through a mouthful of toothpaste and saliva. He gets off the chair. "I've got to go spit."

Bill drags the empty chair over, scraping the metal legs over linoleum, and sits heavily on the seat. He gazes at me. How about it Yayoi? Do you want me to try?"

I can hear Jemma tapping her fingernails on the stainless steel top of the bench. Tikka-tikka-tikka-tikka.

"It sounds okay. That's if they don't mind."

"You know—you could stay with me at Paul and Carol's. What I mean is—you stay with them for the long weekend. Then you could come back with me when I return to Wellington."

I nod my head. Stay with him? That's what he said.

I see Jemma and Bill sneak a look between them. There's a responsibility that weighs heavy on them, behind all the goodwill. I can see now that Bill is politely refusing my request, and I feel ashamed of myself. It's time I got back to the hotel and I stand up "Look, I'm sorry for all the bother!"

Jemma stares at me in surprise. "You are going to go with him, right?"

"No—I think it best I go back to the hotel. Thank you, Bill-san and Jemma-san for allowing me to stay over last night. I will call a taxi."

"No-no, wait a minute," Bill says. "You are welcome to travel up north with me. I'm sure Paul and Carol won't mind at all. Just me a few minutes to make the phone call. Really."

I look at the two of them, and when I see I had it all wrong and I feel a huge sense of relief.

15

"All set?" He asks me.

I look up from my phone. "Do I have time to make a call?"

"Go ahead."

"Just a few minutes," I promise him. I wait for Shizue to pick up her mobile, but when I get a recorded message, I text her that I'm going to be in touch and will send her more details soon. She rings moments after I press send.

"I was enjoying my first sleep-in for ages," she complains. "What's up?"

"Shi-chan, I'm about to leave Wellington with Bill-san. I will be staying with his friends on the East Coast."

"Where?" She asks in dismay.

"It's a small town called Opuhunaki. Please don't tell anyone. I don't want Nori to find out where I'm going."

"I told you I'm on your side, didn't I?"

"Thank you. Koga-san is going to ask you if you know where I am."

"I'll tell him that you called and that I tried getting more details, but—you know—Yayoi's head is like a stone. You can't get information from a stone.'"

"He's going to go on about contractual obligations, and that you work first for J-Big and second for me."

"Shi-chan, don't worry. I won't tell him where you are, but are you sure you don't want to be on the plane with us? Remember, we fly out in two days."

"Everything's fine. Relax. I'll contact you once you're back in Tokyo."

In the car, Bill tells me we're pretty much going to be cutting diagonally across the North Island, from one coast to the other. I settle back in my seat. Finally, I feel myself begin to relax. Let the adventure begin.

The coastal highway from Wellington runs through countless gray towns clustered along the edge of the road. They are sleepy settlements with only a handful of houses, perhaps including a derelict gas station and a shop that seems to sell everything from ice cream to rubber boots. In two hours, we are making our way inland amid gently rolling hills where sheep cover the slopes like maggots on a green carcass.

"There is so much empty space," I exclaim as we wait at a rail crossing for the barrier arm to lift. "Is Opuhunaki as quiet?"

"Much more lively and prettier, with the kind of beaches and mountains people from Auckland like to play in during their summer holidays."

"It all sounds beautiful."

"When you see the town you are more likely to think it quaint. People used to ride horses through the main street of the town when I was a kid. There were hitching rails outside the pubs. After the hitching rails were taken down continued to ride their horses down the main street. They just tied them up at the power poles."

"Do they still ride them through the town?"

"No, now they have bylaws forbidding horses in the town center."

"They can't be as dangerous as cars," I tell him.

"Well, that depends on how drunk the riders are when they leave the pub," he tells me laughing.

We have been climbing steadily higher for an hour when we pull into the last township before we enter the dry central plateau. He turns the Nissan into a gasoline stand.

I gaze at him in the side mirror as he leans against the car waiting for the tank to fill. He is lost in his thoughts.

My phone rings. It's Shizue again. She tells me she's been worrying. Now she's panicking over the idea I am alone with the gaijin. "Shi-chan, you don't know for sure what he has in mind. It's not like there's anyone you can turn to for help if things really go wrong. There's only the two of you in the car. Please be careful!"

"Oh for goodness' sake! Stop freaking out! I speak English! I have lived in America for four years and survived."

"But the place he's taking you to—it sounds remote."

"I was born in the countryside."

"That's not what I mean, and you know it!"

Nothing I say is going to stop her worrying. "Shi-chan, how about we go out for lunch together just as soon as I get back to Tokyo?"

She forces a laugh and suggests we go to a hot spring for a long weekend. We could make plans for our future.

I like the idea.

Bill peers through the open window at me as I end the call with Shizue.

"There you go with that frown again," he says.

"Oh, I was talking to my PA. Work stuff. Hey, you can talk." But I don't want to upset him, and I don't tell him how unhappy he's been ever since I arrived at his house. He might tell me I am the reason. He might even decide to leave me to my own ends. For whatever reason, I don't want him to do that.

"What's that? He asks.

"Nothing. Sorry."

He waves his hand in the air in as much to say it doesn't matter, and points to a restaurant next door.

"Are you hungry?" He asks. "Let's get something to eat."

16

"Do you have fresh fish?" Bill asks.

The waitress runs her pen down the large plastic menu Bill has in his hand. "We have Fish of the Day," she tells him.

"What is it today?" He asks her.

"Tarakihi," the waitress tells him. She points her pen at a whiteboard on the wall.

"Is it good?" I ask Bill.

"You want the fish?" She asks me, impatient to fill our order.

"Yes, please," I tell her.

"Porterhouse steak for me," Bill says.

She limps away on a bad hip. The swinging wooden doors close with a loud bang, and we hear shouts and the clatter of plates from the kitchen.

Bill pushes the condiments aside and pulls a map from his pocket, spreading it out on before him on the table.

"Let's take a look at where we're heading."

I don't really care what roads we take. What I do care about is cheering him up, so I tap him on the hand. "Do you know that a Japanese-American co-production was filmed in the North Island? The movie starred Tom Cruise and Watanabe Ken-san."

"I saw it," he says, looking up from the map.

"You look a bit like Tom Cruise. A little bit." I gesture with finger and thumb to show him how little. "You have the same smile."

Bill grins like a maniac and jumps to his feet, and for just a moment I wonder if I should be afraid. Then begins to dance. When he sees my puzzled face he tells me he's imitating the actor. Bill watches me laugh with a look of delight. "You liked that?"

I nod and his grin grows wider.

We pass by tall forests, still blue lakes, and scatterings of houses. The bones of townships. Pretty spots in sleepy hollows. The sun is hanging low in the late spring sky as we wind down a steep gradient. As we come around a bend in the road, we see the sparkling Pacific Ocean.

I catch my breath. "Oh, it's beautiful."

"Isn't it just," he agrees, and he begins to hum a tune.

The car hugs the log lazy curve in the road as we enter a tunnel of big brooding dark trunked trees that remind me of Japanese cherry trees. Pohutukawa, he calls them. They spring from both sides of the road, the leafy branches intertwining over us in a marriage of convenience. We drive out of the corner, leaving the trees behind us. Then I see them. They appear suddenly as if apparitions.

Two small children are standing like silent, bare-chested sentinels beside their stocky horses. The children hold the reins loosely, nonchalantly at their sides as though the animals are only an extension of them. They watch us pass with studied disinterest. Only their wide eyes betray the curiosity they attempt to hide behind their stern expressions.

I turn to look back and see a small girl in a cotton dress sit upright on the bare back of her mount. Her hands grasp the horse's mane. She must have been hiding behind the animal's thick neck as we approached the turn in the road. She straightens up to see us leave. When the Nissan comes out of the bend in the road, I look back to see the girl staring back at me. She tosses a long black tangle of hair over her thin brown shoulders.

17

I wake with a start as the car bumps over a metal cattle guard and onto a gravel driveway. Sunlight flickers through the bright foliage overhead, and at the end of an overgrown hedge, we pull into a large carport, next to a long white painted weatherboard house.

"We're home," Bill announces, his voice lifting like that of a child anticipating a treat.

At the edge of the concrete floor stands a muscular white and tan dog, that stares at us with pink-rimmed brown eyes. The creature stands as still as if it were carved from stone. The face is white but for a black patch around one eye lending it the air of a savage clown. Saliva drips from a mouth open just enough for me to see the bottom row of sharp white teeth.

Bill thumbs his sunglasses up his forehead, and with both hands on the steering wheel, he straightens his arms and yawns. He's in no hurry to open the door.

A tall man steps outside of the house. "Shut up, Max!" He yells at the dog. A small white terrier bounces about as its owner struggles to get his foot into a white canvas shoe while balanced precariously on one leg. He gives us a cheerful wave and bends to cuff the dog with his open hand. The broad-brimmed hat he wears drops from his head to reveal a pink pate barely covered by thin wisps of sandy hair. The terrier barks even louder, delighted by the action and the attention.

"I thought you would be here after dark," The man says. "You were driving like a demon, I suppose."

"We struck it lucky with the traffic!" Bill replies with a laugh.

The big that until this time has remained motionless lashes the air with his tail.

Bill walks up to the animal, and crouches before it. The dog stares at him and closes its mouth. Bill reaches over the snout and rubs the center crease in the scarred head with his knuckles. "Jasper! You're a big boy, aren't you now. Yes-yes, you are."

The mutt snorts in excitement. He wags his tail so vigorously his whole rear end sways to and fro. He lurches at Bill and slops a lick across the man's face.

"A big kiss for me, eh?" Bill laughs as he wipes off the saliva with the back of his hand.

He gets to his feet to shake his friend's hand, but finds himself enveloped in a bear hug instead. "Well, you've not changed much," Bill gasps. He turns to point at me still sitting inside the car. "Yayoi, this is Paul. Come on out. The dogs won't eat you."

Paul stretches out his hand to shake my hand. They are the hands of a man who works the land, coarse and strong but warm. They remind me of my father's. "Welcome to our Opuhunaki," he says with a shy smile.

I give him a bow.

"Aw, you don't need to bother with a bow," he chuckles. "Hasn't Bill warned you about how rough I am?"

Bill shakes his head. "Not a word."

"But—you know it's true," Paul tells him.

"I haven't been drunk enough to tell her any stories yet."

"He can't hold his drink," Paul tells me in a mock whisper. "He becomes a pussycat, once he's had more than a couple. You end up having to carry him home."

I look from one to the other. The likeness can't be an accident. They both have the same stupid grin plastered across their faces.

"You two could be brothers!" I tell them.

Paul looks delighted and claps me on the back. "Hey, your English is good," he tells me. "You sound like you could be an American."

I smile despite being a little annoyed at his unintentional put-down. "I'm Japanese. But, yes, I speak Californian English."

"Oh, I thought… ah—anyway, glad to meet you," he says quickly.

I catch a flicker of self-doubt and an attempt to mask

it with a smile. As always, I notice the eyes first. Paul's are the clearest gray. I don't doubt they could might cold in anger, but today they sparkle like the surface of a still lake on an early morning.

He's the picture of health. Skinny, perhaps even a little too gaunt, with arms and leg muscles that are striated with muscle, and the prominent veins of a long-distance runner. He also has the fresh complexion of someone who lives on a diet of fresh vegetables and fruit.

"Carol ought to be back from town soon," he tells us.

We follow him into the house.

18

Bill pulls two stools out from under a thick timber bench dividing the kitchen from the living room. He sits down close enough to me that our elbows touch. I don't move my arm, and neither does he.

"We took out the wall last year," Paul tells us. "It makes a difference, eh?"

He turns on the jug and lines up three mugs.

"It really opens the place up," Bill agrees. "How's the orchard's going?"

"It's up and down, bro," Paul tells him, spooning instant coffee powder from a large tin. "The last few years were a bit rough, but it looks like we might be in for a good season."

"Our kiwifruit vines caught the virus, and what with the national payout falling because of the international competition from Chinese and Italian growers. Nothing stays the same."

Bill gets to his feet. "Oh, wow, I've been guzzling bottled water all the way up here. Where is it again?"

"It hasn't moved since you were last here," Paul says, gesturing with his thumb.

He places a plate of biscuits and a mug of milky coffee in front of me. He takes a seat and drops two spoons of sugar into his mug, stirring it noisily, and watching the swirl chase each whisk of the spoon as if it's the most interesting thing he has seen all day.

"Sorry, if I annoyed you when I mentioned how good your English is," he says quietly, gazing at me with an uncertain smile.

"I wasn't annoyed," I tell him, but he doesn't look convinced.

"Carol and I did a trip to the Gold Coast ten years ago," he says. His face lights up at the memory. "That's a place in Australia," he adds quickly. He clears his throat. "It was our honeymoon," he continues. "That's about the full extent of my international traveling experience. And Carol's too."

I laugh. "Really! I wasn't annoyed, Paul-san."

I turn to see Bill join us again. "Did you two grow up together?"

They stare at each other. The matching frowns are hard to miss.

"He grew up, but I never did," Bill replies. "I thought I'd get that one in first before you did," he said to Paul.

"That's your excuse for not getting a proper job," Paul replies, and they laugh together.

"I'm not the farming type," Bill tells me. "I'm a city boy."

"Your law degree must be paying for itself, eh?" Paul says, serious once more.

"Mm, I guess I can't complain," Bill replies. "Well—actually that's not true. The company just finished trimming its staff. I was one of the unlucky bastards who got laid off."

"No way," Paul says with a sudden look of concern. "When did that happen?"

"They told me a while back. Oh, they tried to make it pleasant by giving us extra notice. I've just spent the last month wrapping up my project."

Bill glances at me. "I got a couple of days in Tokyo out of them. You know—they told us there were going to be retrenchments," Bill continues. "But, you know, you hope you aren't going to be one of those."

"I thought your outfit was doing well."

"The downturn's carrying on too bloody long," Bill replies. "The international market has dried up. Profit margins have taken a tumble."

Paul shook his head.

"Ah—shit! That's a blow. I don't know what to say. I thought you were sure to tell us they were promoting you to CEO."

"Yeah, right," Bill says, rolling his eyes. "I guess Uncle Hemi is going to be saying the same to me."

"As it happens, I plan to head out their way, so I guess

he will have that chance," Paul says, pushing the plate of melting chocolate biscuits towards me.

"Good one!" Bill replies quietly.

"Aunt Margaret's been asking after you heaps!" Paul adds quickly. "And Uncle Hemi's been missing you too. But, you know, he's a grumpy old bugger and never admits to having those kinds of feelings."

"How can you tell then?" Bill asks, looking sharply at Paul as if to search for a hidden truth.

"He talks a lot about the time we were kids. It's all silly stuff. We have a laugh about those times. Yeah, but he's been asking me what you're up to in Wellington. I always say I haven't a bloody clue."

"How are they—health-wise?"

"Good on the whole. They're getting older."

Outside the kitchen window, I can see two avocado trees and a broad-leafed giant towering over the front gate, the foliage ringed in the gentle red glow of the setting un. The hills beyond the road are a blur that runs along the horizon in the soft evening haze. I think about the sea and how far away it must be. At least there are the hills between the house and the coast.

The men talk on, and I am left to make my calculations. Bill told me in the car the house was about four miles from the sea, and just over forty feet above sea level. That does not ensure it's safe, but then again this isn't Japan.

I listen to the chirrup of a tree frog. Or is it a cricket? The sound reminds me of a farm a long time ago. A place where three generations of my family had lived together. I remember going home on the school bus. It dropped me off on the side of the main road after school finished. There I crossed a small bridge and made my way down a narrow road to the village. In late spring and early summer, the farmers filled the rice fields with water from the stream running down the old concrete feeder drains I walked beside on my way home.

The place was full of critters. Small birds dived around my head, feeding off the bugs of all kinds that crawled, swam, and flew among the bright green shoots of the young rice plants. Every so often, the muddy surface erupted with tadpole trails and the splash of frogs chasing food as I walked past the flooded fields.

The way down to the edge of the flooded field was a muddy ramp used by farm machines. I dumped my school bag on the dry concrete, pulled off my shoes, and tucked-in my skirt. I was careful not to step into the soft mud, or I'd likely disappear below the surface. No matter how fast the frogs were, my quick little fingers were faster.

One day, I arrived home with my jacket dripping water in the entranceway of the old house. I sat on the wooden step in the vestibule to take off my shoes, unable to contain my giggles as I thought about how I was going to surprise Grandfather with my catch. My mother had heard the sound of the screen door opening. She called out to me to hurry so she could show me what she had bought in town before she started preparing a meal for us.

I found Mother in the *tatami* room holding out the new pair of jeans for me to try on. I set the jacket on the floor. That's when my mother ran out of the room. She returned with a broom, screaming and swiping, and slipping on all the wet spots because my escaping prisoners were leaping everywhere. She hated frogs.

Grandfather had been lying on the rice mats behind the low *kotatsu* table watching the national high school baseball game on the TV, but the performance in his living room was proving far more interesting. He howled with laughter as he watched Mother's antics with the broom.

I saved a handful of the poor creatures. They were the lucky ones I found crouching in the shadow of the table, shielded from the decimation meted out by Mother. Grandfather and I set them free in a drain outside the back door.

19

Paul's wife sets her groceries down on the step and runs into the kitchen to envelop Bill in her arms. Then she catches sight of me. "You must be Yayo-eye," she says, letting go of Bill. She stretches the final vowels of my name until it was unrecognizable. "Is that how you say your name?"

"It's Yayoi," I tell her. "Ya-yo-i."

"Ya-yoi?"

"You got it," I give her two-thumbs-up. "Perfect. I'm pleased to meet you, Carol-san."

"Plain old Carol will do fine," she says with a laugh.

She looks at me as if she has never seen anything like me before. "You're so beautiful," she says.

Carol's long wavy hair falls sun-bleached and gray-streaked onto her broad shoulders. Under her baggy faded shorts and T-shirt, she's tall, sinewy, and deeply tanned. She is like a female version of her husband.

She stares at the table. "Jeez, Paul, the biscuits were all you could find to eat?" She switches on the jug and drops a tea bag into a large orange teapot. "Have you two eaten anything since breakfast?" She asks us.

"We stopped off for lunch in Turangi," Bill tells her. "But, we will eat anything you throw our way."

"All right, give me time to have a cuppa then I'll fix us some dinner." She flicks on the light switch beside the front door. "I almost forgot. I better show you guys where you're sleeping." She glances at Bill. "Are you two an item —or is it separate bedrooms?"

"That's no to the first and yes to the last," Bill tells her with a laugh.

I wake to see sunlight streaming through a hole in the thin faded curtain above my bed, and I throw off the blanket. I lie on my back with one arm shielding my eyes the glare and listen to the rattle of a tractor engine outside my window. The familiar sound unlocks more memories of my childhood, and I close my eyes and watch them like they are a movie playing in my head.

During the school summer holiday break, I sat with my two best friends on the floor of my bedroom listening to CDs. It's strange, but what I remember most of those days was the scent of the ocean drifting through the open window. The house was several miles from the coast, but when the wind was coming off the saltwater, the village might as well have been within sight of the sea. That's how it seemed.

When the wind blew the right way, my school friends complained of the scent of dead fish and rotten seaweed. They begged me to close the window, to turn on my air-conditioner. After they had returned to their homes, I opened the window again and dreamed how one day I'd travel over the watery expanse to the exotic lands that lay beyond the narrow confines of my country.

The old wooden farmhouse was the center of the most cherished memories of childhood. The two-story building had been a home for generations of my family. It was built in the old way, without any nails. Instead, the huge hardwood beams were notched to firmly locked together, one inside the other. The tiled roof was so heavy, that if a wall collapsed, it would have crushed the house. The idea of a heavy roof was simply to prevent the house blowing away in an occasionally catastrophic typhoon.

The house was big enough to hold the entire local community of sixty-some people. Whenever a powerful storm bore down on the village, and every few years a bad one hit our area, the old farmhouse was the place people knew to take shelter. For more than a hundred years it protected generations of villagers.

On calm midsummer evenings, during the lull just before harvest time, our grandparents and our uncles and aunts gathered around the long, low *kotatsu* tables assembled in the center of the *tatami* room. They drank beer and rice wine, ate barbecued river fish and pork, and supped the hot noodle soup noisily to show their appreciation.

While the adults drank and talked, my little sister and I chased our young cousins silly around the rooms. When we had run ourselves out of energy, we collapsed behind our parents who by then had reached a state of happy somnolence. That was when Mother sang and played *Tsugaru jamisen* accompanied by an uncle on his instrument. The old man sat cross-legged and straight-backed on the rice mat beside my Mother, who was dressed in the white and black silk kimono she wore in her public performances. They struck the *bachi* in unison until they reached the break, then the two players became locked in a duel. The sound of the instruments combined with Mother's keening voice filled the room with aural dervishes that whirled in our heads.

Mother's song told of an Aomori woman who pulled vegetables from the hard frosted earth as falling snow caked her bent form. She dreamed of her lover who had returned to the sea to catch fish to feed the family with enough left over to sell in the market, but he never returned.

She had a dreamy sad smile as she stood balancing the weight of the *shamisen* in her arms. Even the way she held the instrument was a part of her act. The long neck of the instrument with its massive tuning pegs turned provocatively away out from her body. *Shamisen* players posed like this, long before any rock chick guitarist of today thought to posture with their Fender.

Later, Mother would have me stand before the family and our neighbors to sing with her. When I was in my teens, I sang duets with Father. The tone and the pitch of my voice matched perfectly with his. Father was a popular singer in his own right before I was born. When Mother found fame, Father had returned to the family farm to take over from Grandfather, by then too frail to work the fields.

J-Big always insisted I take part in the NHK Hall for the New Year's Eve concert in Tokyo, more than a hundred miles from my hometown in Tohoku. It helped put me in the mood to think of my parents performing their duet in front of the family in the old farmhouse.

Nori always insisted we spend the New Year holiday at his parent's home since we were in Tokyo after all. Every year he promised the next New Year we could visit my home. He didn't keep his promise.

"Hey, Yayoi, are you joining us for breakfast?" Bill calls from outside the door.

"Sorry, I need time to get dressed."

"Breakfast is going on the table. We have a big day ahead of us."

"I'm up," I reply. I drop my feet on the floor and get dressed.

20

C arol tells me I am welcome to stay with them for as long as I like. I give her an envelope of large notes and tell her it's for my food and power. She hugs me and pops the money into a jar above the sink. I am going to have my chance to finally shed Yaya from my life. The only way is to step outside of Japan, Nori, J-Big, for long enough to find me, Yayoi, again. Time away from everything and everyone that stops me from getting out of the deep hole I have fallen.

My feelings of relief don't last long. After breakfast, Bill tells me he and Paul have decided to go into the forest for three days as soon as he comes out, he will return to Wellington to find a new job. He is not going to waste any valuable time procrastinating over his decision.

So begins my first day in Opuhunaki. The sun is yet to

breach the line of the garage roof when we climb into Paul and Carol's new Toyota Hilux.

Bill has heaped so much praise on the new truck that Paul finds himself defending his decision to buy it. As we drive onto the main road, his feelings of guilt at spending on the extravagance surface. "It's the 2010 model," he tells Bill. "It's not like we bought a brand-new truck. It's just what we needed," Paul says enthusiastically warming to his own defense. "If I forget the fence posts in the back, all Carol has to do is throw the hardback cover on, and she's good to go."

Carol gives snorts her derision beside me. "Yeah, right, and all I have to do is throw the bloody cover on. Good one, Paul."

Paul stops outside a pretty little white-painted bungalow on the side of the hill. "We'll pick you up in the evening," he tells her.

"Don't worry. I can get a ride back," Carol replies. She hesitates before she closes the door behind her. "Yayoi, are you sure you don't want to come in and meet my friends?"

"We were thinking Yayoi might enjoy seeing some of our beautiful coastline," Bill tells her.

"But aren't you carrying on to the farm to see Hemi?" She asks.

"Hemi and Mākere will be rapt to meet a friend of Bill's," Paul tells her.

"Oh, yes, they will too," Carol says and waves goodbye.

"We're picking up Rawiri, right?" Bill asks him as we turn back on the road.

"Yeah, man. It's been a while since you have seen each other, eh?"

"Sure is. He was a big boy back then. I bet he's changed."

"Rawiri? He's twice as big these days!" Paul laughs, then he glances up into the rearview mirror at me.

I take my phone out of the top pocket of my shoulder bag and run down the list calls. Most are from the crew asking me why I didn't show at the end-of-shoot party. Shizue has emailed me my return ticket. Koga asks me to call him. I return my phone to the bag and settle back in the seat.

Perhaps, I can start to get rid of the demons that plague my sleep, and begin to heal myself, heart and spirit. If all I achieve by my little disappearing act is to return to Japan stronger than before I left, it will be enough.

We find Rawiri waiting for us in front of his house, a tidy bungalow that looks as though it recently received a fresh coat of paint. The road ends a distance way at the entrance gate to the *marae*, the community meeting house. There are few small buildings inside the fenced-off area along with the long community meeting house and its exquisitely carved entrance.

The gate is a tall, thick beamed arch with ornate

palisades that run off either side. Both beams are decorated with intricate carvings depicting gods with saucer-
like eyes and long curled tongues that twist their way out
of the wood to confront us as if to demand we state our
business.

The *marae* is surrounded by the mowed grass of the
hillside, floating against the vast blue backdrop of crystal
clear sky and the Pacific Ocean. Behind the green hill is a
long bay that stretches like a scythe into the distance. Paul
tells me we are standing on the eroded rim of an ancient
volcano.

When Rawiri climbs into the back he's so large he
has to hang one arm outside the open window of his
door. He's bigger than the sumo *rikishi* I have met on
occasion with Nori. The man's head brushes the cabin
roof, and he's so heavy the backseat sinks under his
weight.

"You ought to buy your wife an SUV, bro," Rawiri
tells Paul. "You could have written that off to the taxman
as part of your business, eh?"

"You ought to look after Carol-san better, Paul-san," I
say.

Rawiri gives me a bemused look and nods his head in
agreement.

We pull over onto the shoulder of a cliff that juts out high
above the ocean. It is a short walk through tall dry yellow
grass to an old farm fence we must cross. The thick rusty

wire hangs in loose loops from twisted gray posts carved by the salt-laden winds off the ocean.

"Be careful going over," Rawiri tells me. He presses his thumb down on the single rusted barbed wire running along the top of the fence and lifts a heavy leg over the barbs. I watch as Paul and Bill squeeze themselves between the lower wires under the barbed wire.

"Hey wait for me!" I call out as the two men walk off.

Paul turns back and steps on a wire to make a gap for me to climb through. "You probably have never had to cross over a fence like this before," he said with a laugh.

"They usually have a gate," I answer tersely.

We follow in single-file a narrow dusty track worn into the side of the hillside by the hooves of countless animals. It is on a steep incline, strewn with tiny crushed marbles of dried droppings, and sometimes covered by wide sharp blades of flax, the color of caramel and blood. Over the shrill drone of crickets, I hear the swell sloshing against the rocky wall below.

Rawiri stops in the track with his hands on his hips and peers over the lip of the cliff. He points to a flat rock shelf that projects out into the water. "We are going to dive off of that," he tells me.

I turn away from the sea to look in the other direction. Over the top of the road that disappears down the side of the hill, I can see in the distance scattered groves of dark trees and a wide river that flows into the sea. A line of dark mountains etched into the sky beyond the curve of the bay.

Paul stops and taps my back and I turn to look at where he's pointing. Down at the water below.

"In winter, the sea really pumps here. The waves form stacks of long lines that are speckled with surfers. It's hard to believe it when you see it looking dead calm like today."

I take a step closer to the edge of the drop and dare myself to gaze down into the deep green water at the base of the cliff. I can see tiny shadows flickering back and forth beneath the surface.

I can hear Bill talking to Rawiri around the corner of the hill. "The hammerheads look like they enjoying lunch."

"They are not interested in eating right now, Bro," Rawiri tells him.

"What are they doing then?" Bill asks.

"Making friends with each other," Rawiri relies with a giggle.

"Are you sure it's a good day to go for a dive here?" I hear Bill ask.

"Relax," Rawiri replies. "They're too interested in each other to be looking at your miserable bones. We're on the other side of the rock. It's no problem."

My runners slide on the trail and I have to grab the sharp-edged broad leaf of the flax plants to keep my balance. When they aren't there I drop to the hard track.

"Take it easy," Paul chuckles from behind me.

"Are the sharks always there?" I ask him, breathing deeply to slow my racing heart.

"No, They don't usually hang out in big groups unless they are feeding. Hammerheads are solitary animals."

The goat trail takes a sudden dip as we turn a bend, and I feel the smooth soles of my sneakers slide over hard marbles of goat dung and loose grit. If I fell on my backside, I would not be able to stop myself from sliding into the sea. I should have taken up Carol's invitation to stay with her for the day.

Paul's voice is soft and calm behind me. "You know we've had science boffins from Wellington up here to study the hammerheads. A couple-a-years back an Aussie film crew flew into town to do a story on them. They reckon this is an annual mating ritual."

I give a nervous giggle in reply.

"Don't worry, I'll grab you if you look like you are going to fall," Paul calls to me.

I peer down at the water below us once again. "Are you sure this is safe?"

"Shit, I'm joking, Yayoi. You're doing fine."

21

The big man sits on the edge of the slippery rock shelf, dangling his legs in the swell, taking slow, deep breaths. He pulls the mask over his head and bites down on the rubber mouthpiece of the snorkel, pauses for a moment to gaze into the blue depths below him, then steps off the rock. Seconds later, he pops up and sucks in a lungful of air and flips back beneath the surface.

The sea is calm around the rock. It quietened on our arrival. I don't trust it at all, but I steel myself to enjoy the adventure. I peer down into the depths, and I see him colored in fractured lines of green and yellow light. He's clinging to the rock shelf. "I can see Rawiri!" I call out.

Bill squats beside me and stares into the clear water. "He doesn't waste any time, does he?"

"Half fish, half-man," Paul says in admiration. He stands next to Bill, holding his mask to his face, and does a backflip off the rock.

"I'm out of practice," he sputters when he surfaces. Bill drops in beside him and comes up coughing. When he recovers, he gives me a thumbs-up before he dives to chase after Paul.

I slip off my running shoes and walk to the edge of the rocky ledge when Bill and Paul break the surface together, both sucking in lungfuls of air, then they are diving again. I watch their bodies descend dappled in green light for some two yards until they vanish beneath the overhang.

I am alone listening to the damn sea slopping and splashing against the shelf. I look at my hands and see they are bright pink. The sun is vicious. The floppy cloth hat Carol gave me barely covers my bare shoulders. I take out the tube of sun cream from a side pocket of my jacket again and rub it over my bare skin.

Bill is the first to clamber out of the water. Paul surfaces after and holds onto the rock with one hand, gasping for air. His forearm is striped with red scrape marks. "Hey, Yayoi, can you take this?" His gloved hand comes out of the water holding a crayfish. The tail snapping uselessly in the air.

I screech and fall back onto the rock.

Paul laughs with delight at my shock and hands it to Bill, who grasps the creature delicately by its blue antenna and drops it into the plastic net sack at his feet. He wipes the saltwater from his face and clears his nose. "The bastards move into the cracks fast. They are so difficult to catch."

"Rawiri is still down there, isn't he?"

"Yeah, he hasn't come up yet, " Bill replies. "How long you reckon he's been under, Yayoi?"

"Maybe two minutes. Is that possible?"

Bill shakes his head. "That's a decent set of lungs!" He peers into the water. "I can't see him."

Paul slips his mask over his head and pushes himself away from the rock shelf. We watch him perform a slow spin with his arms outstretched before he brings himself upright and breaks the surface with Rawiri beside him.

Rawiri coughs and gasps for air. His eyes are glazed, the whites pink with blood, and for a time, he just stares at us as if we are not there at all. Then he lets out a whoop and raises his arms over his head. "Look what I got for the table!" He holds a blue spiny crayfish the thickness of one of his forearms in both hands. "Whoppers, eh?" He chuckles. "It's getting harder to find the big fellers."

"Shee-it." Bill takes one from his hand.

"Awesome!" Paul exclaims. He reaches over to grasp Rawiri by the forearm to help him out of the water but the big man shakes his head. "Nah, I'll break your back, bro."

He launches himself onto the rock and lands on the rock like a majestic bull seal. He wipes a towel across his face and over his matted hair, then gazes down at the net bag. "Sweet as…"

"How do you do it?" Bill asks.

"I'm persistent," Rawiri tells him.

"I guess those little bastards will always out-persist me," Bill replies with a shrug.

Rawiri pulls on his T-shirt. "Yeah, well—I've been diving since I was a puppy." His face crumples into a smile. "That's the secret sauce."

Rawiri told us he wouldn't be joining us for lunch at Uncle Hemi's. He had promised his wife he would be back home in time to babysit while she went to netball practice. So we drop him back outside the front gate of his house.

A small runny-nosed child with long tousled red hair runs out the open front door and down the path with his arms outstretched.

Rawiri leans over-the-top rail and reaches down to the kid and hauls him up and over the gate. The child squeals and grabs at his daddy's hair as he's gently placed astride the broad shoulders.

Rawiri calls out to the Bill and Paul. "Tell Uncle and Aunty I'll drop by next week. Okay?"

"Yeah, will do," Paul replies.

"Outstanding, bro," Bill says through his open window. "They are going to be rapt when they see their dinner."

It isn't long before we are in the hills and on the way to the farm. I reach into my bag and switch off my phone.

22

The Hilux winds its way through a gully edged by thick native bush. The heat in the cab has steadily built up since we left the coast. Paul has kept his window open so to enjoy the moving air. He strips off his shirt, presses it into a ball, and pushes it into the small of his back while holding onto the steering wheel with the other hand. For the rest of the journey, he drives in his black singlet with one tanned hairy arm dangling out the open window. "Love it," He says to no one in particular.

"It's a bit windy back here," I complain.

"You might as enjoy the free air-conditioner for the moment," he says. "Over the rise, we hit the gravel road, and from then on it's windows up all the way."

Minutes later we are trailing a dust cloud behind us. The fine grit leaks into the cab even with the windows closed, and I breathe through the cotton sleeve of my shirt.

"I always thought you and Carol would have moved to Auckland by now," Bill says to Paul.

"If you hang around here long enough, you might find that you want to stay here too," Paul replies. "Opuhunaki is home, bro. It's not sweet all the time, but it's not all bad either. We love it here, so why move? Why don't you consider working the farm with Hemi for a spell? That'll give you time to think about what you do next."

Bill glanced at Paul then turned to gaze out his side window.

"Farming is not a bad life either," Paul tells him. "I reckon over the next few years we are going to see a lot more farmers driving Mercs."

Bill turns to pull a face at him. "Dream on."

"Dairy farming might be where you can make big bucks. Lease some land, start with a couple of cows, and build the number up. Make money. Buy the land. That's how you get started."

"You make it sound so easy," Bill mutters.

Paul slows the Hilux as we come to a neat wooden rail fence. We pass a large signboard announcing the Kingi Family Dairy Cooperative, and Paul pulls off the road and into a long gravel drive.

Uncle Hemi's home sits atop a rise. The house is old and grand. The iron roof and tall brick chimneys blackened by a century of winter fires stand starkly against the rolling green backdrop. It's a splendid farmhouse all the same with the weatherboards glistening under a fresh coat of white enamel.

The old hedgerow almost runs the length of the homestead. We reach a group of corrugated iron buildings. A dusty car and an old jeep hide in the shadow of one of the buildings. In the next shed along, a tractor stands next to ancient rusting farm machinery. Paul turns the truck in front of a stable and parks under a large European tree.

I can see the grave drive continues past a galvanized farm gate and up a rise to some lonely looking sheds in the distance.

An old woman pushes open a gate in the hedge and gives a friendly wave as she walks up to meet us. Her gray hair twisted into a bun and spiked through from the top with a bone comb. Bill opens the truck door and hops out. "*Kia ora*, Aunty Margaret," Bill hollers his voice filled with affection.

Her brown hands clasp his wrists, and she pushes him back to gain a better appraisal before she embraces him. "*Kia ora*, Billy Manning. Look at you!" She exclaims. "You are bigger than the last time you were here. Welcome, home."

"He's twice as stupid too," Paul says, and he kisses the old woman on the cheeks.

"I have just about given up on you lot making it in time for lunch," she says.

I close the truck door behind me.

The old lady suddenly notices me, and she pokes Bill in his chest. "Well, introduce us."

"This is Yayoi, Aunty."

"I am pleased to meet you, Aunty Margaret."

Her face crinkles into a warm smile. "*Kia ora," she says.* Come here and give me a hug." When she pulls me to her chest I discover she is much stronger than she looks. "I suppose Paul drove like a mad bull all the way here."

"He drove quite well," I tell her with a laugh.

"Doesn't sound like Paul," she replies. Her eyes have never left me, flicking over every detail of my face, capturing a sense of why I'm here.

"Hey, Aunty," Paul calls from the back of the truck. "Wait until you see the catch!"

He reaches under the blue plastic cover in the back and pulls out the net bag, holding it aloft, saltwater dripping over his feet.

She claps her hands in delight.

He drops the bag on the grass and lifts out a crayfish for her to see. "Fresh from Makara Point," he says proudly.

"*Kapai!*" She utters in wonder as she looks into the crate in the back.

"Rawiri caught two of them," Paul tells her.

"There were heaps of hammerheads on the cliffside," Bill adds.

"You boys were careful though?" she asks, raising her eyebrows.

"Rawiri said it would be okay," Bill replies. "They were busy around the other side in front of the cliff. They didn't pay any attention to us at all."

"I'll put these in the pot for lunch," she says lifting out the dripping crate. "We'll eat the roast beef for dinner tonight."

"The roast will do fine for lunch," Paul says, resting his hand on hers. "Save these for your dinner."

"There's enough here for breakfast as well," she says over her shoulder as she starts for the house. "*Haere mai kite kai.*"

"Where's Uncle Hemi?" Paul calls after her.

"He's up in the milking shed with Atawai and Haimona," she calls back to him from the porch. "How about you boys go up there and tell him to get a move on if he's hungry. He'll be telling stories to the youngsters because milking finished ages ago. Tell him to stop stuffing around." She turns to look at me. "Hey, girl, come on inside and tell me all about yourself."

Aunty Margaret slides off her shoes at the kitchen door.

"We do the same in Japan," I tell her cheerfully as I place my own by the door.

She picks up the crate again. "Just a minute and I'll sort these out before we sit down to a cup of tea."

I follow her inside and watch her empty the crayfish into the sink. The creatures clatter around as the fresh-water splashes over them, frantic to escape. She opens a huge polished metal refrigerator and slides out a plastic drawer. By the time she lifts them out to place them into the chilled drawer, the fight has already left them. "Ngaire is visiting me. She's in the living room if you'd like to go in and introduce yourself. I'll be in with a pot of tea to join you both in a minute or two."

We sit around a wooden table in front of the bay window, sipping the hot brew and not saying much. I concentrate on the loud ticking of an antique clock on the sideboard, feeling the two women studying me. Just when I am beginning to feel awkward, Aunty Margaret places a warm hand on my arm and taps it with a forefinger. "I can see something is going on with you and Billy."

Ngaire brings her hand to her mouth and chuckles. "Mākere, you are going to scare the poor girl."

While Aunty Margaret was in the kitchen Ngaire and I talk. She told me they are cousins. She is eighteen years younger, and endures the old couple treating her a lot like a granddaughter. She's also the mother of the two boys who are outside with Uncle Hemi.

"We are not together!" I say attempting to end the interrogation before it begins.

"You be careful he doesn't take advantage of you," Aunty Margaret tells me. He didn't learn a lot in Auckland," she say, shaking her head. She turned to Ngaire. "All they ever did for him was pack him off to boarding school."

I have no idea what she's talking about.

Ngaire nods her head in agreement and takes a long sip of her tea.

Aunty Margaret sets down the half-eaten biscuit, and she smiles her eyes seem to dance like she's about to tell me a joke.

"He wouldn't like me saying this to you."

Ngaire giggles as Aunty Margaret's grip on my hand tightens. She lowers her voice to a whisper and leans her head close. "I'm telling you this just in case. You know?"

I nod my head in reply.

The old woman releases my hand and taps it again. "I bet he hasn't said anything to you about him and Hemi," she says. She picks up her cup and watches me over the rim as she sips.

"No," I say.

"Hemi made mistakes with Billy," Aunty Margaret continues. "They argued a lot. The old man is stubborn. No one will ever get the silly bugger to admit to those mistakes if he doesn't want to."

"It would be good if they could just make up," Ngaire says turning to Aunty Margaret.

I smile politely and swallow my tea in silence. I wish I was in the milking shed with Bill and Paul. I stand up and excuse myself, telling them I must check to see what is going on. In case I'm offending them by leaving the table, I quickly add that I've always wanted to see a New Zealand milking shed. I tell it's probably because I'm a farmer's daughter.

They look at me with sympathetic expressions and Aunty Margaret tells me to pass on the message that she expects them all to come down to house immediately or lunch is canceled.

23

The cows meander down the dirt lane from the milking shed, following the fence line back to their paddock. They stroll along, taking their own good time as though lost in their daydreams.

On the top of the hill, I can make out two figures leaning over a metal railing in front of the long open tin-roofed shed. The men appear engrossed in their conversation. Shoulder to shoulder, their heads almost touching, as they share their thoughts. Once I draw closer, it's clear why they are standing so close to each other. The noise from a thumping diesel engine together with the syncopated rhythm of reggae combines into a cacophonous racket that resonates off the corrugated metal walls.

A stocky gray-haired man pushes a long pipe gate across the wet concrete surface. Uncle Hemi's face is half-hidden under the shadow cast by the broad brim of his sweat-soaked stockman's hat. He pauses after closing the gate to thumb his hat up enough to allow a draft of air to cool his shiny brown head. His large blue eyes peer at me under long bushy gray eyebrows, and after he's seen enough, he drops the hat back in place. "Hey, Atawai!" He calls out. "Haimona! Turn off the main."

I hear the disembodied voice of a child over the noise. "Okay." The music stops and after a time so does the engine.

The old man greets me with a wave. "Phew! It's a hot out, eh?" He pulls a crushed packet from his top pocket and shakes out a cigarette into his callused palm. He sticks it in his mouth and bites down as he lights up. He glances across at Bill and Paul. "It must be lunch. You two hungry?"

The two men nod together.

"Mākere will have a meal on the table, so we better get a move on." He looks up at me.

"Hello," I say.

He nods in reply and smiles at me, the creases around his eyes deepening, and walks on by past me toward the parked cars.

"A man of few words," Bill says with a chuckle.

Two small boys appear round the corner of the building hooting and hollering as they run. They circle the silver Hilux before they run straight into Paul. The boys step back and square up to him and laugh when he makes a show of blocking their punches. The three dance around each other until Uncle Hemi hollers for them to stop.

The old man stands by the driver's door of his small red open-decked truck and slaps a leg in his impatience. "Come on. It's time to eat."

The older boy's mouth hangs open. "Awl, let us go with Uncle Paul!"

Paul points down to the cow manure all over the boy's gumboots. "Aren't you going to brush the cow shit off first?"

Haimona looks around for something to wipe his boots. "Yeah, I was gonna do that."

"Mine isn't so bad," Atawai says gazing down at his jeans and gumboots.

The old man eyeballs the boys. "Hurry up!" He shouts, pretending anger.

"We wanna go with Uncle Paul," Atawai cries out.

"You will get cow shit on Paul's shiny new seats," the old man says. He stabs his finger at the opposite side of the red truck. "The two of you get over here, right now or you're walking back."

"Go on," Paul laughs, slapping the back of the eldest boy.

"Awl, shii…" Haimona moans under his breath. He grabs his brother's hand and pulls him to Uncle Hemi's truck.

"You stayed for cookies and tea, didn't you?" Paul asks me with a broad grin.

"I told them I was giving you two the hurry up," I reply.

"Hear that?" Paul asks Bill. "She came to give us the hurry up."

The two of them look at each other and laugh, and I feel my face burn. If there's one thing I hate it's being made fun of. "Did I say it wrong?" I ask Bill.

"No, you said it right," Bill tells me. "Only, that's exactly what Aunty Margaret always says."

Paul turned to me. "She's recruited you, Yayoi. That means she's taking a liking to you."

Uncle Hemi is sitting on the wooden steps of the porch, pulling off his gumboots when Bill walks up the path after securing the farm gate. The old man slaps the sodden socks on the edge of the floorboards and grabbing hold of the veranda post the pulls himself upright.

The shine of the artificial foot poking out from a trouser leg catches my eye, and I find myself staring at the faded orange-pink of a plastic limb until I realize what I'm doing and look away.

The plastic foot makes a clicking sound on the boards as he limps to the door. He pauses there to glance back at Bill. "Are you still driving that old Datsun?"

"It's a Nissan."

"Thought you'd be earning yourself enough to buy a new car by now."

Bill grimaces and flashes a sheepish smile at the old man. "I'm still paying off my study loan from the government."

"You must be doing alright with the company," the old man asks, looking at Bill with a quizzical expression that said he knew something was up.

"I finished with them on Friday," Bill says and looks down.

"You quit?"

"Hell no. I was made redundant."

The old man shakes his head and pushes open the kitchen door. "Well—come in and eat then you can tell us about all it."

24

Later, when I'm back at Paul and Carol's house, Shizue calls to tell me our office received a call from the Japanese police who are investigating a possible kidnapping in New Zealand. My husband made the complaint in person at a local police station. Nori has upped the ante in his game of cat and mouse.

She tells me J-Big has reassured the police that I haven't been kidnapped, that they still have contact with me. I guess they are letting me know through my PA that they don't buy into Nori's kidnapping story. Shizue pleads with me to send her my address. I send her a thank you text, but I don't send her the details she wants. I don't want Nori to know any more than he already does. I don't trust J-Big to keep my address from him, even if they promise Shizue that they won't tell him where I am.

. . .

The rows of kiwifruit vines in the orchard enjoy a tropical microclimate on the slopes below the house. There, the air barely moves between the high shelter belts. When Carol and I return to the house after a long walk through the orchard, we are both red-faced and perspiring. We leave the men to their conversation at the table in the living room and sit together on the front doorstep to sip our long glasses of orange juice over ice chunks and enjoy the early evening breeze that cools the top of the hill.

Carol tells me how she and Paul have struggled through many tough years of mortgage repayments to the bank with little return coming in from their meager harvests. She tells me how they had to keep borrowing to pay for tractor breakdowns, building repairs, and new seedlings to plant, when season after season of crops continued to suffer from the kiwi fruit virus.

She rolls the side of the chilled glass across her forehead, then turns to give me a wistful smile. "A life like yours must be wonderful," she says, popping a ringlet of gray-streaked hair behind one ear.

I shake my head. "No, you don't want my life. Always having to put up with people wanting to know every little detail about your days and nights. A celebrity in Japan is lucky to have any secrets at all. "

We laugh together like sisters. Even if she doesn't have much idea of what I am talking about. At least, she doesn't probe me for details.

My phone rings on the bench inside the house, and I run in the door, but before I even glimpse the display, I get the sinking feeling inside that tells me it's Nori. I stop at the table. My gut was right once again. When I turn around, I see Bill watching me.

"Could be important," he suggests with a grin.

"It's him," I reply.

I walk out the door and pick up my glass from the step.

"You hungry?" She says to me and gets to her feet. "Come and help me make dinner. It'll be fun."

"I'm sorry, Carol-san, I need a few minutes by myself."

She gives me a puzzled look. "Sure, okay."

I close the bedroom door behind me and stare a long while through the glass at the haze enveloping the fruit trees. I sit at the edge of the bed and gaze at the red dot beside his name. I know ignoring him will only make things worse, so I tap the screen to read his text.

Are you too busy with your boyfriend to answer my calls? I know where you are staying. I will see you there tomorrow.

He has to be bluffing! How could he possibly know where I am? I text him back and tell him to not be so stupid. I tell him I won't be here when he arrives, that I'm leaving tomorrow. So, he need not bother making the long trip. I add that I will see him when I'm good and ready.

I probably shouldn't have added the last bit.

A half-hour has passed since I sent the text. There is only the ghost of daylight remains in the evening sky as darkness falls on the orchard. I don't know how long I've been sitting on the bed when Bill's knock on the door snaps me out of my thoughts.

Without waiting for a reply, he peeps around the corner at me. "You okay? Can I come in?"

"Yes, sure," I look down, not wanting him to see my teary eyes.

"Carol wants to know if you're going to eat dinner with us. Are you hungry?"

I hear him closing the door. He's chewing over what to say to me.

What can he say? He knows I want to go with them into the mountains.

I look up and see him standing there looking awkward with his hands thrust in the pockets of his cargo pants. He is eyeing the phone I left lying beside me on the bed.

"You can talk to me if you want."

I don't look up.

"If you feel like it," he adds. "You know you are acting a bit weird."

"*Gomenasai.*"

"I should go back to Japan," I say, and I force a smile to my face. "I think it best."

"Best for who?"

"Bill-san, I'm very sorry for causing you trouble." I didn't mean the words to come out as a whisper, but they did.

Shit! I'm sniffling like a baby.

I rub the heel of my hand across my face.

"Hey, perhaps it will help if you tell me." He hesitates a moment before sitting down next to me on the bed. "Tell me what's wrong."

I notice him looking at an old teddy bear sitting slumped over at the end of a shelf of children's books across the room. At the other end of the shelf is a faded photo in a wooden frame of a smiling young couple. They watch two toddlers playing beside a parked car. The pride in their faces is obvious.

"Nori won't accept I have left him. It's as simple as that."

"He rang you?"

"He sent a text telling me he knows where I am."

"How——? What an idiot!"

"He's a jealous man."

"Do you think he will turn up here?"

I shake my head.

"No, he won't do that—but just in case, I think I must leave. If I could go into the mountains with you…" I glance across at him.

"You can't," he says, leaping to his feet. "It's not a weekend hiking trip. We're on a hunt."

I know that it's a ridiculous idea, but I have to get out of here, and I do want to spend time with him. I don't think I've ever met anyone like him before.

"And it's dangerous!"

"Not as dangerous as he may be to me."

"What are you talking about?"

I tell him how Nori had insisted I meet with him at my hotel, and then I tell him that Nori struck me.

"You have to go to the police."

"Why can't I go with you tomorrow morning?"

"Because—it's—dangerous!"

"I would be with the two men who know exactly what they're doing."

"No. You won't be with us, because we will be chasing after our dogs. Where they go we go too. That means sliding down slopes and into gulleys so steep you can easily break an ankle or worse and running through bush that tears your skin. Does that sound like fun?" He stops to take a breath. "A wild boar will do serious damage to you if it can. The only way to escape them is to find a tree you can climb—that's if you are lucky enough to find the right one before the boar reaches you."

"You're just trying to scare me."

"No, I'm trying to give you the facts. You get lost for days. Do you have any experience in the mountains? You can die out there."

"I can wait for you to return to your campsite, can't I?"

He puts his hand on my arm. "It's better that you stay here with Carol. She's looking forward to getting to know you. Tomorrow you both go to the police station and report you are being harassed. That should put an end to it."

"I want to go with you."

Bill shook his head. "You are so stubborn! Why don't you ask them what they think?"

Carol glares at Bill when she sees my reddened eyes.

"Tell them," Bill urges me.

After reading Nori's text tonight, there's nothing any of them can say that's going to change my mind. So, I steel my resolve, and I give them the story I told Bill. When I've finished, we watch Paul cut lumps from a block of melting butter and layer the thick slabs of yellow fat over his white bread.

"The mountains are nothing like you imagine," Paul tells me. "The tracks get washed out after a hard rain. Sometimes we have to get off our horses and walk through the mud. It isn't supposed to rain over the next few days, but if it does, we will have to wade through streams that will rise fast. A flash flood can sweep you off your feet."

"Can you swim?" Bill asks.

"Yes, quite well."

"Why can't Yayoi stay at the hut while the two of you go on your hunt?" Carol asks Paul.

Paul folds the buttered bread and takes a bite, chewing slowly and swallowing with loud gulps. He glances across at Bill while he eats.

"Can you ride a horse?" She asks me.

I nod my head again. "Good enough."

"Well, guys, what's the big problem?" Carol asks the men.

"You are going to get very dirty and smelly," Paul tells me.

"I told her it isn't safe, but she still wants to go," Bill says.

"I'm sure I'll be safe with you two," I tell them.

Bill grimaces and slumps in his chair. "Okay, I give up," he says and turns to me. "But don't say we didn't warn you."

"Jeez, Yayoi, you are full of surprises," Paul says with a shake of his head. He slaps his hands on the arms of his chair and gets to his feet. "Right! I better give Uncle Hemi a call. We're going to need another horse."

25

We sit around Uncle Hemi and Aunty Margaret's table, looking at the empty dishes.

"*Kapai-kapai!*" Bill slaps his stomach contentedly. "That was an awesome meal!"

Aunty Margaret nods her head happily.

"Has this one hunted before?" Uncle Hemi asks, pointing his finger me.

"I'll be fine, Uncle Hemi," I tell him indignantly.

"Girl, you've no experience in those hills," Aunty Margaret says, shaking her head. "It's best if you leave it to them two."

I give her a small bow from where I sit. "Thank you, Aunty Margaret, for your concern. I trust Billy and Paul will look after me. I'm sure I'll be okay."

I notice Bill frowning at me.

The old man works his tongue around his mouth to dislodge the food caught between the gaps in his teeth.

He turns to Paul. "Take my dogs. Just make sure you don't bloody well use your rifle when they bail. I want them back without any extra holes." The old man belches loudly.

"Why don't you go into the mountains by helicopter?" I ask them.

"There are plenty of tourists that hire choppers to take them in. They are looking to get a trophy stag head. They shoot them from the air. There's no sport in it. When you're hunting pigs, like these two are, you need dogs. And a knife is what you need when you end up in the steep gullies where the dogs corner the pigs."

Bill rubs his hands together. "Hope we get a big old boar."

"If you smell them, you might! But by hokey, they're smart. They are fast too. If they think they're cornered, they come at you like that!" He thrusts his hand like a knife at Bill's stomach. He points out the bay windows. "You can take the one with the black-tipped ears. But you got to keep him in line. And Bilbo next to him is a good one! Take her as well."

"What's the white dog called, Uncle Hemi?" I ask.

"Dunno," he said, waving his hand in the air. "Got him as a pup from the neighbor's bitch last year. Pretty useless right now. I haven't had a chance to train him properly."

Uncle Hemi turns to Bill and Paul. "Blackie will clamp onto an ear," he says. "Then Bilbo goes in and grabs the pig by the snout, and holds on tight. You might want to bring Whitey with you and try him out." Uncle Hemi's piercing blue eyes fixed on Paul. "Make sure you take the Kevlar jacket for Bilbo and put it on her every time before you go out. I don't want her getting ripped up. Don't forget!"

"I won't," Paul answers nodding his head.

"Blackie can have the collar," Uncle Hemi says. "It'll do for him. Billy—you watch out when you go in to stick the porker. Cause—I seen big porkers that will gore you, even with the dogs all over them!"

"In case you forgot how to hunt, Uncle Hemi means," Paul adds with a hoot.

Suddenly the lines of the old man's face deepen, and his eyes sparkle as breaks into loud laughter. "Yeah, that's right. You can get out of practice."

"They will head straight for your balls, right Uncle?" Paul asks him, grinning at the old man.

"That's right," Uncle Hemi says laughing hard. "No little *tamariki* for you."

Paul raises his eyes to the ceiling. "Carol wouldn't like that."

"You leaving it a bit late for kiddies, Paul," Aunty Margaret tells him.

Pauls pulls a face at the old woman. "We're still trying, Aunty."

The old man frowns at the change in subject. "Just finish it quick with your knife."

I know I can't back out now, and my stomach is a knotted ball.

Bill rolls his eyes. "Yeah, those boars sure make a mess of the dogs," he says, taking a noisy sip from his mug.

Uncle Hemi gives a solemn nod of his head. "Fucking oath they can!"

Aunty Margaret fixes Uncle Hemi with a withering glare. "Old man, you don't use that language in my house!"

We hear Ngaire laughing in the kitchen.

Uncle Hemi waves his hand at his wife and lowers his voice to a conspiratorial whisper. "Did you two hear about that bloke over Parata Ridge? He got himself gored by a boar!"

"He had a big hole in his leg," Aunty Margaret says. "Lucky he made it to a house with a phone."

"Watch out for the young ones running between your legs if you get below them," Uncle Hemi informs me with wide eyes. "Their tusks slice as clean as a knife. So you end up like this!" The old man raps with his knuckles on the plastic leg beneath the cord fabric. He glances at me and chuckles at the look on my face.

"And big ones just hit you like a truck," Aunty Margaret adds.

"Did you boys hear what happened to old Fiedler?" Uncle Hemi says, and not waiting for a reply he breaks into wheezy giggles. "I was talking to a bloke in town, and he said it wasn't even the pig that did the damage. Old Fiedler lopped a ball off with his own knife."

"He's always rushing in," Aunty Margaret adds as she gets up from the table with a stack of plates.

"We'll be taking the more cautious approach," Paul says, grinning at Bill.

Uncle Hemi jabs a thick forefinger down hard on the table. "Now, here's the thing." He looks sharply up at me to make sure he has my attention and draws an imaginary line across the surface towards his stomach. "It doesn't matter if it's sow or boar. It's going to run downhill looking for cover. And—if it's an old bastard, it will probably see you as one of the top dogs in the pack that's chasing it. That means it will make a line straight for you!" He turns to Bill and Paul. "So, my advice is to leave the old boars alone." He peers through the glass at the sky. "Youse'd best get on your way if you want to make it to the first hut on the flats before dark."

26

Bill and Paul size up the three horses. A big unhappy gray stallion twists its muscular neck against the orange braided plastic rope, securing it to the rail. Two smaller horses pull at the grass around the base of the fence behind him, chewing contentedly, not close enough to catch whatever is afflicting the gray.

"You boys watch this one," Uncle Hemi warns as he runs his hand down the flank of the stallion. "He's a bit touchy, but he's good on a hunt. Once you let him know who's boss, you'll be fine."

"I'll take him," Bill calls out. He's on the other side of the car, packing his saddlebags with supplies.

Paul stands by the old man and shakes his head. "Could be a handful for you, bro."

The old man's fingertips brush the edge of the straps around the horse's girth. He passes his hand under the belt. The animal stamps the ground, and Uncle Hemi straightens up like a much younger man. He grasps the buckle and tightens the strap one more notch. The horse rears and kicks.

"Hey, calm down!" Uncle Hemi roars. He grabs the reins and jerks them down hard enough to pull the horse's head into his face, so close the two are eyeballing each other only inches apart. "Don't you try that on me!" The old man's thick muscles standout on his forearm as his grip remains steady.

The stallion rolls its eyes, and it flares its nostrils. The veins stand out along its neck as it braces its legs, whinnying a warning before it wrenches itself free of the old man's grip. Then it seems to give up, dropping its head and shaking its mane. The protest is over for the time being.

Bill takes the reins from the old man and places a foot in the stirrup, ready to swing his leg over the gray's back, but he has to balance on one leg when the horse snorts and steps to the side. He tries again and, this time his foot slides into the stirrup and he sinks into the saddle. Holding the reins high, he swings his mount around in a tight circle.

"Just take no shit from her," Uncle Hemi growls, his hands on his hips.

"I won't," Bill tells him. "We'll get used to each other, won't we, buddy?"

"Always make sure the straps are tight. He bucks hard if so much as a saddlebag slips on his flank." Uncle Hemi turns to me. "I have something to show you," he tells me.

"Oh, here we go," I hear Bill say under his breath.

I watch the old man walk through the gate in the hedge and stop at a lemon tree. He places his hand in the small of his back and stoops to pick up an object. He holds up the lower jaw of a pig with still shiny curved tusks protruding from either side.

Bill wheels the gray around and leans over the side for a look.

"Wicked, eh?" Uncle Hemi says to me. He cups his hands under the jaw like he might be showing me a precious trophy. "This is a boar that was sniffing around the sheds one evening three winters ago. I shot it right between the eyes."

Paul brings his horse around on the other side to inspect it.

"It came down off the hills, right?"

"Yeah. I don't know who was more surprised. Her or me."

Bill gives him a look, pretending surprise. "And you shot it with a gun."

The old man appreciated the jibe and smiled. "I wouldn't go near it with a knife. These days I leave all that kind of thing to you boys." He sets the skull down on the gate post. He turns back to the gray and lifts the Velcro top on the black canvas scabbard sitting under

Bill's knee. He pulls out the rifle and turns it over in his hands, squinting to see the details better.

"I've told him it's only good for goat and possum," Paul says with a laugh. "I even offered him one of my rifles, but he wanted to bring his shiny toy with him."

Bill ignores Paul, and watches the old man turn the rifle over again.

"A twenty-two caliber Marlin," the old man says, whistling his approval. "It's a real beauty."

Bill's chest swells with pride. He glances over his shoulder at Paul with an expression that says, I told you so.

Uncle Hemi chuckles as he holds it up in front of him. "This barrel must be longer and thicker than your donger, eh, boy?"

"Sure is," Bill nods, looking a little embarrassed. "I bought it from a South Islander."

The old man feels the weight in his hands. He places the stock against his shoulders and peers down the sights at the distant milking shed. "It may be a varmint gun, but you could bring a deer down with this if you were close enough. Maybe a young pig if you hit it just right."

He swings it around to line up a tree on the hill across from the milking shed. "It's a little heavy, but shit, these sights are good!"

"You'd have to be bloody close to bring down anything bigger than a possum," Paul says, not at all convinced.

"Well, sometimes, you get lucky!" Uncle Hemi says, sliding the rifle back into the scabbard. He looks up and winks at Bill.

Bill flattens the tab down with the heel of his hand. "Eat your heart out, Paul."

Paul rolls his eyes. Then he turns to me like he had forgotten that I was there the whole time. "Hey, are you going with us or not?

"Of course I am," I tell him, with as much certainty in my voice as I can muster.

"We better get going," he says. "She's yours." He points to the docile brown mare, saddled and ready on the grassy verge of the gravel drive.

"The last time I was on a horse was on a set," I tell him and give a nervous giggle.

The two men stare at each other.

"There was a handler nearby," I admit in a fit of honesty. "I never had a problem though," I add a little too quickly.

Paul shakes his head. "I thought you said you could ride?"

I grit my teeth. "I can…" I take the reins from Uncle Hemi and reach up for the saddle and my foot slips easily into the stirrup. I feel confident as I swing my leg over the horse's back, but my shoe catches on the edge of the saddlebag. The animal snorts and turns in a slow circle. I try again, but the horse keeps turning.

"Looks like we only need two horses after all, Uncle

Hemi," Bill tells the old man. "Yayoi can ride behind me."

"Better you switch with Paul then," Uncle Hemi tells him. He watches as the two men swap horses. "Don't forget to bring my saddles back," he tells them.

"We will," Paul replies.

I grasp Bill's outstretched hand, and he swings me up behind him.

Paul brings the gray beside us and punches Bill lightly on the arm. "You two look cozy. You know, I wouldn't mind you riding up behind me, Yayoi."

"I bet," Bill laughs.

"You're kinda gutsy to go into the hills with us," Paul says to me. "Don't you think, Bill? She is, eh?"

I glare at Paul. "Gutsy for a girl, you mean?"

Uncle Hemi is fastening all the catches of the thick, wide band of studded leather on Jasper in silence. He straightens up when he's finished to watch the three dogs run off barking and jumping over one another in a sprint to the end of the stable. Paul gives a piercing whistle, and they bound back to the horses.

"Uncle Hemi, what's its name?" I ask him as I pat the warm flank of our mount.

"Bennie," he says.

"Bennie—Bennie," I repeat. I smile at the old man, and then I see something in his face. Perhaps it is doubt.

We ride the horses down the drive and onto the grass strip beside the road. Paul shifts around in his saddle to look over his shoulder, and I turn to follow his gaze. We see the old man standing beside the farm gate with his hands at his sides. He's watching us without a word.

When I turn back again, he's still by the gate. A distant figure, standing at the end of the road. He lifts his hand, and I wave back.

27

The hut stands on the edge of the oval clearing, surrounded by forest. A simple structure of plywood walls and a tin roof, it's built strong enough to withstand the kind of wind and rain commonly visited on the area and painted green to match the forest. A lean-to to one side shelters a rail for the horses, and a neat stack of firewood piled against the wall.

The dogs pee their mark on everything upright and roll in the scatterings of horse dung around the hut. They snap at each other, playfully at first, but then they turn mean, snarling and snapping. Once the pack hierarchy is re-established, the dogs collapse in the grass to lick their sore paws.

Paul swings himself off his horse and pushes on the door. It hits the wall with a hollow bang, as he peers into the gloom a moment before he turns around again to survey the hills from the top step. "See the track past the chimney?" He says to us, pointing at a path leading down from the clearing to the slope and into the trees. "That's where we get our water for drinking and cooking. The river's down there."

I slide to the ground, pound my numbed backside with clenched fists to win some feeling back. The long ride has left me bruised and exhausted.

"How about we leave the saddles on?" Paul calls out to Bill.

"It might be worth a scout along the ridge," Bill replies as he surveys the hill range opposite the clearing.

"Yeah, I was thinking we might surprise a sow with its litter catching a late afternoon snooze on a slope," Paul says.

"How about we leave the saddlebags in the hut?" Bill suggests.

"I wouldn't worry about it," Paul replies. "Your horse is a lot lighter now."

"Hey, I got that!" I cry out. "I'm not so heavy."

They laugh.

I reach behind the door frame for the light switch to discover there isn't one. I take a step inside and stagger back out again to breathe the fresh air. It takes a few minutes before I can stomach the reek of wood smoke and old bacon grease inside. The only source of illumination in the hut is sunlight coming through the open door and a small window above a stainless steel sink unit. The furniture consists of a long heavy table, two wood benches, a bunk made of hewn wood planks with two thin black-and-white striped plastic mattresses strewn over the top platform, and a large chest on the floor. Four aluminum mugs and a large battered metal pot sit upturned on a thick slab of timber bench-top.

I step back outside into the sunlight and sit down on the top step with my back against the warmth of the wooden door frame.

"Will you be okay to stay here if we go for a short hunt?" Paul asks me.

"No problem," I tell him.

"We are going to trek across that ridge." He points to a large hill above the river bed. "We should be back before it gets dark."

"Okay," I say squinting against the glare of the sun to try to see where he's pointing.

"We'll start from other fork you probably saw when we came in, and then once we are on the peak, we'll work our way back across the ridge." He turns to check if I'm following him.

I nod my head silently. I'm too tired to complain.

Bill follows the line traced by Paul's pointing finger, chewing on his bottom lip.

"Whatcha think?" Paul asks turning to Bill.

"Yeah, let's do it," he says. Then he sits down beside me. You might want to take a nap on a bunk," he says. "Or, you could try your hand at catching a trout."

"Catch them with what?" I ask. "My hands?"

"That's what I said," he said and smiled. "You'd be surprised how easy it is once you practice a bit. The hard part is sneaking up on them. You have to be real slow and quiet." He uses his hands to show me how it's done. "Then, when they least expect it—you toss them over your shoulder and onto the rocks. Like this—wham!"

"You're joking, right?"

He laughs. "If you were hungry enough, you might surprise yourself."

"I would starve if I had to survive out here by myself," I tell him.

"Don't worry. We will bring back fresh meat." He grins at me and winks. "If we don't, well, there's always the tinned beans in our packs."

They spend a few minutes checking the straps on their horses. The gray animal snorts his annoyance and Paul quietly cusses him.

"Hey, do you want to ride my horse?" Bill asks Paul. "I'm heavier than you, anyway."

"If you want," Paul says. "He's a handful, though."

Bill shoulders his rifle and mounts the big gray, turning in the saddle to give me a cheerful wave.

I smile and wave back.

"Good luck with the fishing," Paul tells me as we reach the center of the clearing. "We'll see you soon."

The dogs have reached the edge of the forest. They lift their snouts and flare their nostrils to catch a sign in the light breeze. The leg muscles twitching as they stand alert, whining with excitement.

"They're onto a porker already," Bill calls out, already he's fighting to control the big gray wheeling under him.

"I bet it's a runaway bitch in heat," Paul says. He gives a piercing whistle to get the dogs to return.

Hemi's dogs gaze back at him, their tongues lolling from their ridiculous grinning mouths. Then they are gone, vanishing like sprites into the trees.

Paul curses at them, but they don't return. Jasper whines and yelps his frustration.

"Okay, go on then, you buggers!" Paul exclaims when he sees his own dog staring plaintively up at him. "Go on. Get!"

With a joyous grunt, Jasper bounds off.

"That's it," Bill yells. "We're off!"

"Hope you got a rocket under you," Paul yells to Bill. "Cause once we get up on the ridge… woo-hoo, the fun starts!"

Soon their voices are absorbed by the forest. I walk further past the fork in the trail. Their route through the trees betrayed by the lumps of broken moss and turned black slivers of the forest floor cut and scattered by the hooves of the horses. I take a few more steps into the silence, tempted to walk on after them. Suddenly, I don't want to be alone.

I decide to go back to the hut and take the track down to the river. I find it in minutes, my sneakers sinking into the thin layer of composted rotten leaf and twig matter. The trail collapses in places into a ditch. The bright orange clay chopped out by sharp hooves and washed out during the winter months. I learn to avoid the trenches. Better to be scratched by the bushes than to slip on the clay and risk a broken bone.

Before long, the trees thin out, and I hear the sound of running water. I see a grassy bank and a sand bar bathed in sunlight. A few more paces and I stand on the edge of a quiet lagoon. The long pool is fed by water splashing over a ridge of boulders beyond which lies the river, almost hidden from view. The place is peaceful and beautiful, and quickly I realize how tired I am.

I linger in the doorway of the hut, but the still-warm air inside is tolerable to breathe. The urge to sleep is over-whelming. I knock the dust off a thin mattress, pull it from the top bunk, and heave it onto the bottom bed.

The plastic surface feels sticky against my skin, but it doesn't matter. I'm too tired to care. I ignore the dust, and curl up like a cat with my head on my arm, and let sleep carry me away.

28

I'm damn sure I saw a movement. There it is again! A shadow runs across the floor and up the wall. I sit up and blink my eyes to clear them.

The hut door is ajar. Was I so tired that I fell onto the mattress without thinking to close the door? Did I close it or not? If I didn't, it would be most unlike me.

I rub my hands my arms and feel goosebumps. I reach over to my bag beside the bunk to find my jacket. Someone coughs outside the hut, the moment my feet touch the floor. I freeze for fear a board creaks under me. I take one step and then another as I inch to the door and the shack does not betray me.

A horse snickers in front of the hut, and I immediately relax. They would have opened the door and seeing me asleep, they decided to leave me that way for the time being. I put my pack down on the table and take a couple of gulps of water from my bottle, then tip a little into my palms and running my fingers through my hair. Heavy objects are hitting the ground. I'll do my best to hide my disgust when I see the bloodied pig carcass and praise their hunting prowess instead of complaining.

I notice the sun has slipped low in the sky. It is almost behind the hills. I must have slept for several hours. It's going to be dark soon. I notice a pungent blend of hay and horse sweat heavy in the still evening air. It smells oddly familiar and a lot better than the inside of the hut.

I walk out the door as nonchalantly as I can without looking up at them, readying myself for the sight of their kill. But I am not prepared for the sight of the two strangers. They are bulky men dressed in thick, dark woolen shirts that hang loosely on them. The late afternoon light runs in beads of gold down the barrels of their rifles they wear over their shoulders.

They are not looking at me, but I know they are aware I stand there staring at them. I guess if they had any ill intent, I would know about it by now.

The reins of their horses dangle in the dirt, but the animals are content to stand patiently while their riders attend to their tasks. One man pulls a blanket off his mount, and drops it on the saddle at his feet. The other man squats beside his horse, his broad back turned to me, peering down at a fetlock. The horse submits to its examination without fuss, content to pull on the grass within reach.

The younger man, tall and wiry, glances down at his friend and mutters a few words. When the other lifts his head, the younger man gives a quick nod in my direction. The man gets to his feet and turns to regard me with a serious countenance. He is a powerfully built with thick shiny hair that is gathered up tightly at the back in a short ponytail. His face is adorned by a magnificently thick mustache curling down over the corners of his mouth.

They are both of wild form and fierce appearance, and there's no getting away from it. I should be afraid, but I'm not. They look like have stepped out of a black-and-white photograph of two Japanese samurai snapped more than a hundred years in the past. Except that all three of us are alive in the present, in the mountains of New Zealand.

The grim features of the mustachioed man soften into a toothy grin. "*Kia ora*. I'm Tama," he says. "We didn't expect anyone to be here."

"Oh—I'm sorry." I hesitate before I step to the ground. "I am Yayoi."

Tama gestured with his thumb at his friend. "He's Noel."

Noel stares back at me with a distinct look of suspicion, then he gathers up the reins of both animals and leads them into the lean-to.

I stand to the side of the steps as Tama walks past into the hut without another word.

Noel throws the canvas saddlebags over his shoulder and stalks past me and up the steps in silence, but I catch a hint of curiosity in the flash of his dark eyes.

I sit down on a gray log lying beside the remnants of

an old fire a few yards from the hut. I've no idea what is happening. I'm sure Paul didn't mention anyone else would be joining us in the hut. My bag is still inside, and I wonder whether I should just walk in to claim it. Should I wait for Bill and Paul to return? If I were to run up the track they took I would surely get lost in the dark looking for them. There's a light shining through the open door of the hut and as I gaze at it, I see it glow brighter. Then I see Tama's large frame filling the doorway.

"Hey!" He calls out. "Do you want a mug of coffee?"

The light is from a hissing soot-blackened propane lantern they have hung from one of the beams. I sit on a bench seat they have pulled up next to the hearth and watch Noel feeding wood into the fire.

He ducks back and to the side to avoid the sparks that sometimes burst from the wood. He has a bud of black hair under his bottom lip and what looks like two days' worth of stubble on his shaved head. As I gaze at his back, I notice a long, angry pink scar that runs from one ear to the base of his skull.

Tama winces as he offers me a mug, holding it by the metal rim. "It's a bit hot," he complains. He shakes his hand when I take the mug from him.

The brew is milky and sweet. It is hot, but it tastes good, and I smile my thanks.

"It's from my thermos," he nods his head in the direction of a flask on the bench. "Made it before we left camp."

"It gets cooler up here in the evening, eh?" Noel says, but he doesn't turn his head.

"Yeah," Tama replies. "Not much of a start to summer so far, is it?" He grasps the leg of one of the two wooden benches under the table. "Let's bring that bench over to the fire."

I stay where I am, watching him drag over the other bench from under the table. He spins it around to line it up with the hearth and sits down heavily.

I get up and stand beside the open door. The fire is warm, and the tea probably tastes good, but I still don't know why they are here, or what they are doing in Paul's hut.

"Smells good!" Bill says as he stands in the doorway, and sizes up the two hunters.

"*Kia ora*," Tama says in greeting. "You're just in time for *kai*."

Noel barely glances at Bill only for a moment before turning back to his cooking task. He lifts the lid of the large battered aluminum pot he has hung on a thick wire over the fire and peers at the bubbling stew inside.

Bill drops a saddlebag on the floor, spilling water around the leather before it disappears between the gaps in the floorboards. He slips the gun from his shoulder, snaps the bolt open, and palms the round that springs from the chamber. He drops the bullet and the magazine on top of the saddlebag and leans the barrel against the wall.

"*Kia ora*," he says, finally returning the greeting. "I'm Bill."

"You don't recognize me?" Tama asks, leaning out from behind Noel to shake the offered hand.

"Ah… no."

"My youngest brother James was in the same class as Paul at High School. They used played rugby together. The same team. I used to see you at their game every weekend before I shipped out."

"Oh, yeah. I remember James!" Bill declares. "You were in the Army, right? I remember—you had a lot less hair back then."

"I looked more like Noel here, I bet," he says, pointing to Noel's stubbled scalp.

Tama catches Noel's eyes. It's brief. Almost as if something that isn't up for discussion at the moment has just been confirmed.

"*Kia ora*, bro," Noel says cheerfully.

Perhaps he's had a sudden change of heart. Maybe he takes a while to warm to anyone. But, he returns his attention to the burning wood on the hearth, poking a red ember back into the fire a blackened stick.

I feel Tama's eyes on me as I duck my head. I don't want him to know I saw the glance he exchanged with Noel.

29

"You got venison or pork outside?" Tama asks. "We saw you two up on the ridge," Tama tells him. "Your dogs were onto something, eh?"

Bill slips off the heavy leather belt around his long yellow checked Swannie jacket, the hilt of a long knife inside its sheath hits the floor with a loud clunk. "We shot a small boar. Paul has it across the back of his horse," Bill says. He hooks the metal buckle of the belt over the head of a thick nail behind the door. "On the way back, the bloody horse threw me off," Bill tells him.

"Looks like you missed most of the water when you landed," Tama points out. "Bad luck."

He pulls off his wet socks and tosses them against the wall next to his gear. The stink of wet wool and river mud from him is overwhelming. Then he sits down beside me "I guess we'll find it grazing along the edge of the river."

"It could be halfway home by now," Tama tells him.

Bill shoots him a glum look. "I hope not. Someone might catch it on the road. I don't want to lose the saddle."

Tama gets up and lifts the lid off the pot. "Looks like it's ready, cuz," he says. "Okay, let's do this," Noel says. He lines the metal mugs up at his feet, filling each to the top with stew, and carefully hands them out.

"*Chotto*, Bill-san. Do you have a spoon in your bag?"

Bill reaches into his pack and unfolds a small metal spoon. He locks it into place and drops it into my hand.

"You guys need sleeping bags or blankets for tonight?" Tama asks. "We got plenty in the chest." He gestures at a large black painted wooden box at the foot of the bunks. For the first time, I notice the chest has a heavy padlock that hangs open from twisted metal brackets.

"You own this hut?" Bill asks with a look of surprise.

"We do," Tama says between quick breaths as he blows on the hot liquid in his mug. "In a manner of speaking,"

Bill nods his head. "Got it."

"Anyone's welcome to use it—so long as they look after the place. Some people don't appreciate it as much as others." He pointed at the battered chest. "Paul knows he's always welcome, so that means you too, right?"

"Thanks," Bill tells him. "We appreciate it."

"No worries, cuz," Tama replies. He pats the pockets of his baggy bush shorts, finds the pocket he's looking for, and pulls out his tobacco. He pokes two large fingers inside the pouch and produces a thin packet of cigarette papers.

I watch them roll lines of tobacco in the palms of their hands.

Tama offers the tobacco to Noel.

"Nah, told you I quit, cuz," Noel replies and mutters under his breath.

Tama licks the edge of the paper and runs his fingers along the cigarette to seal it. He looks up at Noel with one raised eyebrow. "I notice you haven't quit dac," he tells his cousin.

"Yeah, that's right," Noel laughs. "And I won't be giving that up anytime soon."

Bill points a thumb over his shoulder toward the back wall of the hut. "That's a sweet stack of wood outside."

"Help yourself, cuz," Noel tells him.

"You two should get a little fire going outside and watch the stars come up together," Tama suggests with a smile.

"What do you think?" Bill asks me.

I shrug, and I'm surprised to see my disinterest disappoints him.

Noel picks a strip of scrap metal off the hearth and uses the end of it to slide the empty cooking pot away from the heat. He pokes at a battered kettle, pushing it across the ash-covered bricks until he has it positioned over the red embers. He gathers up the mugs and spoons in one hand, but Tama stops him.

"Cleaning up is my job," he tells him. He walks the

cups with water from a pot on the bench and swishes them around in the sink. He takes a rag from under the kitchen sink to hold the hot kettle and fills the mugs with the strong black tea Noel has brewed.

"Sorry," he says as he passes me a mug of tea. "We don't have any milk."

Bill stands up and walks over to his saddlebags by the door. "Well, as it happens, I do have something we can enjoy in our tea." He pulls out a large bottle of rum and waves it at us.

Tama eyes the label. "Bundaberg!"

Noel smacks his hands together. "It's OP, eh?"

"Yee-up," Bill says happily.

Noel gives him a thumbs-up. "Good one, bro!"

Bill breaks the seal on the cap and spins it with his thumb sending the metal top tumbling into the ashes at his feet.

I pick it up from the hearth, blow off the ash, and put it in my pocket. Stupid man He'd get badly drunk if he drank the bottle, even with some help from the other two.

He pours several shots into Noel's mug and then into Tama's.

"She—it!" Tama exclaims, raising his hand. "Two fingers are enough. You're going to give me a headache."

Noel laughs. "That's not your attitude when you smoke da herb, cuz."

"Good bud is a whole different story," Tama nods his head in agreement.

Bill pours for Noel and turns to me with the bottle in his hand.

"No-no," I say, shaking my head. I'm not at all comfortable about getting drunk with three guys when I'm in the middle of nowhere. Especially not when I have only just met two of them a few hours before.

"One wee shot isn't going to hurt anyone," Bill says gleefully, and he pours into my mug, ignoring my protests.

We raise our mugs together and drink.

"Paul should be kicking back in the hut on the flats by now," Bill says.

"With your horse, you hope," Noel laughs.

"Yeah, I hope so," Bill says and takes a long sip. "So, where are you two planning on heading?"

"We're heading for the flats," Tama says to Bill. "And from there to the ranges out the back."

Noel draws deeply on the marijuana he has rolled for them. I watch them pass the joint around until it's nothing but a sticky brown stub.

Tama taps me on the arm.

"Hey, do you know the story about how Stumpy got his name?"

I can feel Bill tense up beside me. "Awl, don't tell that story."

"Who's Stumpy?" I ask.

Bill looks at me with an expression that begs me not to expect an answer from him.

"Tell me," I plead when I see the delight in the faces of Tama and Noel.

"That's Uncle Hemi's nickname," Bill says unhappily.

Tama waves a hand in the air to still any further interruptions. "Back in the day, they used dynamite to blow stumps out of the ground to clear land for cattle grazing."

"Big stumps!" Noel adds.

"From the original forest," Tama nods. "That's right. Anyone who knows Hemi has heard how he used some of his dynamite to catch fish in the river. He would wait until the fuse burned almost to the end, then he'd toss the stick into the middle of the stream. Bang!" He says, throwing up his hands. Any around fish just floated up to the surface. They were stunned or dead, you see? All Hemi had to do was wade out and scoop them up with his net, eh?"

Bill groans. "Awl, please-please don't tell this story."

Tama ignores him Bill's protest and continues. "One early morning, Hemi was at his favorite spot, a little further around the coast. He and his ten-year-old boy."

"He had this old flat top Bedford truck, right, cuz?" Noel asks.

"Yeah, that's right," Tama confirmed. "It was a battered, rusty thing, but he saw to it that it never broke down."

"Yeah, old Bedfords keep on going forever," Noel says, nodding his head enthusiastically.

"The kid's playing behind the truck. And Hemi, he's been drinking rum for breakfast."

"Would have been whiskey," Bill interjects.

"Whiskey—anyway, he—"

Bill interrupts again. "He was drunk."

"He'd have a bottle in his pocket. So, the routine was to take a swig and throw in a stick," Tama continued.

Bill gazes into the fire and nods his head in confirmation. "That's apparently what he did, alright."

Tama gets to his feet, his back to the fire, and he starts acting out the story. "He waited until the fuse burned almost to the end just like he always did, readying himself to throw it. Then he steps on the whiskey bottle he's dropped, and it rolls under his feet. The next thing he knows, he's lying on his back. Whaaa…? He sits up and sees the stick of dynamite beside him. The fuse is almost burned into the stick." Tama gazes around at his audience with the melodramatic flair of a seasoned storyteller, his thick black eyebrows jumping like excited caterpillars.

Bill groans once again and scowls.

"He hits it with his hand but he doesn't knock it far, so he kicks and—kaboom!" Tama claps his hands together and I jump. He drops to the floor, acting out Uncle Hemi struggling to sit up. "The smoke clears and he looks down and it's—hey!—No foot! He's blown it clean off."

"Stupid mistake," Noel says.

"So Hemi is hopping around like this," Tama says as he mimes the injured man.

"Nah, he wouldn't be doing that," Noel says, shaking his head. "He'd be lying on the ground screaming in pain."

"Alcohol is a good anesthetic," Bill says, grim faced.

"Yeah, it is that," Tama says. "So—then Hemi pulls the belt from his pants. Makes a loop with it and straps it around the stump. He has the kid pull it tight and help him to the truck." Tama turns to me. "You know, the little bugger is hardly tall enough to see over the dashboard, but he drives all the way back to town with his dad bleeding all over the floor of the truck." Tama imitates a child peering over the dashboard of the truck as he steers it on a winding route.

"He was lucky to be alive!" I say quietly.

"He was," Bill agrees. He glances at me. "The ten-year-old was Paul."

Tama laughs. "Yeah. Ol' Hemi. He's going to live forever."

We watch the two men pick up their gear from the floor. They buckle the belts over their outer garments, the contents of the square leather pouches rattling. The dull metallic clink that ammo makes.

Bill gets up from the bench. "You're not staying the night here?"

"We're off to the DOC hut," Tama replies. "It's only an hour up the river." He grins at Bill and me. "You two should sleep well after that rum, eh?"

He's out the door and down the steps before either of us has the chance to reply. Noel turns and nod his goodbye to the two of us.

"You know, we don't mind sleeping on the benches, or the floor," Bill jumps to his feet. "We can sleep outside. You two don't need to go."

"Nah, we were planning on being further ahead anyway," Noel says, and he walks down the steps.

We listen to their horses snorting and stamping in anticipation, and their hooves clattering across the clearing. When they are enveloped by the forest there's only the sound of our breathing.

Bill tosses a piece of wood into the fire. It sends a cloud of sparks exploding up the chimney and the flames jump over the top of the embers. "That should keep the fire going," he tells me. "It'll keep the mosquitos outside. It'll get chilly soon."

"Why didn't they stay?" I ask.

"I don't know. Maybe they want their own space."

He gazes through the open doorway of the hut. "I'll tell you one thing, though. I'm surprised they didn't have their dogs with them. They must be after deer. It's not deer hunting season, but I guess they don't care about that. I would've known there were hunters in the hut if pig dogs had run up to check me when I rode in."

"Maybe they are still in the forest—like your horse, Bill-san."

He laughs. "Hey, you are the cheeky one! How about we take a look at the river while there's still some sunlight?"

"Good idea. It's really hot in here, and I'm feeling a little dizzy."

30

"Watch out for the ankle breaker," Bill tells me. He pointed to a tree root as fat as a man's leg looping out from the side of the sticky clay. Long sections of the trail were little more than a trench where the ground has been chopped by horse hooves and washed away by the rains during the long winter months.

"*Kuso!*" I exclaim as I slide on the slick surface and catch a layer of dirt on my backside.

"Told you," he says.

"Oh, shut up!" I tell him.

He waits for me where the undergrowth becomes tall. The black, burned looking shrub spikes straight up from the forest floor. Sharp branches catch my clothing and scratch any exposed skin, but it is the final barrier to the river, and it doesn't last long. We emerge out of the scrub, walking side-by-side listening to the sound of flowing water rattling and splashing through the valley, and there it is.

The narrow lagoon shimmers through the trees, the horizon of smooth rounded boulders providing shelter from the breeze coming down the river. The last rays of the sun shine through the leafy canopy above us, striking the shifting crystalline surface and playing with the shadows on the stony bottom.

Bill barely stops to pull off his boots, then his socks as he wades out until the water is lapping his knees. He looks back at me. "Aren't you coming in?"

"I don't have a towel."

"You don't have togs either, but what does it matter here?"

"Togs?"

"Americans call them a swimsuit."

I crouch down on the bank, crossing my arms over my knees, and resting my chin on my forearms, and sniff my T-shirt. It stinks. "Are there hot springs up here?" I ask.

"You'll be surprised how warm this water is!" He assures me.

I peel off my shoes and socks, roll up my cargo pants, and wander to the edge of the water to dip my toes. "This is cold, Bill-san."

I am surprised to see he's on the bank again and stripping to his boxer shorts. I turn away quickly. Then he runs by me and dives into the pool. I shriek and stagger back to onto the bank, water dripping from my face, hair, T-shirt, everything. I'm soaking. The idiot!

He emerges at the furthest point of the lagoon among the exposed roots of the trees, wiping water from his face and laughing as though he was looking at the funniest thing he has ever seen. "What are you waiting for?" He calls. "Jump in."

I wring the water from my pants. "I was going to do that—before you splashed water all over me!"

"Oh, come on," he laughs.

"I'm not going to now," I yell. I try to sound angry, but his grin is infectious. "No, way," I add a little lamely.

"We are both very stinky," he tells me. He screws up his nose to show me how just how stinky he thinks we are. But he has stopped laughing. Perhaps he's worried that I really will walk back to the hut. "This is only the first day, and we already smell like horses," he adds.

He's right. I strip off my cargo pants, placing them over a dead tree trunk, and toss my T-shirt on top. I cross my arms over my chest and glance back to see that stupid little-boy-grin of his. "Can you not stare at me?"

I can feel myself blushing—dammit!

"Sorry," he says, and he disappears below the surface.

I walk in until I am submerged up to my waist and sink down to my chin, searching with my toes for small round stones. When I find them, I roll them under the soles of feet and begin to work the soreness out them. He's right. The water already feels warm. It was a good idea. I feel the grit of the day falling away from me, and I close my eyes. I open them again to find he has snuck up on me. I splash water at him as he draws closer, but it's a halfhearted effort.

"I would prefer a hot spring," I say.

He scowls and slaps his neck. "Little bastards," he exclaims.

"They're not biting me," I tell him.

"Not yet, but they will if you come over here into the shade."

"No, thanks."

"Then I'm coming over to you are."

He only stops when he's so close we could touch toes.

"I will bite your nose," I warn him taking a step back.

But he ignores me, leaning forward to kiss my cheek.

"Quit that, Bill-san."

"What's with this 'san' you keep calling me?"

"What should I call you then?" I ask, but I don't wait for an answer. I push myself off the river bottom and swim out into the deeper end of the lagoon where the water does a slow swirl under the bank. I turn to face him again. "How about I call you Billy?" I giggle.

He rolls onto his back without giving me an answer, floating under the green ceiling of leafy branches.

"Uncle Hemi and Aunty Margaret are nice," I tell him. Perhaps I've offended him.

"Yeah, they're alright—Uncle Hemi's my dad."

I hadn't expected him to tell me that. "You don't look alike," I blurt out, feeling stupid.

"We don't look much alike, but people say we have the same eyes?"

"Yes, you do. That's right!"

"My mother left when I was one," he says as he's talking about the weather.

"Do you keep in touch with her?"

"Not really. She moved back to Melbourne not long after I was born. I've thought of looking for her, but I figure since I've never heard from her, she doesn't want me to find her. Uncle Hemi raised me until I was seven. Then a couple from Auckland adopted me. That's why my last name is Manning."

"You don't remember your mom at all?"

"My mother? Only vaguely. Uncle Hemi married Mākere—Aunty Margaret when I was sixteen."

"If he's your father, why do you call him Uncle?"

Bill swam in a circle and stopped to face me. "He told me right after he filled out the adoption papers, 'from now on you call me Uncle'. That was what he said." He splashes water at the bank. "I call the Mannings, Mom, and Dad."

"Why did he give you to another family to bring up?"

I know I shouldn't ask, but he doesn't seem to mind talking about it.

"The state gave him no choice. Hemi was drinking. He got himself into trouble with the courts and he didn't bother to argue with them. He has a few convictions for things he did when he was drunk. So—the courts of the land made their decision because he never thought to decide for himself. He thought he was doing the right thing at the time. Mom and Dad Manning sent me off to a boarding school in Auckland as soon as I turned thirteen. I got to spend holidays with the. With Mum and Dad Manning I mean." He floats on his back with his arms outstretched as though he might embrace the scattered patches of sunlight. "I made plenty of friends at Boarding school."

I swim up to him and kiss him on the nose.

He blinks in surprise and stands up. For a long moment, we stare into each other's eyes, and suddenly his lips are on mine, and they are warm and soft. He runs his fingers down my shoulders and my back. Our chests and legs drift together, and his arms are around me. It feels good, but I quickly come to my senses and push him away.

"That was fun while it lasted," he says.

I shake my head. "That was my fault. *Gomen, ne.*"

He wades to the edge and walks onto the bank.

I stay in the pool for a short while, watching him sluice the water off his body using the edge of his hands. Then, I stepped onto the bank and did the same.

A cloud of mosquitoes quickly envelops us, and they are merciless. With our backs to each other, we smack at them uselessly. The kamikaze insects attack by the dozen, and we hurry to pull on our clothes.

I twist the river water from my hair and use my T-shirt to wipe my damp skin, sneaking a look over my shoulder at him. He's skinnier then I thought he would be, but he looks strong, with ridged stomach muscles, and strong thighs and calves.

"Ah... I don' know why I told you all that stuff," he says. Then he turns to catch me staring and looks at me in surprise. "We better get back to the hut before we are eaten alive by these little bastards," he says.

Caught out, I let my hair fall in a curtain over my eyes. Even so, I glance at him through the strands and see him pulling on his shirt and wearing that stupid grin again.

31

W e sit shoulder-to-shoulder on the doorstep, enjoying the warmth of the wall against our back. Silently sifting through our unstated declarations and conflicting notions. Gazing at the last rays of sunlight over the hills highlighting the tops of the grassy peaks across the river.

The cool high country evening air descends quickly when the sunsets. It feels like a frosty blanket settling over the clearing. I put on the cotton slacks Carol gave me to discourage the mosquitoes, but they find the fabric only a minor challenge.

"Let's bring the fire on the hearth outside!" He says with the enthusiasm of a schoolboy at Summer Camp. He walks to the lean-to, reappearing with an armful of cut branches he dumps on the ground in front of the log. Then he walks into the hut, and moments later, reappears in the doorway, holding a chunk of smoking wood.

"Out of the way!" He shouts, and he leaps off the steps. "This is bloody hot!"

"Stupid!" I call after him, but I laugh at his excitement.

"Oh, you think I'm stupid, do you?" He calls back at me. "Why don't you come over here and watch a skilled bushman at work."

I shudder from the chill as I sit on the log beside him. On his hands and knees, he places the smoldering wood in the center of the bare ash-colored earth and builds a teepee of fine twigs over it. When he's finished, he tilts his face so low his hair is in the dust and blows on the small structure until thick white smoke begins to rise. He keeps blowing, and suddenly flames burst from the kindling. He sits up and looks back at me, expecting my praise.

"You cheated," I told him.

"What do you mean?"

"A real bushman would rub two pieces of wood together to make fire."

"Yeah, but real bushmen don't live in the city," he replies.

We watch the flames flicker in the breeze for many minutes, without saying a lot. I think about what Bill told me. I just don't know what to say to him now that he's said all that. I don't know what kind of reaction he expected from me. It was more than I wanted to know or even needed to know.

Then, he announces he has an idea, and he walks off to the hut to return with Carol's red checked bush jacket. He drapes it over my shoulders and from behind his back produces the bottle of Bundaberg. "This is going to warm you us up!" He tells me.

"I think I had quite enough before."

"No—you need it."

"I need it?" I giggle. "Like how?"

"To take the chill away."

"I'll be sick."

"It's just a few drops," he says and pours a generous quantity into my mug.

"That's a lot of drops!" I protest.

"You will have a good night's sleep," he says. He quarter fills his cup and twists the cap back on the bottle.

I throw more wood on the fire, and we watch the shower of golden sparks as they rise to join thousands of pinpricks of light in the black expanse. "Oh, there are so many stars," I say. "You never see them like this in Japan. Not unless you're in the mountains. Even then, they never look so bright."

"Too much smog?" He asks.

"There is too much light from the cities and towns."

"Wait until you see the Milky Way," he tells me, pointing up at the firmament. "It'll come around soon."

"What about the Southern Cross?" I ask. "Where is it?"

"I'll be there along with all the other stars."

The breeze picks up and kicks life back into the dying

fire. I draw my knees up under my chin, pulling the jacket tighter around me, and give a long yawn. "I'm tired."

He passes the flashlight to me. "Here, you better take this."

I aim the white beam his way, and see that he's lying on his back in the grass with his arms behind his head. "Are you sleeping out here tonight?" I ask in surprise. "It is too cold."

"No, I'm going to lie here a while and watch the shooting stars."

"Really? Do you think there will be any?"

He laughs. "There are always shooting stars. Stay here with me we can watch them together."

"Bill, I'm so tired!"

"Okay," he replies with a laugh. "See you in the morning."

"*Oyasumi*," I tell him, wishing him good night.

His laugh is gentle. I like the sound of it very much. I am happy that he's disappointed I didn't stay with him. Maybe I should, but I really feel so tired.

The paraffin lamp is still hissing when I walk inside the hut. I look back and only just make out his face and hands reflecting the red glow from the fire. I wave to him before I shut the door, and he waves back.

I pick up a piece of wood from the hearth and place it carefully on the embers. I lean close and blow on them. The cloud of sparks hit my face like a thousand tiny pins. I sprawl on the boards, the acrid smoke stinging my eyes.

When I collapse onto the rancid sleeping bag on the

bottom bunk, and almost immediately I drop off to sleep. It's sometime later I wake to hear him open the door, and I watch him tiptoe across the floor through my half-closed eyes.

He stares at the ash scattered over the hearth and the floor, and finding a brush under the sink, he sweeps the debris onto the hearth. When he's done, he turns off the lamp.

I listen to him pad across the floor in his socks. The bunk above mine creaks as it takes the weight of his body.

32

My heart is pounding. I might have just finished running a race. That was a bad nightmare. I lie still on top of the sleeping bag, staring into the darkness as I control my breathing. Through my nose and out my mouth. Deep breaths down to my belly and out again.

I turn my head and see a gleam of moonlight running along the edge of the table. I wriggle out of my jacket and slacks and throw them on my feet, then find the open end of the bag and snuggle inside. It stinks of the sweat of men and probably their dogs as well, but I don't mind.

"Yayoi—are you okay?"

"Yes," I reply. My voice sounds small and uncertain like that of a child afraid of the dark, and I clear my throat.

"You screamed," he says.

"Oh, did I? *Gomen*. It was a bad dream. That was all."

I hear him shift about above me. "You want some water?" He asks.

"I don't want to get out of the sleeping bag," I tell him.

He swings his legs over the end of the bunk, landing with a thump on the boards. "It's okay. I'll find my bottle."

He pads over to the door and picks up his damp saddlebags. "I have a spare flask someplace here," he says, rummaging inside them. He squats beside my bunk and passes me the flask.

He's close enough I can feel the warmth of his breath on my cheek. "It's just water, right?" I ask, reaching out a hand until I bump his and take the container from him.

"Just water," he says.

I take two small sips and hand it back.

He stands beside the bunk and takes several gulps. The aluminum cap squeaks along the thread as he screws it back in place. He drops the bottle on the floor. "I used to have a lot of bad dreams when I was a kid," he says.

"What about?"

"I was always in a car being driven through a forest. The road overgrown by trees and it was dark. There was someone I never got to see chasing us. We were always being chased."

"Who else was in the car with you?"

"My mom. My Australian mom. I don't remember ever seeing her face in my dream. That's weird, I kind of remember it when I'm awake, but I never can when I dream."

I flick back my hair as if he were able to see me do it. "Was it always the same road? The same forest?"

He hesitates before pulling climbing back into his bunk. "I can't remember."

I can see his profile silhouetted in the moonlight and feel his eyes on me.

"You should try to get some sleep," he says. But still, he doesn't move.

"Do you still have those dreams?" I persist.

"No, not anymore."

"Oh."

"Are you going to be okay? It's chilly standing out here."

In the moonlight I can see the angles of his face. The shine of his eyes. I feel my skin tingling. "Why aren't you wearing a shirt?"

Couldn't I think of anything cleverer to say than that?

"These sleeping bags are meant for winters. It's too hot inside for inside them this time of year. But it's bloody cold standing out here half-naked!"

I can see him wrap his arms around his chest.

"You do look cold."

He pulls down his sleeping bag. It falls over his head and he curses softly. He scrunches it up and walks over beside me. "Move over," he says. "And don't worry, I won't try anything."

I shuffle across the mattress surprised that he just

comes out and tells me to move over, and even more surprised that I let him.

He spreads the open sleeping bag over his feet and lies still beside me.

"Do you have enough room?" I ask.

"No," he tells me with a chuckle. "It's bloody cramped. Do you mind if I stretch my arm out? You can use it as a pillow. That's if you don't mind."

"Mm, sure," I reply. I lift my head and he slides his arm under it. Then he rests his hand on my shoulder. For a while, I am sure he's going to try something, but he doesn't. He just falls asleep.

I listen to his slow steady breathing, and in the dark I stroke his curls, and rub the ends between the tips of my fingers. His hair is softer than I imagined it would be. I want to taste his lips, but instead, I brush mine against his forehead. He doesn't stir.

I wake to the sounds of the entire wood instrument section of an orchestra playing in the clearing. The dawn chorus of native birds is a combination of bells, chimes, and throaty bassoons.

He stirs beside me, and slides quietly off the bunk and pulls on his clothes.

The latch on the hut door lifts, and minutes later, I hear the clatter of wood as he drops an armload on the hearth. I half-open my eyes at the click of a lighter, and hear the dry kindle crackling as it catches fire. I listen to him pouring water from the pot filling the kettle and smell the crisp spicy scent of the wood gum in the crisp air.

When he hear him walk outside again, I jump to the floor and stretch my arms out above my head. It takes me a minute or two before I realize, it's gone awfully quiet. I feel the vibration in the air moments before I can hear the dull thumps beating the hut like a drum. The sound of a turbine engine bouncing off the hills. Then I hear the rotor blades as they cut through the vortices of churned air they create. The machine is hovering above the clearing.

He is standing behind the saddlebags he has laid on the grass to dry in the morning sun. His rifle lies at his feet, beside the cloth he was using to clean it.

The shiny red monster floats above the center of the clearing, but it doesn't land immediately. The pilot takes it up again and does a wide sweep over the line of trees. Midway across the clearing, he comes back on a steep incline and stops a few yards from the front door. Beneath the cockpit, ash forms into tiny twisters in front of the log we had sat on together.

"That pilot knows what he's doing!" Bill shouts to me over the shrieking machine.

I don't reply or move. I know what I'm looking at. It would be hard to mistake a McDonnell Douglas Explorer for any other kind of helicopter. The chunky single-engine turbo has no back-mounted tail rotor. The thing is big, being large enough to carry six passengers. Why should such a beautiful and expensive machine land here?

The pilot throws the kill switch and the whine of the turbo ebbs.

A thickset bearded man wearing wrap-around black sunglasses drops out the door as lightly as a cat. He turns and pulls down a set of steps. Although the rotors are high above his head, he still stoops under the spinning blades.

This doesn't feel right. The man standing guard by the door doesn't move to greet us and I can see his mouth is set in a tight line. Even though he still wears the shades, I know his eyes are fixed on Bill. A second figure appears in the door, and my stomach sinks as I watch my husband step down from the cockpit.

33

I think about running into the trees to hide in the forest, but I don't. I run into the hut and slam the door shut behind me.

"Yayoi, bolt the door," Bill calls out from the other side of the door. "Don't let anyone in!"

"I can't see a bolt," I cry out. "What can I do?" It doesn't matter much what I do, because if they want inside the hut, I can't stop them. I'm trapped. I back myself up to the end of the table.

Bill bursts burst in, a frozen scream of anger on the bone-white mask of his face. A thin red bead dribbles from his nose and tracks over his top lip. He smears it with the palm of his hand. "The bearded fucker snatched my gun off the ground," he screams. "Right in front of me!"

The door creaks open, and we see the bearded man

standing cautiously on the second step with only his hand inside the room. When he sees we are the only people in the room and that we have no weapons, he removes his sunglasses, slipping them into his shirt pocket, and steps inside.

He blinks his pale eyes in the low light to get used to the dim light. Then he gazes around the room, taking note of the broken chest, the two bunk beds, and finally, he directs his attention us. Satisfied with what he sees, he examines his fingernails and stands where he is with his feet apart, nonchalantly picking each in turn. There's a total lack of interest on his face. It is as if Bill and I were not present at all.

He's dressed in a short-sleeved cotton shirt, casual slacks, and black cross-trainer shoes. He might be about to take a Sunday stroll on the ocean boardwalk. All he needs is a straw boater to complete the outfit. He might be in his late thirties or even his early forties. He has the weathered skin of a man who has spent a long time squinting under the glare the sun with deep lines that stretch from his eyes to his mouth.

Someone has taken a cheese grater to the side of his face. A mass of thick scarring runs from the cheekbone down to his chin, and there are several long, deep nicks in his neck, like those the claws of a bear might make. It is not his best side, but he doesn't care.

He raises his head to gaze out the open door, to reveal large black letters, part of a partially visible word tattooed on his neck just above his shirt. A slight stockbroker's jowl and a thick girth betray a liking for rich food and probably for beer. But the heavily muscled body is not that of an office worker's.

When he moves it is in a straight-backed, efficient manner. I've seen bodyguard's move like that. The kind with a military background. The kind Nori used to like to have around him.

As if he knows we are staring at him, he glances up at the two of us and grins with obvious pleasure. He pulls back his lips over an expanse of broken chipped enamel. It's the jagged smile of a predator. But, it's only for a moment, because that's when Nori swaggers into the hut just as he would if it were his office.

Nori's eyes settle on the two sleeping bags scrunched together on the same thin mattress. He sniffs loudly and stalks past Bill without so much as a glancing at him. He pulls a bench out from under the table and brushes the surface with the edge of his hand, and sits down.

Nori presses both palms flat on the tabletop and gives Bill his best sharp straight-backed bow. "My name is Shimano Noritake. I am Yayoi's husband."

He intones the words slowly and deliberately. Acutely aware of his own stilted and heavily accented English, he does his best to avoid a mistake. He must have been practicing those opening lines for days.

Nori clears his throat and gestures with a small movement of his hand, inviting Bill to sit beside him. "*Dozo,*" he says softly. "Relax, please," he adds in the awkward machine-like way he has when speaking English.

He wears his shoulder-length black hair, glistening with camphor oil, and swept-back against his skull and tied at the back with a small topknot. The *chonmage* was the preferred style adopted by Japanese male artists twenty years ago. College students and character actors today have brought it back into fashion amongst intellectuals and artists. Nori is not among the first group, and I haven't seen him with one since the time we first met. Perhaps he's trying to impress me. If so it won't work. He probably thinks he's acting out a scene from one of his movies.

The passing years have not been kind to Nori. In the harsh cast of morning light, his skin looks as though it's drawn too tightly across features that might have been cut from stone. His cold heart finally reveals itself in his face. How fitting.

He slides to the end of the bench and gestures once more for Bill to sit down next to him. Gentleman Nori. Gentle Nori.

Bill presses closer to me. He refuses to sit down.

When the bearded man lays a hand on his shoulder, Bill shakes him off without lifting his eyes from my husband. It's a big mistake.

"Sit down!" The bearded man barks, and this time his hand comes down heavily on Bill's shoulder to force him onto the bench beside me.

"How did you know where to find us?" Bill asks Nori.

Nori returns him a thin smile and reaches into the inner pocket of his windbreaker for his silver cigarette case. He turns it in his hand, enjoying the feel of the etched surface before he opens it. He always goes through the same ritual whenever he weighs a decision. My husband is a book I have read many times over, and it turned out to be boring the first time I reached the end. Poor Nori is a narcissist, and as a result, he is entirely predictable. I would have warned Bill if I had ever known they were going to meet.

Nori offers Bill a cigarette and snaps the lid shut with a shrug when it's refused. He taps down the end of the cigarette on the tabletop. I almost have to stifle a giggle. He is a caricature of a Hollywood movie gangster. A De Niro character who makes each draw of nicotine look as though it hurts. I watch Nori squint and cock his head, as if he was examining the cigarette he holds between thumb and forefinger in minute detail while, of course, still thinking deeply about the topic at hand. It is such an elaborate routine, I'm sure he isn't even aware he's doing it.

"How did you know where——?" Bill begins again.

"Easy," he says, cutting him short. "My wife can't seem to leave home without her iPhone."

He studies our faces with his gangster squint, allowing the words to sink home, and when he turns away to blow a stream of smoke, he watches as the toxic swirl unfurls.

The situation feels like it might easily spin out of control. I try not to look at Nori because I am afraid I will burst into giggles. I find him funny in a way I haven't before, but at the same time, I also want to get up and run because he's terrifying. "Is that how you knew where to find me?" I ask Nori. "My *keitai?*"

"That's right," he says switching to Japanese. "I had others trace you because I couldn't do it by myself. It's easy to find the people you need if you know how."

"But I turned off my GPS," I said in English.

The bearded man leans over to me. "Triangulation," he says, in a mocking voice.

The corners of Nori's mouth turn down. His *gaijin* employee's uninvited contribution has irritated him, but his eyes never leave me. "Japan and New Zealand both have hills and mountains making tracing your phone more difficult, but it's still no problem for the right people." He gives a vague wave of his hand as if not wanting to burden me with technical details. "And, certain officials were helpful once we explained the situation."

"We?"

"The company explained to them," he says. "I explained."

I had always suspected that J-Big would eventually line up beside him. His family pulls their strings after all. I was right to be cautious, yet it did me no good. "And what situation are you talking about, Nori?"

"They located the town. Then the house. I paid two locals to find you. Perhaps one of your friends even knows Tama-san and Noel-san. I told them to organize whatever they needed and they found a satellite phone. So, you see? I was able to track you right to this dump."

His expression is the picture of smug self-satisfaction. "They are—how do they say it in English." He glances across at Bill. "Ah, yes— my eyes on the ground," he says.

Bill turned to me.

"Did he just mention Tama and Noel?"

I nod my head in confirmation.

"They work for him too?" Bill asks me in astonishment.

Nori leans across the table. *"Hai! Sou desu."* He switches back to English.

"You never had a chance. I pay them to find you. The pilot, Tua-san is also a local. And Rick-san—he has special talents. It is easy to get help when you can agree on the price, and the price was cheap. They all work for me," he says matter-of-factly, raising his eyebrows and opening his hands as if anyone with eyes could see as much. "You know—what they say? Money talks."

34

W e can hear the sound of metal grating and clanging against metal as the pilot tends to the helicopter. Inside the hut, the hot tin roof expands under the sun even at this early hour, creaks and cracks noisily. Nori flicks the sweat from his brow and stands up to peel off his windbreaker. He folds it carefully before placing it on the table and moves close enough to me that the stink of tobacco on his breath makes me want to retch.

"Why him?" He hisses in Japanese. "Don't tell me you are content with this shit-hole to stay in? Why do you think you can up and leave me—just like that? Do really think it's that easy?" He gets to his feet and turns his back to us, staring out the tiny window over the sink with his arms folded. After a minute of silence, he swivels around to stare at me. "Are you too tired to talk?"

There's a sudden rawness to his tone, and I know he expects me to reply, but then he shifts tactics. "Anyway, it doesn't matter now," he says with a sigh. "At least I have you back again."

"We're not together!" I shout in Japanese.

Nori blinks in surprise, then I see the blood drain from his face, and he comes back twice as mean. "You talk to me like that in front of them?" He exclaims spitting out the words between curled lips. "You bitch!"

"You can't make me go back with you," I shout, getting to my feet to confront him.

"You behave like a child," he hisses, his face inches from mine.

"Oh, you have to be talking about yourself," I say. Then I take a step back, shocked at my outburst. I realize with a sudden stab of fear where this argument is going. It's too late.

He grabs my face between thumb and forefinger with a force that jerks my head back. The veins in his temples look as though they are going to burst as he presses his contorted face to mine, daring me one more act of defiance.

Angry tears well up in my eyes, but I bite my bottom lip in an attempt to regain control. "You can't make me!" I shout.

"We are going home together!" He bellows, spitting out each word. He releases his grip on me, and I fall back against the bench.

"Don't you hurt her!" Bill says in a low, guttural tone I haven't heard before. He steps in front of Nori and gives him a push before the startled minder can separate the two men.

"Bill-san," I say, grabbing his wrist. "It's okay. I will go back with my husband."

Bill jerks his arm free of my grip, and I jump to my feet, desperate to pull him back from Nori.

Rick gets there faster and stands in front of Nori, chest-to-chest with Bill, blocking him, with his chin jutting and his lips set in a thin bloodless line. "You, sit down right now!" Rick bellows at Bill. Not waiting for his directions to be followed, he shoves Bill to the bench.

But Bill bounces back onto his feet just as quickly as Rick pushed him down.

I grab at Bill's arm once again, but he's already moving forward, and he jerks his arm free of my hand once again. "Bill-san! Please. Do as he says."

"Last chance!" Rick says, stabbing an index finger at the bench. "Sit down!"

Bill swings his fist in a wide arc. Too wide. Rick is ready, and he's fast. He moves without expending any more energy then he might squashing a fly. He shifts his weight to the side without moving away from Bill, deflecting the blow with a casual flick of his thick wrist. At the same time, he flicks the back of his hand into Bill's throat. It makes a sound like a soft slap.

Bill coughs and gasps as his legs collapse under him. He falls forward into a straight forearm to the chin. I hear the clack of enamel against enamel, and Bill's head snaps back. When his body hits the floor, it's with the dull thud of a shop mannequin toppled in a department store.

Rick bends over the body and pulls back one eyelid to peer at the pupil, and then pulls back the other. He straightens up to gaze down at his handiwork, as if to take a trophy picture in his mind of the damage done. Then, without a word, he drags Bill across the floor and out the door.

I am on my feet, but I am unable to move from the spot. I hear Bill's boot heels bounce off the steps. The chopper door slides open, and Tua cursing loudly.

Nori looks as shocked as I am. The rapidity of events caught him by surprise. When he moves to the door, I launch myself at him, screaming, and pummeling him with my fists and feet. I want to hurt him badly, and he barely attempts to fend me off. He stops on the top step, and when I try to push past him, he turns to grasp my wrists so tightly, try as I might, I can't wrench my hands free.

"Everything is fine." His voice is much calmer than it should be. But, if everything is fine, why doesn't he look at me? "We will take him to a hospital. You don't need to worry."

I stop struggling, and he lets go of me. I push past him, only for my legs buckle under me, and I fall to my knees and vomit. I am only faintly aware of him gathering me in his arms and carrying me to the helicopter.

35

N ori tells me Bill is lying on a bench at the rear of the helicopter as he buckles me into the copilot's seat. I plead to sit with Bill, but it is like talking to a robot working through its program of algorithms. His mind is made up, and nothing I say moves him.

Tua glances at me across the cockpit. It is the vague curiosity shown by someone who is committed to doing a job. His eyes speak of experiences he would rather not talk about. Not ever. They are set deep in a thin face framed by graying curls that might once have lent him a boyish look. However, the lines around his mouth speak of years of steeling himself to all types of extremes, most of them probably terrifying. He turns his attention back to his instrument panel.

I concentrate on the noise of the helicopter as it springs into life, counting off each stage of the takeoff. I find refuge in routines, and right now, that's what I need

to do. Each mechanical note is a thin thread attaching me
to sanity.

One. The tick-tick of the igniters.

Two. The whine of the starter.

Three. The thud of fuel into the engine.

Four. The vibration of the rotors picking up intensity.

Tua brings us around in a sharp climb over the clearing, and the hut becomes a small box below. I feel the old
fear return as I realize how thin is the metal skin of the
helicopter. That's all the protection we have, should the
machine fall from the sky. Years of training and bundles
of my father's money has not conquered my fear of
heights. Only the exhilaration of being in control of a
helicopter could overwhelm the dread. Long before I
became a professional singer and an idol, I dreamed of
becoming a chopper pilot.

Now I am only a passenger, and I realize that is all I
have ever been, ever since Yaya was created and Yayoi
was crushed. Me. I. Yayoi. I feel anger and I know I must
hold on to it. Anger is better than fear.

We descend in a twisting arc, and the familiar G-
forces push me into my seat. Below us is the river. The
horizon flips, and now the rugged slopes of the hills are
floating above my head.

"Look to the port side—ahh—to ya left!" Tua yells
into the mic fixed to his headset as he straightens up the
helicopter.

We are flying a little below the ridge. Paul is riding
along the trail close to the top. I make out the dark bulk

of the pig tied across the rump of his horse. The trail Paul rides on follows the line of the ridge, just below the hilltop.

Rick appears behind the pilot's seat. He's holding a long shiny object in his left hand. Unless I release my harness, there's no way I can turn to see what he's doing.

Paul gazes up at the helicopter roaring above. He's wondering what the hell the chopper pilot is playing at. The shadow of his hat falls over his eyes. He gives a friendly wave, squinting behind his outstretched hand, trying to better make out the pilot. Paul would know all those who were locals.

I can hear the pilot snapping at the voice in his headset. Someone in the back is not happy with Tua's flying.

"Hold on!" Tua yells into the mic. The engine roars as he takes us into a high climb at a diagonal. It ends in a sudden wall-plastering turn. We are heading down again. He is taking us to a position above and behind Paul.

I watch the small figures of the horse and rider zoom-up below us as the helicopter comes in fast and low.

The bay horse is terrified. It twists its head to see the source of the noise, staggering on the hardened edge of the narrow track, but it is able to regain its footing.

Tua holds the helicopter steady as he watches Paul turn the horse for the tree line.

There is the sound of the rear door opening behind me. I snap off my harness. As I rise from my seat, Tua turns his head and catches my eye. It is only for a brief second, but I recognize the look of a troubled man.

I hear a loud crack from the door, then Nori's voice shouting over the noise of the engine. I can't make out what he's saying, and I've never heard that tone outside of his acting. He sounds hysterical.

I pause by the window in the cockpit to glance down at Paul and see him drop his head and shoulders behind the neck of the horse. He hangs precariously over one side, his mount threatening to break a leg as it charges down the slope toward the safety of the forest.

"Hold on!" Tua yells for a second time into the mic.]

As he rotates the machine, I grab my seat with both hands to steady myself. I hear a second loud crack behind us. Then the chopper is soaring over the tree line.

Too stops the machine over the trees and rotates it so that we face hill top again.

I make it to the open door. We are hovering over some three yards above the rippling, flattening sea of grass. My husband stands in the doorframe, holding the rim of the frame above his head, screaming into the maelstrom. The words are unintelligible. He's focused on Rick who is securing a harness around a crumpled, motionless Paul.

I fix my eyes on the gap between the transfixed Nori and the edge of the doorframe. I hear, Tua shout a warning, but it's too late. I hit the ground hard, tumbling over the uneven slope. It breaks the impact, I roll to my feet, and run for the thicket of trees below the craft.

I stumble and fall, but quickly I'm on my hands and knees, scrambling forward, and springing to my feet again. I run faster than I have ever run, crashing my way through the first of the low bush growth, slipping and sliding down the slope. I bust a path through the tangle of undergrowth in front of me using my shins, thighs, and chest.

A tree branch whips my cheek, and unable to see through the tears, I stumble blindly. My foot catches on a stump, and the ground smacks me in the face. I smell moist earth, and stunned I lie still, listening for the noise of the rotors, dreading the craft breaking through the foliage.

I lift my head. I see a mass of ferns, tangled and thick in front of me, but I can also see that the slope levels off a little ahead. I get to my feet again, running on nothing but adrenalin, I no longer feel the sting of the coarse fern fronds that whack my legs and scrape my bare heels.

I fall face down again. This time into a matted carpet of damp rotting leaves. I twist my head to the side, but I can't hear a sound save for my breathing, the warble of the bush birds, and the clatter and splash of rapidly moving water. There is a bright light sparkling between the dark tree trunks. The river is just a few yards ahead of me. I get to my feet.

Where the fast-flowing floods have cut deep, the river-bank has dropped away in a tangle of roots that hang like mummified limbs.

Above the sound of the water, I hear them. The metallic rhythmic beating. The rotors shake the forest ceiling. Tua is opening breaks in the tree canopy so they can see me. I look up to catch the glint of reflected sunlight, but my eyelashes are full of grit. Fuzzy dots blot my vision. I rub my eyes with the sleeve of my shirt. That's when I panic. I am a deer in the undergrowth, aware too late that the hunter is on to me. I leap to my feet and sprint.

The helicopter swings in a low turn as I run along the edge of the riverbank, trying to keep what sparse cover there is between my pursuers and me. I know the lagoon is close. As I run, the noise of my pursuers fades. They didn't see me after all.

I duck behind a thick trunk and bend double just to get air into my lungs. Blood is pooling between my toes. I suddenly realize I am barefoot. I pull up a trouser leg and peer at the cut. It's long, but not so deep.

I strip off my clothes and step into the lagoon, and walk to the center of the pool where it is deepest. The heat of the sun has yet to warm the water, but it feels clean and soothing, like a balm soaking my torn skin. I crouch lower still until my shoulders sink beneath the surface.

Shadows are darting through the beams of sunlight. I watch the metallic flicker just beneath the surface as the trout chases its breakfast.

The air erupts overhead with the sudden and loud arrival of the machine. They must have swung around behind the hills before returning to the hut. They really did lose me.

The trees blanket the noise of the rotors as they touch down in the clearing. I listen to the sound of the turbine power down, and the doors slide open. I hear the raised voices of Nori and his hired thugs, but they are too far away to make out more than the occasional word. Nori's tone is urgent, and he sounds agitated as he argues with one of the men. I don't hear Bill's voice.

I spot the indents of my small narrow feet in the soft ground. My fresh footprints run down from the grassy bank to the water. If anyone comes down the trail from the hut, they are going to see them too.

The river laps at my nose as I press my knees against my chest. My heart thumps in my ears so loud I might not hear them coming down the forest trail.

36

I almost want them to find me. For the chase to be finally over. The minutes tick by, and there is no sign of anyone coming down to the river. Finally, I hear the unmistakable screech and thump of helicopter doors slamming shut, and it lifts off. They are in a hurry.

The beat of the rotors fades, and an overwhelming quiet settles over the valley. There is no movement in the leafy canopy and no birdsong. The only sound I hear is water bubbling over rocks.

I wade out of the pool and start to dry myself with my T-shirt. My teeth are already chattering. I pull on my clothes and sit down on the bank. I feel like I am in a vacuum where time has stopped and bury my face in my arms, the flannel shirt wet and rough against my cheeks.

It is the shrill cheeps of a bird darting around close my head that makes me look up. The tiny creature pivots on its fan of tail feathers before settling briefly on a branch, close enough for me to see the inquisitive black eyes. Now it's on the move once again.

I set off after my new guide as it flits through the dusty shafts of sunlight. Flying to and fro above the trail, it is always a few feet ahead of me.

The door of the hut is standing ajar. I pause at the bottom of the steps and stare at a dark, congealed smear on the dusty surface. I call out, but there's no answer. I touch my fingertips against the weathered door and give it a light push. A triangle of sunlight falls across the floor. There is a trail of small droplets glistening on the boards like beads from a broken necklace.

My fingers come away from the blistered green paint, sticky and red with engine oil. The bangs I heard when I was inside the craft would have been the sound of a mechanical failure. I was lucky the engine didn't seize.

I sniff my fingertips for the acrid smell of engine oil, but the scent is heavy, sweet, and rich. I touch it, and I see it isn't oil. My stomach contracts as I take a step back. I have to force myself to go inside.

A man is lying on the tabletop. His arms are at his sides. His legs are splayed apart. His head is turned away to the small window. There is a strange stillness about him, and I fear the worst.

He groans and coughs. "Is someone there?"

I recognize the voice at once. "Paul-san?" I ask, but I already know.

"Yayoi?" Paul calls out. "Is that you?"

I expect to see Rick's handiwork. A broken nose,

swollen eyes, and lips, a broken tooth or two. His face looks unmarked.

"I guess I lost Hemi's saddle, after all," he says. He stares at the square of light in the wall.

His shirt has been ripped open to the waist. Only strands of cotton hang where the buttons had been attached. Bandages wrap his chest, right shoulder, and right arm. But, even I can see it is a hurried effort. Blood already seeps through the cotton.

"Do you see my fingers? Are they moving?" I place my hand on his upturned palm to comfort him and lean over him so that he can see me.

"Are they moving?" He asks with urgency. "Tell me the truth!" He sees the answer in my face, before I can look away. "Nothing, huh? That's it then. I'm stuffed!"

"Why did they leave you here?" I ask, sniffling like a child.

He coughs, and his lips and chin speckle with bright red spots. "Maybe because they shot me. I don't know."

I stroke his cheek. "Can you feel this?"

"Feels good," he replies. He opens his eyes and smiles. "Can I have some water?"

I pick up Bill's water flask and bring it to his lips and watch the water trickle into his mouth.

When he coughs again, the whites of his eyes roll back in his head.

"Paul?" I ask, then I turn to look around as I hear a heavy object hitting the ground outside. I stand the water bottle on the table beside him and steel myself for the moment they walk into the hut, but instead, it's Tama's wide frame that fills the doorway.

"Is he alive?" He asks in a hoarse voice.

"Yes," I reply.

Tama leans over him. "Hey, cuz. I've found you," Tama says. He turns and grabs one end of the bench, slamming it against the side of the bunk. "The fucking bastards!" He exclaims.

"Uh—you noisy bugger," Paul tells him opening his eyes.

Tama's face is twisted as he stares at the floor, fighting to control his emotions. He turns back to Paul. "What'chu been up to, cuz?" He leans over Paul and looks him up and down.

"Oh—you know…" Paul says. "The regular stuff. Catching a bullet or two."

"I already checked with Rotorua on the radio," Tama says, turning to me. Tua called the medivac team. They should be arriving soon."

"Tua was flying the chopper?" Paul asked in a voice of disbelief.

"Yeah, I could hardly believe it myself," Tama replies. "I shouldn't be surprised. His *hapu* is seriously screwed-up."

Paul sighs, and he closes his eyes again. "Even so…"

Tama gazes down at the bandages.

"Hey, you don't mind if I check out the dressings, do you?"

"Yeah, I do," Paul growls. "But you are going to anyway, right?"

"Hold tight," Tama says.

"Okay," Paul replies unhappily.

Tama pulls the thick hooded bush shirt he is wearing over his head and tosses it over the upturned bench. Perspiration shines on his shoulders and arms, making his black woolen singlet stick to him like it was a second skin. With slow, careful movements, he lifts Paul's shirt and separates the flannel from the sticky bandages. Paul groans and then he falls silent.

Tama leans over the prone body for a moment then looks up at me. "He's gone bye-bye. Right—I'm going to start with his arm." He slips the blade of his hunting knife under Paul's sleeve, slitting the fabric up to the shoulder, he pulls the shirt away. As he unwinds the bandages, he tells me to stand beside him and pay attention. "You see this?" He points to a small round hole in Paul's bicep that is oozing blood. He turns the arm, peering at the strands of pink muscle that hang from the gaping exit wound. When he feels me slip back, he pauses and looks back at me, "Are you okay?"

I take a breath and nod my head silently at him.

"Good," he says. "Because I am going to need you to help me lift him." He re-wraps the bandages in a careful crisscross over the arm. When he's done, he pulls apart the sodden binding around Paul's chest.

We see a neat round puncture wound on Paul's right side. Tiny bright red bubbles gather as the air escapes in a fizz with each fall of his chest. Tama sucks in his breath and straightens up, "Oh, you've caught one in the lung. Shit!" He presses the palm of his hand down on the chest puncture.

Nausea is sweeps over me, and the room begins to spin around me. I reach out for the corner of the table to steady myself.

"Hey, don't you go and faint on me," Tama snaps. He glances over his shoulder. "I need you conscious, okay?"

I concentrate on each breath I take and count until the feeling passes. "I'm alright."

"Good. I can't take my hand away, okay?" He says. "Bring that over here." He points to a canvas satchel that hangs on a peg above the window. "There's a medical kit inside. I want you to empty it on the table."

I shake out a red nylon zip-up bag embossed with a white cross. Plastic envelopes of gauze pads, sticky sheets, and rolls of surgical tape tumble onto the tabletop.

He works quickly with the skill of someone only too familiar with tending to trauma wounds. As he treats Paul, he continues to talk to me as though he were sorting through a suitcase.

"Stand behind him and place both your hands under his head. Slide them along his neck. Until your fingertips touch his shoulders. Like this."

He shows me with his free hand. "Only you do this with two hands, Then you got to lift him, but you got to do that really slowly. Okay?"

I nod my head.

"Don't you drop him!"

"Okay."

I take Paul's weight in my arms.

"I can't see an exit point from that chest wound," Tama says. "His spine must have stopped the bullet. Ah, there you go..." He points to a plum-sized purple swelling protruding from the base of Paul's neck.

"Good thing it wasn't a larger caliber. We wouldn't be needing the bandages if that was the case. Okay, now you got to let him down gently then come around here to the other side."

He stands beside me and places my hands, one on top of the other, and presses them down over the bubbling hole in Paul's chest.

"Use this amount of pressure, and whatever you do, don't lift them. You got that?"

I nod my head in silence.

"Alright. We gotta do this right so he has a chance. They just slapped those bandages on him before. Clueless!"

I watch Tama's hands move with precision.

"Are you a doctor?" I ask.

"A medic. That's how I know those two in the chopper with your husband. The three of us were in the same unit. Tua—he's a hard fuck—a professional prick." Tama looks up at me. "We used to play together at school. That was a long time ago though. Rick is different. He's a mean fucking asshole! He'd cut off his mother's head if you offered him enough money. Nori didn't have a fucking clue when he hired those two." He gazes up at me. "He wouldn't have known, right?"

I shake my head. "I don't think so." I don't want to think about that too much. I feel a fluttering under my hand like a baby bird is inside Paul and trying to break free. I will him to be strong, for him.

Rivulets of perspiration running lines down his face, sticking his glossy black hair to his forehead. He screws up his eyes and rubs them with the side of his hand, smearing his face with red. "He has a collapsed lung, and he's lost a lot of blood." He walks over to the sink and tips the remainder of Bill's water bottle over his hands. "He's probably not going to make it," he says quietly.

He gazes back at me from the doorway. "I'm going outside to wait for the medivac chopper. Do you you can keep your hands on his chest?"

"Yes."

I look down at Paul, lying still, white and bloodied. His spirit struggling under my palm like a butterfly trying to free itself. "*Gomenasai*," I tell him. I know it's useless, because it can't change a thing that has happened, but I keep saying sorry to him, over and over again.

37

The medivac helicopter is on the ground for only a few short minutes before they and Paul are gone. The late morning sun is warm, but I shiver in my damp clothes. I pull off my wet gear inside the hut and rummage my way through the backpack for something clean and dry to wear. I find a pair of cotton longs and a T-shirt. I wear Carol's jacket over the thin clothes. It's the cheap fragrance of her perfume that still clings to the fabric I appreciate most of all.

I try not to look at the tabletop. The bloodied lengths of bandages and clumps of cotton wool drying under the warming tin roof. I hurry outside and breathe in the fresh air.

Tama drops an aluminum pot at my feet.

"We need water from the river," he says. "I thought you might prefer fetching water to cleaning off the table."

I pick up the container. "How did you meet my husband?"

"Tua came to me first. He invited me to join the team. He told me your husband wanted to rescue his runaway wife and return to Japan with her. It sounded like easy money for a good cause. When I found out your kidnappers were Paul and Bill, I told him to bugger off. But then—you know—Noel and me—we needed the cash…"

"So, why are you helping us now?"

"We never thought there would be any shooting involved. I should've known better. I can tell you one thing for sure though…" Tama looks down for a moment as he fought his emotions. His face darkens when he looks up. "Rick's not getting away. He's going to get what he deserves!" He takes a breath and I see him softened. "I was talking to Noel on the radio while you were changing your clothes. He's got Bill with him. They'll be here before dark."

"Is he okay?"

"Yeah," he says, and he smiles at me.

"Oh—*yokatta!*"

Inside the hut, I find Bill's flask and take mine from my backpack and drop them both into the pot. I hurry by the cloud of angry flies buzzing the tabletop.

The path still glistens with morning dew. A little fantail bird joins me on the narrow trail. Perhaps it's the same one that kept me company earlier. The thought it might recognize me is comforting. The bird dives and darts ahead of me, piercing the quiet with shrill excited chirps.

I think of it as a tiny forest spirit that has chosen to wear the form of a lower animal to guide and protect me. I silently ask it to petition the gods to heal Paul.

I remember walking with Grandmother along a narrow path behind our farmhouse. It wound through a rock garden that could have been as old as the house. It was filled with clipped bushes that were no larger than my diminutive figure. A small, ancient stone statue stood at the end of the path. A shrine dedicated to the white snake god that protected our farmhouse and all within the walls.

The stone figure was so weathered in places the surface had few features. Whatever details remained hidden by moss. Yet, I could see a small creature with personality and grace. The statue was no higher than my six-year-old knees from the top of the serpent head to the stone feet.

Every New Year's Day, I watched her place a fat round rice cake and a large orange in front of the statue. We clapped our hands two times to wake the god. We bowed our heads, to ask our house to be protected for another year.

I watch a fish glide in and out of the shadows in the lagoon. A silver ripple breaks along the surface and bright metallic red and blue erupt as a trout breaks free of its watery world to snap at an insect. I step onto a large boulder and fill the pot, careful not to let grit from the bottom swirl inside. When the containers are full, I set them on the bank and push my hand deep into the wet sand to rub away the blood.

When I reach the top of the track and see the hut I come to a stop. From the other side of the clearing comes the fall of hooves and the snort of a horse. A tall figure walking beside a horse walks out of the shadow.

I run up the steps and drop the pot of water and the flasks on the floorboards. The table has been scrubbed clean. There's a scrabble of claws on the hard ground, and I feel a wet snout pressing into the back of my leg. Jasper grins up at me, excited at the fresh smell of Paul. The dog presses past me and peers into the gloom of the hut. The big head swivels around the empty interior as he sniffs the air. Then with a plaintive whine, he runs down the steps and crawls under the hut.

When I see Bill sitting in the saddle I gasp at the sight of his face. His mouth is hanging open, saliva trickling in a rivulet down his chin. He attempts a smile, but his swollen face manages only a sneer.

Noel holds the reins against the animal's neck as Bill to slide to the ground. When he turns, I wrap my arms around him, but I bump his chin.

Bill pulls himself free and stumbles backward. "Chris-sakes, tha... hurts!"

"*Gomen.* I'm so happy to see you," I tell him.

Tama appears around the side of the hut carrying an armful of long green herbs that drip muddy water.

Bill and I sitting on the top step.

"Hey, bro," Tama chuckles as he walks past, slowing to peer down at the damaged face "You took your time getting here," he calls out to Noel.

I'm excellent, cuz," he replies quietly. "Thanks for asking," Noel replies as he edges past us dump the saddle-bags on the hut floor.

When Tama drops the plants into the sink he squats beside Bill. "You look funny."

"He has a broken jaw," Noel informs him from inside the hut.

"It's a good thing you got Yayoi to chew your food tonight, bro," Tama says, "You might be able to do that yourself sooner than you think because it looks like a dislocation to me."

"Don't worry, I'm not hungry," I tell Bill.

"Make sure you remember to add salt," Tama calls out to Noel who is busy preparing the watercress. "Because the last time you forgot."

"Hey!" Noel exclaims. "I didn't forget the salt. Your problem is you smoke so many cigs you can't taste shit."

Tama places a hand on Bill's shoulder and straightens up. He unhooks the paraffin lamp from the ceiling, places it on the table, and beckons Bill over. "Come and sit on the bench with me."

"You okay?" Bill asks me, ignoring Tama.

"Can we talk a bit, later on?" I ask him.

He looks at me, but I turn away. I don't want him seeing my eyes tear up all over again. He doesn't know about Paul.

Tama calls out as Bill sits down at the table. "Is there any more rum left in that bottle?"

I pick up Bill's saddlebag still lying on the grass where he dropped it earlier in the morning.

"It's one-third full," I tell him when I set it down on the table.

"Me first," Tama says, pouring two fingers from the bottle into a mug. "This is going to take a steady hand." He tells us before he tilts back his head. He bangs the mug down on the table and burps loudly when he's finished.

"Shee-it!" He pours another shot of rum into the mug and slides it over to Bill. "Get that into you," he orders.

Bill puts the metal rim to his lips and upends the contents. He breaks into a fit of coughing and groans with the pain, touching his swollen jaw with his fingertips.

Tama pours into the mug again. It's more than before. He slides the mug across to his patient, but Bill holds up his hand and shakes his head.

"It's bush anesthetic!" Tama tells him.

Bill stares at Tama with glazed eyes, considering the implications of the words. "Wha' you think you're doing?" He asks regarding Tama with a look of suspicion.

Tama waves his hand at the mug. "Knock that back first, bro."

He watches as Bill takes a sip of the whiskey. He stifles a cough and pushes the mug aside.

"If you have a dislocation, and you do, then it has to be reset," Tama explains.

Bill pulls back from him the outstretched hand. "It'll 'ee okay—"

"No-no, it's not. It's going to get worse. If you don't fix it straight away, there are going to be complications."

Bill shakes his head. "You're not touching 'ee."

"Drink the damned whiskey, bro!" Tama shouts in exasperation.

I sit next to Bill and take his hand in mine, and squeeze it tightly. "Tama knows what he's doing. He does!"

Bill stares at me. "How the hell would you know that?" He shrugs when I don't answer him and gulps the contents with a grimace and a shudder.

"Bro, don't worry," Tama tells him. "I've fixed a ton of dislocation back in the day. As a medic in the field, I always got one go at getting it right. That's all the Army allows. I slotted it back in place the first time or the soldier dealt with it until we reached the base. Which might have been a long while. I had to be good at doing it right the first time. I can fix you. Let me do it."

Bill sees me nodding my head. "Go ahead and do it."

Tama slides closer to Bill. "Bro, listen. I'm going to stick my thumbs in your mouth—but they're almost clean, so don't worry."

He chuckles at his own bad joke.

Noel snorts as he hangs the pot over the fire.

"Hey, Noel!" Tama says in irritation. "Concentrate on what you're doing, and I'll concentrate on fixing goofy here!"

Tama inserts a thumb into each side of Bill's mouth, using his fingers for support under the jaw, and manipulates the mandible back and forth. Sweat beads across his forehead as he works the jaw, ignoring Bill's gasping and gagging until he finally hears it pop into place. He pulls his hand out just in time.

Tama leans over the body sprawled on the floor to inspect the damage then sits back down with a look of satisfaction. He pats down his mustache. "That had to hurt!" He says, and he laughs loudly.

Bill sits up with his hands pressed to his face as if it might have fallen apart and glares back through teary eyes. "Fuck off, you bastard!"

"You could thank me," Tama replies with a grin. "Now you will be able to say your name again."

38

"Why is Jasper under the hut whining?" He asks without turning around. He has been staring into the fire since we finished eating. "Tell me what happened."

Tama sighs. "Paul's in Intensive Care in Rotorua Hospital. Medivac flew him out this morning—They shot at him from a chopper and he took at least one bullet."

"Shot?" Bill asks. He turns around to stare at Tama with a look of despair. There was no question that Tama was telling him the truth.

"I talked to Tua over the radio," Tama says. "He was piloting the chopper with the shooter."

Tama explains to Bill how he and Noel tracked us for Nori.

"What kind of man is your husband?" Bill asks.

"No!" I say shaking my head. "Nori would never have told them to do that."

"Nori didn't have a clue what he was getting himself into when he hired Rick," Tama tells Bill. "You can't expect a wolf to be a sheepdog for a day—and all that." He turns away from Bill's accusing eyes.

"How long ago was it when you last talked to Tua?" Bill asks. "We got to call him again."

Tama climbs onto the top bunk and lands on the mattress with a heavy thump. "I will first thing in the morning," he says, and he covers his face with a thick forearm.

"Why not give him a call now?" Bill asks.

"We've organized to talk in the morning, bro! The batteries have bugger all charge left in them."

"How come you couldn't tell us you were working for Nori the other night?" Bill says with a contemptuous sneer. "If you had told us, this wouldn't have happened."

Noel who has been sitting on the doorstep walks inside and closes the door. He takes a joint he has finished rolling from between his lips and crouches over the hearth to light it on an ember. Bill waves him away, and when he takes it to the bunk so does Tama. But Tama changes his mind and lifting himself on one elbow, he calls him Noel back and takes the joint from him.

Noel blows a thick cloud of blue smoke into the air and turns to Bill. "We thought we were helping Nori get his wife back. We would have told him to get lost—if we thought anything like this was going to happen."

Bill turns away and pokes at the dying fire with a stick without replying. After several angry jabs, he tosses the wood into the flames. "You happily both took his money, right?"

"Why else would we tramp all over these hills doing someone else's work?" Tama says.

"It was strictly biz for us, eh?" Noel says, and he takes another puff at the joint before he passes it back to Tama. "There's no work in the forestry. The mills have cut back on production. And then this rich Jap…"

He glances at me. "I'm not saying you're all like that."

"Well, Nori is rich," I reply with a shrug. "Most Japanese aren't."

"He shows up with a fat roll of hundred dollar notes. American bills! It was ours he said if we help him search for his runaway wife," Noel continues. "What are we supposed to do? It wasn't like anyone else was offering us work."

"I've got to go see Paul!" Bill says, his voice breaking. "What if Carol doesn't know yet?"

"The cops would have already talked to her," Tama says. "We wait until the morning and go out together. Hey! He's getting the best care in the world. Don't worry."

"How do you know Tua is going to talk to you in the morning," Bill says in a tone of despondency.

"Tua will talk to us—I promise, bro. Paul is going to be okay."

"Are you promising that too?" Bill asks.

Tama lies back on the bunk without replying.

Bill doesn't reply. He watches the fire for several

minutes before he gets up and walks out the door into the night air.

I move to follow him outside, but Tama calls out. "What can you do? It was your husband that found Rick. Let Bill have some time to himself. He'll come back to you."

"It was me," I say quietly.

"What do you mean?" Tama asks.

"Paul would not have been hurt if I had not pushed Bill into taking me with him."

"He wouldn't have said, yes to you if he didn't like the idea," Tama says. He rolls off the bunk onto the floor. "You take the top bunk. Bill on the bottom. Noel and me can sleep on the floor."

In the dim light of dusk, I watch Noel pad out the door in his wool socks. He sits on the doorstep and ties the laces of his boots. The dogs have started to whine.

Noel reaches behind him and drags over his saddlebags. He swings them over his shoulder and pulls the door closed behind him. I listen to the sounds of leather squeaking and the heavy hooves of his horse as he rides it down the slope in the direction of the river.

I can hear Bill's soft snoring in the bunk below. He climbed into the bunk late in the evening, sometime after Noel turned off the flame on the burner.

I know he's been awake most of the night because I have been too.

I watch the fluffy white clouds moving past the window. The sky is blue and the sun will be hot. By the time I stand on the boards, my T-shirt is already sticking to my skin.

Tama paces from one side of the clearing to the other, crisscrossing the open space as he tries to find a good connection to the satellite. When he settles on the best spot, it's can't be more than fifty yards from where Bill and I sit together on the steps sipping cold tea.

My knee rests against Bill's shoulder.

"I wish I could lip-read," he tells me as we watch Tama hunker down over the radio. He runs his tongue over a chipped front tooth.

"You still don't trust him, do you?" I ask.

"I don't know who to trust anymore," he replies, gazing at the forest on the other side of the clearing.

"You don't trust me either, do you?" He doesn't reply but at least, he's still able to sit beside me. That's got to count for something.

His hair smells of smoke and horse sweat. I would have found the odor offensive in a past life. I would have preferred a guy who thought enough of me that they would always bother to splash on a little cologne. Now, I don't want to move away from him.

"You didn't tell me Noritake was your husband."

"Why should I? It doesn't matter, does it?" I ask him.

"It might have," he says.

"I don't think it should matter," I continue. "We haven't lived together for months. He hasn't been my husband for a long time, not in his words or his actions."

His hand rests on the step near my foot. When it brushes my ankle I feel a tingle through my thighs. It's like an electric current that passes through the two of us. It's strange, even after the shock of what happened to Paul, I want Bill close to me. When did I start to feel like that? I wonder if he notices the way he affects me as we sit here together?

"Anyway, I will divorce him when I return to Japan."

He glances across at me. "Then you'll be free of him, huh?"

"Yes," I say and I smile at the thought. "Then I will be free of him. What a relief that is going to be."

Suddenly I feel ashamed for thinking only of me. How could he have anything else on his mind, but his brother lying in a hospital bed? I still haven't told him that Paul wasn't able to move. I don't want to either.

Tama walks up the steps, squeezing past us without a word. I watch him set the radio on the table with a heavy thud and stand over it with a frown and his hands on his hips.

He walks up behind us and stares over our heads. "The batteries are dead," he announces finally.

"Did you speak to Tua?" Bill asks.

"Yeah, he's pissed off with Noritake. He said that Paul stands a fighting chance of pulling through. That's what the doctors have said."

Bill stretches his arms in front of him and bows his head. "What does that mean? A fighting chance?"

"He has a chance," Tama says. It's a good chance."

"So what's the bad news?" Bill asks.

"Tua told me the police spoke to Nori this morning, and he says the AOS is on its way."

"Good! Hope they shoot all three of the bastards!" Bill says angrily.

"What is the AOS?" I ask.

"Armed Offenders Squad," Bill replies and glances up at Tama as he steps between us.

Tama steps onto the ground and turns to face us. "They're a paramilitary police outfit. It's smarter to call them what they are—assassins! Most of them come from the SAS."

"The SAS means the Special Air Services," Bill tells me. "They are commandos."

"They are the elite among soldiers," Tama says. "They enjoy the thrill of the kill. The ones who join the AOS can't live without the thrill."

He throws the satchel he brought out of the hut with him onto the bare earth in front of the steps and looks up at Bill. "Anyhow—Tua says Nori and Rick have set you up to take the blame for the shooting. They told the police they saw you and Paul arguing. They said they saw you shoot Paul."

"Yeah, but—you and Noel saw what happened, right?" Bill asks him.

"Damn right! We were both saw what happened. But

our problem—your problem is that Tua says Rick used your gun. When forensics examine the bullet, they are going to discover it was fired from your gun."

He empties the satchel on the ground and starts rummaging through the contents, throwing out everything he doesn't need. "It doesn't matter. We just have to hope local cops arrest your ass before the SAS finds you! We can expect them to drop in on us anytime," he says. He crouches in front of Bill. "What are you waiting for? Grab your stuff! Both of you!"

I stand up quickly, but Bill fingers his swollen jaw with an expression of confusion and disbelief.

Tama's face is only inches from Bill's. "Let me make it really, really simple for you," he hisses. "We got to get out of here. Right now!"

39

Tama is taking us on a straight line to the river, right through the old horse track. He tells us there's good cover along the banks, less chance for them to sneak up on us because we should be able to see them coming, and more chance to lose the police dogs, he's sure they will bring with them. River crossings will have to be quick in case a chopper does spot us in the open before we know it's there.

"Where's your horse?" Bill asks when he catches up to Tama who waits impatiently for us.

"I saddled him up and told him to go home," he says. He swings himself over a dead tree lying across the trail and settles once more into a jog. "If he loses my kit, I make steaks of him," he shouts over his shoulder. "And he knows it! We are best on foot and to stay together."

He places his hand on an old tree stump hanging

exposed over the trench, heaving himself up and over, like it's nothing but a hurdle.

Bill clambers over with an effort.

Tama is taking a straight line to the river, the one taken by hunters and their horses. I struggle through the sticky orange clay trenches cut by countless hooves over time. The clay clings to my runners and weighs me down. I should have had boots for the trip, but we couldn't find any small enough. Now I pay the price for my lack of preparation. I place the heel of my runner on a knot in the damp log to lever myself up, but it slips out, and I land hard, my head bouncing off the floor of the trench. I lie where I fell in the clay and watch Tama's broad back vanish around the curve of the trail.

Bill peers down at me.

"You okay?" He asks.

I feel around my head and find a small lump. "It's just a bump," I tell him.

He looks relieved, but he insists on checking for damage. "There's no blood," he tells me.

I am confronted by an expanse of skin and chest hair through his open shirt and I push him away. "Let's go," I tell him.

"Give me your backpack," he offers.

"I can carry my stuff," I say, standing up and shucking my pack further up on my back.

"Okay—but if you change your mind," he says, looking at me in surprise.

I shuck my pack higher on back. "Shouldn't we catch up with Tama?"

We splash through the shallows of the lagoon and stumble over the slippery rocks of the ridge of what turns out to be a tiny narrow island in the river. Tama stands on a boulder and scans the sky, his teeth bared, his hand eyes shielded by a hand against the glare of the rising sun. He tells us to listen for the sound of a helicopter. Once he is satisfied that there's nothing within hearing range or sight, we set off once again.

There is another island of rocks, silt, and half-buried driftwood running up the center of the river bed. This one goes as far as we can see to a bend in the distance. The water keeps to one side of it. Tama tells us we will stay on the rocks until the trail begins again on the other side. He's worried. He says the river has changed a lot since he has last been this way, and we will be in the open for much longer than is safe.

He leaps from one boulder to another as agile as a deer, covering the driftwood-strewn island faster than we can. We chase after him, but his pace is breakneck. Soon he has disappeared around the bend in the river.

Further down, we come across the remnants of an old bridge. The uprights jut over the rocks and water. Thick twists of wire cables, blotched with the orange rust hang like vines. Somehow the surviving sections of the structure are still embedded in the heavy concrete blocks that remain part buried in the shingle bed, below the dark swirling water, because here, the river runs deep. The bridge is a decaying monolith built by stoic workmen in the middle of nowhere. It is a monument to conquest to be seen only by those the hunters and their prey. Giant ferns and tangles of vines cover much of the metalwork. It looks like the tentacles of the Kraken are pulling it into the depths.

We find him sitting on a boulder turning his head for the phantom helicopter. Tama talks while Bill and I seize on the opportunity to catch our breath. "We've passed the bridge to nowhere. That means I hope, that just around the next bend, we are going to see an old grandfather trunk we can use to cross over and re-join the old track. But we have to move because we are way too exposed here."

The gorge has narrowed to the point the entire floor has become the riverbed from one slope to the other. The water is deep and fast-flowing water, and it runs up against the far bank. Bill tells me if it were to rain, this part of the river would become a death trap. The valley would fill too quickly with water for us to escape. At least it would be quick. Eventually, our bodies would wash out to sea along with the deadwood scattered across the island. I tell Bill to shut up.

"There!" Tama says, pointing to an enormous fallen tree.

The roots of the old Goliath, no longer anchored in the clay bank, reach into the air with claw-like fingers.

The trunk has fallen high above the swirling channel of water to rest on the spine of the island to form a natural bridge. All we have to do is to clamper up the side, and we will be able to make our way to the bank and the old track.

"You first," Tama tells Bill. He turns to me. "Follow Bill! I'll be right behind."

I watch Bill punch his fists into the rotten sides and kick his toes in to stand up. He makes it look easy, and soon he's lying on the top side and reaching down for me to grab his hand.

Tama pushes me from behind, and I am a third up the side. I punch my fists into the side just like I saw Bill do, and kick my toes into the soft moss and bark. I can see his hand above my head, and I grasp it tightly. That's when my foot slips, and I scream as I swing into space.

"You have to kick your toes into the log again," he yells. "Get a foothold."

I do as he says and feel for purchase with my free hand. There's a tearing pain as my nails rip, but I dig in my fingers and pull myself up. It's enough to make a difference.

Bill grabs me by my backpack, and I am on the top lying beside him.

The behemoth tree has cut a wide trench into the muddy earth on its slow-motion slide down the bank into the river. When winter comes, the floodwaters will carry it out to sea, and from there, a storm tide will take it along the coast and back to the land. It will wash up on a lonely beach, broken and bleached. The skeletal remains of a forest giant.

"Don't look down," Bill urges. "Keep your eyes focused ahead!"

It's too late because I've already glimpsed the drop. My old nemesis never let's go.

He holds onto the massive root and gestures to me to take his other hand. "Come on, Yayoi. You're almost there."

We feel the beat in our chests at the same time. A low rhythmic thump as the air pulsates around us. Bill wriggles his fingers, pleading with me to reach out and take his hand.

I drop to my knees, and scrabble forward, digging my broken fingernails into the hard slippery surface of the rotten trunk, and slide forward on my belly. I am almost in reach of Bill's hand.

He reaches out, but he loses his footing and misses my hand. He tries again, and this time his fingers close tight around my wrist and turns, pulling me after him. Together we slide from the top of the trunk to tumble heavily into the mass of wet ferns below.

It is by instinct only that I am quickly able to shield my eyes from the coarse fronds that flay us like metal brushes. The snapping, crunching, and tearing around us is deafening as the helicopter descends over us. We flatten ourselves into the undergrowth, the blast of air buffeting our backs. Wood, rock, and plant material disintegrate into projectiles as the craft descends, the force of its downdraft pulverizing the foliage and shattering the branches of trees, sending the debris crashing to the ground.

Through the blowing fern fronds, I raise my head enough to glimpse the helicopter drawing level with the bank. I can see bulky black-helmeted figures in the open door peering down into the churning water.

Bill presses my face into the bed of rotting leaf matter. Many seconds pass before he lifts his hand. We expect to see black boots on the ground and the rush of large men. The glade is empty. I drop my head and cough, spitting out bits of wood and slimy humus. The branches settle back into place around us, but we are out of trouble. In the distance, we hear voices shouting and dogs barking.

We get to our feet, hunched over to take advantage of what broken forest remains between us and anyone who might be looking from the other side of the river. Tama is nowhere to be seen.

"Let's get out of here," Bill whispers, and without waiting for my answer, he sets off at a fast pace along a barely visible trail in the undergrowth.

I stumble to keep up with him. The trail is nothing but a green corridor overgrown with long grass, bushes of nettles, and a tangle of saplings and thick tree trunks. I'm not used to running in a dense forest or any forest, but I think I am getting better at it. I have left behind the person I used to be. The two of us are not the people we were yesterday. Today we are fugitives pursued by the

state. Criminals to be tried and found guilty. But, guilty of
what?

The only thing that really matters is surviving the day.

I concentrate on the back of his boots as they pump
the ground, and I breathe in short, rasping gasps. Still, I
can't get enough air into my aching lungs. So, to keep
going, I count each footfall.

The trail widens, and we run under the canopy on the
edge of the shadows. We may as well be two vampires
avoiding the sunlight. I wheel around ferns and nettles,
ducking under tangles of the vine Paul called Supplejack.
I remember his broad grin. I remember the pride he felt
in his bush knowledge. I remember that he showed me
how to drink the sap of the vines the day we rode into the
mountains. He told me how in the right season, even the
red berries of the plant can be eaten, and that the root of
the plant boiled in water can treat several ailments. I try
to remember what it could cure.

A sore tummy was one. He said Supplejack will fix
that. Fever was a second. Tea could be brewed from the
vine to lower a high temperature.

I pause to break off an end of hanging vine. I know it
won't fix the pain in my heart. It is only to comfort me
that I chew it now. Because he said it was good medicine.
I wish you were running behind me, Paul.

40

"You are pretty damn fit," Bill tells me. "I reckon you are fitter than me!"

I am bent double with my hands on my knees, sucking in air. I have to force myself to straighten. "Where are we running to?" I gasp.

"A little way from what's behind us," Bill says, glancing back the way we've come. "That's all I know for sure. Let's go."

Each ridge we climb, we drop back down to the river, then we climb another. It's exhausting, and we know our pace is slower than before. We have managed to travel a distance. Already the forest is changing.

We come to a small grassy glade and desperate for a break, I call out to him.

He stops and comes back. "Hey, you're doing okay." He gives me a reassuring smile and it almost works. I know he wants to keep going.

"I—I have to pee!" I'm not even sure can put a sentence together in English. I gesture to him just to make sure he understands.

He nods his head and lets his pack slide to the ground. "There's a stand of birch saplings we passed just around the corner you can get behind."

I retrace my way back down the track a short distance to the grove of thin gray trees and lichen-covered scrub and push between the clusters until I am a few paces off the path.

The canopy overhead is filled with the sound of bells, chimes, clangs, and warbles. It's an avant-garde ensemble of wood instruments playing experimental music, rich and loud. Then it all stops abruptly as if someone has switched off a radio.

I listen and hear the crunch of footfall approaching through the bushes. I sink lower behind the bushes and watch a pair of mud-streaked legs stride past my hiding spot. I wait a few seconds then cautiously push my way back through the thin branches. Ahead of me, there's a burst of laughter and a familiar voice.

When I walk around the corner, Tama spins on his heels to face me.

"Shit! Yayoi!" He exclaims. "You scared the hell out of me." He stares at me and taps his neck then points to mine. "Looks like you got hooked by a branch, eh?"

I wipe my fingers across my grit covered skin. There's swelling, but it's not stinging at all.

"I'm fine," I tell him.

Tama swings the dripping swollen canvas satchel off his back. "This thing's been really slowing me down!" He unbuckles the straps and flips it over, scattering its wet contents over the grass. While he repacks, he recounts to us what happened to him.

Moments before the helicopter flew overhead, he had managed to duck under the overhang of the fallen tree. The current was swirling around his chest, but he was able to stay upright by digging his fingers deep into the trunk. The chopper moved off before his arms and fingers gave out.

In the distance, we hear the bark of a dog. It doesn't sound too far away.

"Hurry up, man!" Bill tells Tama. "We better get going! You were busting to run before! Yayoi, where's your cell phone?"

"It's still on the bunk," I tell him.

"Good!" Bill says as stares down the track. "That means they can't use it to track us."

Tama fastens his satchel and swings his rifle over his shoulder. "They don't need your phone. They already know we are here. They have dogs and boots on the ground. That chopper before—it uses infrared to spot your body heat. Their camera didn't register me because that stretch of water is cold. Pray that when you hear the chopper next time you have time to find water. I don't know how they missed seeing the two of you. It must have been real close!"

Bill shucks my pack higher on his back. "We're basi-cally screwed. That's what you're telling us—right?"

"We won't be able to outrun them for long!" He replies.

"How long we got then?" Bill asks.

"Minutes—probably," Tama replies, and he sets off at a fast run.

"But we don't give up, right?" Bill asks.

Tama swipes a low-hanging branch out of the way. "Cuz, you never fucking give up! Never!" He slows to check we are still with him, but as his strides lengthen, we struggle to keep up.

My head throbs, and I see bright lights popping in front of me. I am tired and sore. I wish the police would arrive and put an end to this.

I don't care about beating Nori at his own game. I will gladly place the mark of my *inkan* on whatever paper he puts down in front of me and return to Japan with him because I just can't do this anymore.

41

The steep inclines of the valley wall clad in thick bush rise above us, the peaks hidden by the branches of tall trees, but the green roof over our heads is already thinning out. As the gorge widens, we know we will soon be out in the open. The ground is strewn with deer scat and the small ball bearings of rabbits. Now it has become a simple matter of placing one foot in front of the other and not tripping.

We are stumbling after Tama on a flat stretch when we hear the low whistle. "Hey!" The hushed voice calls. It sounds familiar.

I feel a heavy prod in the back of my calf, and I know before I look down it's Jasper. The dog snorts with excitement at our arrival and jumps to lick Bill's hands.

"So that's where you got to," Bill says.

Noel is several feet away from the track, crouching

beneath the branches of a large, ancient tree with a twisted trunk he has tied the horses to behind him. His taut features relax into a grin, and he gives Tama a high-five. "Good thing you turned up. I was about to head out of here."

Tama drops the satchel at his feet and leans his rifle against it. He walks over to the horses and grabs the halter of his mount in both hands, nuzzling the animal until it pulls its head away. Then he checks the saddle and nods his head in satisfaction. "Wished you had a cig, cuz. I've run out." He turns to Noel with a hopeful expression.

Noel got to his feet and laughs. "That's too bad."

Tama moans. "I could sure do with one."

"Got a joint thooo…" Noel says, pulling it from his shirt pocket.

"That'll do," Tama says.

I sit on the dry warm earth and close my eyes. I imagine myself back in Tokyo, away from all of this, but Tokyo doesn't seem real to me anymore. I wish I could travel back to the time to the day I first decided to travel with Bill. It might as well have been years ago. So much has changed since then.

"The po-lice flew straight over me," Noel tells us.

"Hope they didn't spot you, cuz," Tama says.

Noel takes a long puff and exhales gradually. He coughs as passes the joint to Tama. "I don't think so. They were booting it. Screaming up the river. Heading to the hut is my guess." He glances up at Bill. "They must think you're a dangerous man, bro."

Tama flicks the burned stub to the ground and grinds it into the dirt with his boot heel. "It's no fucking joke, Noel." He fixes Bill with a grim stare. "You know Sergeant Ray, don't you?"

"In Opuhunaki?" Bill drops my backpack on the track and sits down on it.

"What other Sergeant Ray do you think I mean?" Tama asks. "Jeez! The sergeant in charge at the station. You need to hand yourself over to him as soon as you arrive in town. Nah, make that as soon as you can get to a phone." He gestures up the river valley. "Keep an eye out for the chopper. All the time." He waits just a beat for Bill's reply and looks irritated when he doesn't get one. "Hey! Bill! You hearing me?"

"We are splitting up here, right?" Bill asks to confirm.

Bill picks up a stone and rolls it back and forth in the palm of his hands while he waits for the answer. He slings the stone into the river bed when he realizes he isn't going to get one. He turns back to Tama. "They're going to catch us before we reach the town, aren't they?"

"Maybe—but don't make it easy for them to spot you."

"I won't," Bill says.

"With luck, we'll see Ray before you do and tell him you want to hand yourself in. You only hand yourself over to him too. No one else."

It's almost as though he is telling Bill how to proceed to his own execution.

"Me and Noel are going to tell them we were working

for Yayoi's husband. That we saw everything go down," Tama says, patting down his mustache. "The shooting. The lot."

Bill digs the dry surface clay with the heel of his boot and watches the dust rise. "Simpler to walk out with my hands in the air as soon as I hear the chopper, I reckon. Get it over with."

"They won't shoot Bill. It's me they want," I tell Tama.

Tama doesn't lift his gaze away from Bill. "Hey, bro! I already told you about the AOS. They don't piss about. They take people out."

Bill turns away. "Fuck them."

"Exactly," Tama says. "Hand yourself over to Ray at the police station. That way you're his concern."

Bill glances at me.

"And if the chopper spots you, just make sure Yayoi is not standing next to you," Tama says quietly.

Bill looks up at him. "You mean if I stand next to her, they are going to shoot me?"

"No. If she's standing next to you, she's more likely to get hit, or else catch a ricochet. That kind of dumb luck happens all the time."

"You're winding me up," Bill says in dismay.

"You want to put it to a test?" Tama asks him an edge of scorn in his voice.

"No," Bill replies quietly.

Tama slaps Bill on the arm as he walks by him to the

horses. "You can take mine, bro. Let him go when you hit the beach. He'll find his way home."

But Noel has untied his stocky chestnut and walks it over to us.

"That's your horse," Bill says in surprise, taking the reins from Noel's hands.

"Yeah," Noel smiles shyly.

"Come on!" Tama exclaims, throwing up his hands. "Either it's his horse or mine. Whichever, but hurry the fuck up!"

Noel stares at me. "I wish I never met your husband."

"It's too late for regrets," Tama tells him.

I stand up and brush the dust off clothes. "Thank you," I tell Noel.

"Seems to me they're keeping everything low key at this stage," Tama continues to Bill. He turns to me. "That's because of you, Yayoi. You're some kind of star in Japan, eh?"

Noel's eyes widen. "Like a film star?"

"Like a rock star," I tell him and pull a face. "At least I was."

All that celebrity happened to someone who is no longer me. I can't feel Yaya in me anymore. I've finally killed her.

Jasper lifts his head. His ears prick and swivel.

Tama raises his hand for silence.

The three dogs stand rigid as they stare down the river. Bilbo lifts her scarred face and sniffs the air. The pink folds of her eyelids narrow to slits of ecstasy as she separates each scent. The young dog whines, but Noel silences it when he grabs its snout.

Bill doesn't wait to be told. He leaps onto the back of the chestnut and stretches out his hand to me.

Without a second thought, I reach out suddenly I'm behind him in the saddle. I slide my arm around his waist, but then, I see my backpack on the ground.

"You won't be needing it," Tama says, looking up at me. "Don't worry. We'll carry it out with us."

"What if they catch up with you two?" Bill asks.

Tama shrugs. "We're still working for Noritake, right? So, no problem. We can show them this backpack we found on the track."

And from the tracks you made we saw you were heading in that direction." Noel says with a wry grin pointing further down the track in the direction of the highway. But you're going that way," Noel says with a smile, pointing us in the direction of the sea.

Tama holds the horse by its halter. "Follow the river to the estuary," he tells Bill. "Keep yourselves out of the open. Use whatever shelter you find. The first fisherman's bach you reach, try for a phone. Call Ray at the police station. You keep away from roads! And, don't you go anywhere near the highway. They will have set up roadblocks."

"Okay," Bill replies and pulls the horse around. Before he can say anything else, Tama slaps the horse's haunch. "Go! Go on. Get!"

The horse snorts in surprise but quickly recovers and

starts off at a trot down the side of the bank, its hooves raising dust over the sunbaked silt.

Bill glances back at me, but he doesn't say a word.

I press myself against his back as the scrub closes around us.

42

We search the sky for the dark speck that grows bigger. The tell-tale glint of sunlight off a cockpit windshield. There are only birds gliding in spirals on the updrafts off the hot riverbed. We continue on our way through the river flats and out of the mountains.

He says we would do best to cross to the other side where the cover is better. We find a shallow section of water, and in minutes we are on the opposite bank. The horse is moving at a steady gait, but it's bothered by the broken rocks under its hooves. The added weight of an extra rider is not helping a bit. It jerks at the reins, then it twists its head, warning Bill that it would like nothing better than to wrench them from his hands.

The bush on the steep hill is denser and more tangled then it had looked from the other side. Bill presses his heels into the unhappy horse and encourages it onward, and we continue along the edge of the bank for a way but the mood of the horse is not improving.

Beyond the nettles and dense bush, the sharply rising angle of the hill we ride under means a helicopter might soar over the top without warning. The thought is unsettling, but the horse is our alarm. Noel has trained it well on countless hunts to remain alert to the slightest odd sound. Bill is sure it will hear the chopper before we do, but I see that it's clearly distracted by its own discomfort.

An escarpment comes into view on the other side of the river. Water tumbles over the ridge in a cascade above a spill of small boulders. Beyond the waterfall, the river turns toward the ocean. The line of hills collapses into rows of dunes that disappear in the haze. It's an estuary.

"This may have been a dumb idea," he calls out over his shoulder. "I was wrong. There is not enough shelter over here. We won't be able to take cover quickly. I think we have to cross back to the other side."

Without waiting for my answer, he turns the horse into the river once again. This time the river is deep, and the force of the current is much greater than before. "Hold on!"

The horse blows and snorts, lifting its front legs high, but it's the jarring motion of an animal that's panicking. We begin to roll like a ship capsizing in a storm until we feel the ice-cold embrace of the river. Bill struggles to free his foot trapped by a twisted stirrup under the sinking side of his mount. There seems to be no way to bring the floundering horse around. He concentrates on keeping the animal's head above the waves. He shouts, but I cannot hear his words over the roar of the river. When he turns to look at me, I see fear in his eyes.

The horse snorts as it struggles to keep a straight line in the powerful current, extending its neck to keep its nostrils above the swirling chop. It finds the stony bottom and we lurch forward, the rocks turning and grinding under the stabbing hooves. It fights to clamber up the sharp incline, staggering like a drunk as it seeks a stable surface, but the loose round stones of the bank keep shifting under it.

I feel myself floating free of the saddle and try to wrap my arms tight around Bills waist. The jolting and the water are too much for me. I grab the end of the saddle, knowing my life may well depend on not letting go.

The horse may be be on its last reserves, and yet it has strength remaining. It drags us out of the water and up the bank, and we tumble onto the rocks. Free of the water and its riders, the horse whinnies and shakes the river from its mane. It is too tired to bolt, and after stepping to-and-fro for a while, it quietens enough to allow us to climb onto its back.

We set off over the rocks, feeling each stumble. The horse grunting its exhaustion. Then, when it feels packed earth beneath its hooves, it takes off at a gallop. Only when it reaches the tree line does it finally come to a stop. Under the trees and away from the torment of the river the horse stamps and snorts its fury.

"This horse hates us, Bill!"

He turns in the saddle to gaze at me. "That was close back there, wasn't it?"

"Yes," I reply. "It really was…"

I feel the wetness of his hair on my forehead. I close my eyes as he presses his lips against mine. The heat of his body envelopes me, and I feel a spring inside of me slowly uncoil.

"You did well to hang on," he whispers in my ear.

"I couldn't let you go," I tell him.

The horse flicks its ears and tosses its mane violently.

The forestry drain was always going to be too shallow to contain the flow from the waterfall. The spillage runs along the track to the sweep of a curve. The flow continues in a straight line so that wash tumbles small chunks of soft rock over the lip and down the slope. Long, slimy, streaks of green algae water hang from the track and dangle over the ferns several feet below.

The surrounding forest is dead still, save for the sound of the horse drinking from the stream in rude, eager slurps. It doesn't last. The animal lifts its head when the air turns electric and rears without warning.

Bill's strikes his head on my chin. He stands in the stirrups, tightening his grip on the reins and curses, but he lost control of his mount.

There's a flash of reflected sunlight through the tree

canopy above the trail ahead of us as the machine rotates to face down the trail.

We see the dark shape swell behind the falling leaves, and Bill grabs my wrist and jerks me off the horse. I land on his chest, knocking the air out of him, but gasping he springs to his feet, pulling me up after him. Time moves as slow as treacle dripping from a spoon on a cold winter morning. I see the horse bolting down the track under the helicopter, trailing the orange plastic rope Noel uses for reins. They whip the wet surface behind the galloping hooves so the spray arches into the air behind it.

The helicopter can't have a fix on us, but they do see the horse and the leafy ceiling explodes as the pilot takes the machine up.

Bill's voice is dislocated in space. "Come on!" We leap down the bank, and once more I find myself in ice-cold water, and twice in a single day, his hand pushes my head beneath the surface.

I wrench myself free of his grip to catch a breath of air.

"Get back down," his voice rasps in my ear.

The creek water fills my mouth, and I panic, trying to pull away. I am drowning as I rise once more to the surface.

"Look at me!" His forehead touches mine, and he holds my face in his hands. "Take a big breath. Ready?"

I suck in air and press myself flat beneath the water. It is surely impossible they will miss us twice. They would have seen our heat patterns. This time we are going to hear their harsh shouts and barked orders. Rough hands will haul us apart and drag us over the broken ground. But it doesn't happen.

We lie in the stream until our toes and fingers turning numb, and our teeth chattering waiting until we are certain, the chopper has left before we stagger from the water.

I rub my arms to bring back the circulation, then I cry out with the pain. My calf muscle has spasmed below my knee. It feels like I've been struck by a baseball bat there. I plant my heel down flat to stretch out the muscle, but it contracts even tighter. Years of track work at Junior High School teaches a wise runner always stretches before the race. Too bad I forgot the lesson before we got started this morning.

He crouches beside me. "Here, let me help."

I let him put his shoulder to my leg, and he uses his weight while I press my heel to the ground. All the time, his palms knead the balled muscle until finally all that remains of my cramp is a dull ache.

43

The beech forest is behind us. We stumble on over the rocky river plain, through thickets of thick scrub and prickly blackberries. Seedpods explode in the dry brush with random loud cracks. We press against undergrowth in an attempt to stay hidden. Sharp branches tug at our clothes and rip our bare skin. Our harsh breathing sounds like that of desperate animals on the run. Startled birds fly with squawks of protest into the hot thermals that rise off the stony flats.

The crackle of the radio is faint, but it grows louder as we keep moving. We duck down, crouching in the tangle of dried plant cover, straining our ears to pinpoint the direction of the checkpoint. Bill points to a broad stretch of the riverbed. That route will take us away at a tangent from the checkpoint. We keep our heads low, and we are careful where we place our feet so that we don't knock stones or break sticks. Soon the police radio is left far behind us.

My clothes have dried in the heat. Now I feel perspiration tracking down the inside of my arms and into the small of my back. I don't think I have it in me to keep going. I limp beside him, my hand on his arm. Where does he think we are going? Doesn't he know? There is nowhere safe.

A dry field lies ahead of us. We can see a line of trees at the end. Bill tells me the beach lies beyond the trees. We walk along the beach, and when we are parallel to the town, we only have to cross the fields to avoid the road. There is a chance we can make it to the police station.

He grasps the top of a fence post and steps over the strand of barbed wire, placing his foot on the wire below, then he shifts his weight and drops to the ground on the other side. He makes it look easy. I wave aside his helping hand, but when I'm midway over, a barb snares my slacks and I topple to the ground.

"That was close," he tells me with a tired smile. "You almost had it."

I get quickly to my feet and brush the dust off my slacks and see the rip. I rub my leg until the sting disappears and wipe the bloodied heel of my hand on my leg.

We walk over earth almost bare of grass and dried cow dung to the second fence line. Gray and green lichen cover the old wood posts, and the wires hung loose enough that we can slide between them. The line of old pohutukawa provides us good cover, and we linger under the rich dark-green leaves to listen to the ocean breaking on the stony shore. The rumble of rolling stones tumbled by the waves ebbs and flows on the late afternoon breeze.

We weave around the twisted trees, stumbling on the roots that lie buckled and contorted in our path. My head is pounding, but licking the sea salt from my lips seems to lessen the pressure in my head enough to allow me to keep moving on.

The white-topped rollers crash along the length of the rocky beach, with each unrelenting wave turning the stones and sucking them back after it before the next line arrives with more clattering and grinding. Further down the beach, the arc of the shore almost disappears in the haze. We see where the white chop marks where the river meets the incoming tide. The point where the two bodies of water lock heads in a permanent collision. We stare back at the expanse of coastline. There is the river we had been following running past the dunes and into the hills. We scan the sky and the land searching for a trace of our pursuers.

Bill turns and points up the beach. "We walk to the far end—to the point. There is a tiny settlement where we could find a phone and save us the long walk into town."

"It's endless," I sigh.

We cross a gravel track for farm vehicles and fishermen. We pass another grove of young pohutukawa, the only kind of trees growing along the foreshore, they separate the beach from the empty fields. We arrive at a decrepit house truck hidden in the grove. A boxy structure on a black painted chassis behind an old cab. Overgrown with coarse beach grass, the metalwork looks as though it might have sprung from the ground. There is a trace of smoke rising from a small fire that has been built in a shallow hole, but we see no one.

"Probably a farmworker—or a grower," he muses. He looks up at the blackened windows and knocks on the warped wooden door. He tries several times more, but it's to no avail, and he sits on the step.

"Yayoi, you know what? We could split up. You can walk back to that farm track. It runs onto a road. You should be able to catch a ride into the town. There will be plenty of people heading home."

"I can't believe you are saying this. I want us to stay together—like Tama-san said we should," I tell him.

He throws a stone into the fire pit and gets to his feet "We better get going then."

It is another half-hour of walking when we reach an empty cove. The rocky coastline is behind us, and we are walking on a sandy, flat ground, scattered with beach grass and sheltered by stands of pohutukawa. The type of place a tent might be pitched. A large trunk lies in the center of the clearing. It has been tumbled by the sea, and bleached silver-gray by the sun. A beautiful curving form. One any sculptor might strive to accomplish. Giving into exhaustion, we collapse on the ground in front of the horizontal nude. I close my eyes. It feels so good just to lie on the warm ground. When I open my eyes again, I see him leaning on an elbow studying my face.

"What?" I ask.

"You laughed," he replies.

I giggle like a schoolgirl. "I was thinking how this log looks like a sculpture of a nude."

I sit up in amazement. Behind him the ocean has turned into glittering liquid gold.

"You know, we might see an amazing sight in a few minutes," he tells me.

"I want to see a hot bath and a clean bed."

"If you can find a clear view of the horizon just like we have here, you can catch the exact moment the sun disappears. Then we will see a green flash."

His words float over me. They barely make sense. "I think we've been lucky today," I murmur.

I lift my head from his shoulder. How did I get there? I wiggle back until I am resting against the log. The sun has swollen into a great orange blob, sitting on the fine line that divides sky from the sea where it melts, spreading along the edge of the world.

His gaze softly brush over me. I don't want to push him away.

"I remember my Year 12 physics teacher telling us

about it," he tells me. "A couple of years ago, I was at Kuta Beach and I saw the flash myself!"

The swelling on his face gives a twisted curl to his mouth. He might be the grandson of Elvis Presley with brown curls sticking to his forehead.

"It was like a green laser light," he tells me with the twisted smile. "And it lingered for seconds. You have to be in the right place, at the right time…"

He speaks with the enthusiasm of an eleven-year-old describing how his hero hit a home run. The day the ball traveled right out of the stadium.

What did he say about the right place in time? He is staring at me as if he can see my soul. Does he like what he sees? His hair, his skin, his face, and his arms have a red glow.

He touches a scrape on my cheek, and I flinch. He asks if it is sore, and I tell him, no, not so much. His fingers trace the line of my jaw. Our lips brush, and our teeth crash together. He winces, and I giggle. He kisses my neck, moving to the hollow of my throat. I feel a ball of energy uncoiling deep inside, and I moan.

Against the old tree trunk, our bodies entwine.

Scraped, scuffed, and bloody. My skin is on fire.

And over his shoulder, I can see the shine of a cat's eye. An emerald green that shifts to an intense blue. It twinkles, then it's gone.

Above us, Earth's shadow draws a line in the sky. I know the new world and the old, and only time separates one from the other.

We move as one.

Above us is a vast bejeweled dome studded with a million bright glittering lights.

And I detach.

From the surface.

Falling upwards into the Milky Way.

Something has happened, and it's wonderful.

44

Our world ends when the dawn light eats away the remaining stars.

His steady breathing stops with a sudden intake of breath.

I look into his wide-open eyes.

He sits up with a start, and the beam of a powerful flashlight blinds me. Heavy feet stomp beside my head, and I hear the clink of metal on metal. Then comes a barrage of shouted commands.

"Face down, you!"

"Spread your arms!"

"Hands behind heads!"

"And don't move!"

I do as I'm told. The black boots are inches from my face, so close I can see the individual grains of sand clinging to them.

I hear Bill calling out for me in the darkness. "Yayoi—"

"Shut up, you!" One of the black boots snarls in reply.

A hand pressing down on my shoulder as I try to get to my feet. Then it is gone and I hear a woman's voice. "Are you Mrs. Yayoi Shimano?"

"Yes," I reply.

The flashlight is switched off, and in the pale light of dawn, I can see large eyes and long eyelashes. A mask covers the lower half of her face under the black her black helmet, but her eyes are very human.

"Ma'am, you're safe now. I'm just going to going to check you for any injuries." The beam of her flashlight strikes my face again. She moves to my side, examining my head and working her way down to my feet before she straightens up. "You're hurt."

"No, I'm okay," I tell her.

"Are sure you're not hurt?"

"No."

Once more, the beam of her flashlight blinds me as she checks my face. "You're not hurt?"

"Yes—no—I'm not."

She frowns and clips the flashlight to her waist. She holds out a blanket for me to take. "Put this around your shoulders. We're going to walk that way." She points back up the beach. "Okay?"

"Why are you taking me away from Bill?"

"Ma'am, I have to escort you to a police car."

He's lying face down on the sand beside me with his arms stretched out in front of him. A figure in black body armor grips the white plastic cuff around Bill's wrists with a gloved hand. Another of them kneels on his legs, wedging the butt of his rifle in the small of Bill's back. Yet another officer stands over him with the muzzle of his rifle pointed at Bill's head.

I scream at them. "Leave him be!" I feel the hand of the woman on me.

"Ma'am, you need to come with me now."

"Stand him up!" A short stocky figure shouts and strides past me to step in front of Bill. "Do you have any weapons on you any hidden in the vicinity?"

"No," Bill replies.

"We found your gun," his interrogator continues. "The one you had with you when you went into the hills."

"To hunt pigs and shoot our dinner," Bill informs him. "That's right."

The short man stares into Bill's face with a look of disgust. "Is that right?"

"I didn't shoot anyone," Bill adds, his tone indignant. "They stole it!"

"Describe the weapon?" The man barked.

"It's a twenty-two," Bill replies. "A Marlin." His voice flat, like he has already lost hope.

"A Marlin twenty-two magnum!" The short man barks back at Bill.

"They took it from me," Bill says.

"Did you use that twenty-two magnum to shoot your mate?" His interrogator asks.

"Oh, fuck you too!" Bill shouts in reply. "I already told you—"

His arms are wrenched up behind him, forcing him to drop his head.

"You're hurting my shoulder!" He cries out.

"He didn't shoot anyone," I plead. "I was there!"

The short man glances at me in surprise and gestures to the policewoman. "You were escorting her to the car, right?"

She pulls me to one side, but I twist around to face her. I want her to see I'm not going anywhere with her.

"Ma'am—" she begins in a firm voice, spinning me back in the direction of the beach.

I push back, setting her off balance, but her grip on me is strong, and she recovers. "They'll look after him," she says, pushing me forward.

"I'm not leaving," I reply, and I throw my shoulder against her, forcing her to adjust her grip. When she does, I step sideways and break free. I run to Bill, stopping within arm's reach of the short interrogator.

"I don't want him hurt!" I scream. Now I have their full attention. I feel an arm around my waist, and I am hauled backward across the sand by two officers with such force they squeeze the air from my lungs. I twist my head to catch the woman's eyes. "Please. Stop!"

They hesitate and I drop to the ground.

"On what charge?" I hear Bill cry out.

I can see the interrogating officer take a page from his vest pocket. He holds it in front of Bill's face, shining the flashlight on the print.

"Grievous assault with a deadly weapon?" Bill cries out in shock. "Kidnapping? Attempted murder? No way!"

The man shakes the paper. "Read the rest."

Bill gazes down the rest of the list. "I never did any of this!"

"We have the weapon we believe fired the shots, and we have those in the chopper who witnessed you do it."

"You mean Noritake and his band of psychos? The red-head is the one who shot Paul!"

The short man pushes his face up to Bill's. "You are one lucky bastard," he growls. "Do you know that? You are getting out of here alive—Just so you know. That's not the way things usually go when we are called in."

The woman lifts me to my feet. "Ma'am? We will have a doctor check your injuries in town. Let's go."

"I can walk to the car by myself," I tell her. Even if I chose to run, there's nowhere to go.

She shifts her hand to my elbow and guides me as she might an invalid trying to cross a road. The other officer drops my arm and walks a little ahead of us.

The house truck at the campsite is deserted and desolate. When we reach the gravel track, I see a line of parked squad cars and police vans. I'm thankful photographers are lying in wait. I turn to face the officer. "Bill didn't do it."

She stares back at me. It doesn't matter to her. But, I'm sure she sees I am telling the truth. She holds the door of the car open for me and closes it once I am inside.

45

The patrol car bumps over the cattle guard and roars off in the direction of the town, leaving me standing outside the front door of Paul and Carol's house. She stands barefoot on the kitchen floor, her hand on the open sliding door, waiting for me to step inside.

I don't. I can't even look her in the eye. If I ever had the words in English to even begin to tell her how sorry I am, I can't find them now.

Carol's hair hangs loose and unkempt over her shoulders. Her eyes are red and swollen. She wears a wan smile like it might have been painted on her face, but I know it's a gift for me. One, I know I'm in no position to accept. Betraying the trust of strangers is bad enough. Betraying the trust of a friend is crushing weight I can't bear, and I drop to my knees.

"*Gomenasai-gomenasai*, Carol-san. This was all my fault."

"Yayoi? Stop that!" She crouches in front of me and reaches out, straining to lift me to my feet. "Come on. Come inside."

We sit at the bench table in the kitchen, barely saying a word. She turns the pot of tea. "I need your help," she says. "Paul needs your help. And, you know, if Bill is found guilty of those charges he'll be in prison a long time."

"I've told them Bill didn't shoot…"

"They even want to charge Paul with your kidnapping," she interrupts. "You must talk with your husband. He must tell the truth!"

I tell her that Nori is not the kind of man who would hire an assassin. I tell her Nori doesn't murder people. I wonder though if he is still human.

Carol twists the strands of her hair around her fingers. "You'll have to talk to him, eventually,"

"Of course, I will," I tell her. I gaze at the small pile of plates and cups in the sink. "You've had visitors today. I'll wash those for you."

"I'll do them later," she says. "My friends came over and made me breakfast," she says, and she shakes her head with a smile. "I couldn't eat any of it." She remembers the biscuits they had bought with them and stands up to get them, but she doesn't move. She's trembling.

I would hug her if I knew how to do that properly in

this situation. If I was not Japanese and raised to think hugs were for children, lovers, and warm welcomes, and little else. If I hadn't been taught that grief means respecting the need of the grieving for distance, even if that person is someone close to me.

"They wanted to interview me," she says when she pours the tea. "They said it was only to help them before they began to call in the witnesses. It was off the record. No need for lawyers, and all of that. Tricky buggers, eh?" She sat on a stool and began flicking through a notebook. She tears out a page out and hands it to me. "Nori rang after you left. He gave me this phone number. He said it's his hotel and that I should give it to you. Maybe he's still there."

I reach for the phone on the wall, and as sometimes happens in life, it rings before I tap the first digit. I pause before answering. The synchronicity has unnerved me.

Carol takes the phone from my hand. "Hello? You have Kingi house. This is Carol speaking." She mouths his name to me and passes the receiver back.

I can nothing but silence on the other end. "Hello?" I ask. "Hello?" I ask again then I switch to the Japanese prompt. "*Moshi-moshi*?"

"Ya-chan?" He asks using the term of endearment. It's too much for me, and my stomach tightens. "You tried to kill Paul-san!" I hiss in Japanese.

"I didn't know Rick-san would be capable of committing such a crime. I didn't tell him to do it."

I laugh coldly. "You are nothing but a criminal your-self! Do you know that? And, you can't even control your idiot thugs!" I am about to hang-up on him, but I don't. There is something in his voice. The tone. The delivery. The words.

"I am sorry for what has happened," he tells me in a shaky voice. "I want us to meet and talk."

"I don't have anything to say to you, Nori. You should be in jail!"

"I am staying in Rotorua City," he says quickly. "It's not so far from where you are now." He waits for me to reply. When I don't, he quickly adds, he could hire a heli-copter to fetch me in the morning. We could eat lunch at his hotel. It's such a ridiculous idea that I hang-up imme-diately. The man is completely delusional.

"Well?" Carol asks, searching my face for a clue. "Are you meeting with him?"

I take a deep breath. I don't have to wait long for the phone to ring again. Then something odd happens. I find myself listening to the Nori, I knew a long time ago. The man I once thought I had married.

"Please don't put the phone down," he tells me. "I am sorry for what happened to Paul-san. I know it's my fault. I very much regret the way I acted toward you. I should never have struck you." He doesn't mention what happened in the hotel room, but I let him keep talking.

"Of course, I will pay Paul-san's family reimburse-ment for the suffering I have caused."

"Why are you telling me what you are going to do, Nori? Why don't you just do it?"

"I will—everything I have said! I promise."

Despite my disgust, I am moved by his words. It seems he is still able to speak from the heart about someone other than himself.

"Is Bill-san in jail?" He asks.

"Yes, and I want him out. Carol-san wants him out!"

"I hate him," he whispers.

"You get him out of that jail! He did nothing wrong."

"He tried to take a man's wife."

"I never told him I was married."

"You should have!"

"Nori, I stopped being your wife the day I left you. You stopped being a husband a long time ago—Do you know how long ago, Nori?"

"You are only twenty-three years old. You will change."

"I've changed already. I will never be what you want."

"I can't live without you," he says quietly. Then he adds one more lie to all the others he has told me. "In my heart, I am always with you."

Carol watches me put down the phone and walk outside. I feel sick.

After sitting on the steps and taking several deep breaths, I go back inside the house.

She tells me she will be leaving early in the morning to visit Paul. It will take her two hours to reach Rotorua

by car. Her sister will be returning with her to stay at the
house with us.

I thank her for her kindness and I tell her she's brave.
I tell her I will convince him to tell the police the truth.
It's as much as I can promise.

46

The interview room is a stark windowless box with a table and three chairs positioned in the center. There is also the ubiquitous rectangular one-way glass panel set in a wall. A useless fan rattles in the corner. The room is too warm, and the air is fetid. Perhaps Detective Sean Fender likes things this way.

If so, then that would make him a masochist since he's grossly overweight and already perspiring heavily. Small beads of perspiration gather under Fender's eyes and run in rivulets down his puffy red cheeks. He looks like he's crying, but he's not. Semi-circles of damp darken the white shirt under his armpits.

Sitting opposite him, I want to ask him to reposition the fan. That would require him to move. I think better of it.

Detective Allister McClary is tall with a dry, frizzy brown halo of hair and a pink bald patch in the center that he seems never to stop scratching. He leans against the wall with an attitude that could be mistaken for disinterest. His questions are perfunctory and direct.

Judging from their bored expressions, I've little doubt the two men asked me here to verify conclusions they have already reached. I get the distinct impression they think they have all the facts, and as a result, the conclusion is obvious. That scares me.

"Alright, Mrs. Shimano," Fender says. "We have your statement. I don't believe we have any more questions for you."

He looks up at McClary.

McClary shakes his head. "No, I'm done."

Fender reaches for the plastic jug of water in the center of our table and tops up his paper cup.

"Can I see Bill now?" I ask him.

The two detectives exchange a glance. Fender picks up his cup and gulps the water. "There is one thing. I would like you to clarify one last point in your account." He pulls over the clipboard McClary has placed on the table beside him and flicks through the pages.

"Of course," I reply. I'm relieved I might have the opportunity to correct at least one of their assumptions. "Please go ahead."

Fender licks the end of his finger and pulls out a single sheet from under the clip. He purses his lips and stares at it for almost a minute.

"If you are with your husband in the helicopter, and Mr. Manning is there with you—and he's already injured, why would he have his employee shoot Mr. Manning's buddy?" He stares up at me. "That doesn't make any sense unless I'm missing something."

He glances up at McClary. "You were wondering the same, weren't you?"

McClary grunts in reply. "Yeah, I am a little curious about that."

"My husband is a jealous man, but he never wanted Paul-san dead or seriously injured. As I have already told you, he wanted to frame Bill for a serious crime—the dangerous use of firearms—so he would be arrested. That way, Bill would not be around to influence me. All Nori wanted was for the two of us to return to Tokyo together."

I'm not sure that was all he wanted. Perhaps underneath his calm rational what he desired was revenge.

"Uh-huh," Fender says and leans forward, pressing his palms together under his chin. "Well—explain it again for us, just so we have it all crystal clear!"

"Nori wanted to make it look like I was kidnapped. He wanted the police to believe that after Bill and Paul imprisoned me in the hut, they argued. That's when they supposedly shot at each other. But none of that happened!"

"Why didn't he just have his man shoot Mr. Manning?" McClary asks. He tilts his head and raises an eyebrow.

"I told you already!" I exclaim in frustration. I know I'm overreacting a little, and I don't want to give in to the doubt rising inside me, but I'm beginning to feel desperate.

"You told us you never saw the rifle being fired," Fender says, reading through the page in his hand. "You said you only heard the shots."

"Yes, I was harnessed in the cockpit and Rick was behind me by the door with my husband," I tell him.

"In that case, how can you even be sure the shot came from the chopper?" Fender asks me.

"I was inside the cockpit. It was noisy. But I certainly heard the two shots. They were loud! They came from right behind my head. Two loud cracks. They did not come from outside the helicopter."

The detective reads from the page at a painfully slow speed. "You have told us—and here I quote. 'He has changed. He is no longer the man I thought I married'."

He gazes up at me. "That is what you said?"

I nod my head in agreement. "Yes."

"And you go on to say the following—I feel nothing for him. Meaning your husband." He looks up at me and raises one eyebrow. "You did say that too, didn't you?"

I nod my head again and stare at the thin carpet on the floor. *My marriage is beyond repair.*

I look up and smile. I am wearing my mask.

"Consider this possibility, if you will," Fender says. "You have convinced yourself your husband is a bad man, and you have allowed your emotion to color your memory—because you are so cross with him." He is warming to his theory. "Now, remembering all of that, what if the shots did not come from behind you?" Fender asks. "What if they did not even come from inside the chopper? What if, in the heat of the moment, you heard engine noise?"

"Detective Fender-san. On one hand, you say two crazies—who for some reason took me into the mountains against my will—start shooting at each other. Then, on the other hand, you suggest, I have decided to pin the shooting on my husband." I stare at them both. "I guess I must be crazy too! I mean what are the chances? What a great opportunity. How nicely it all fits together."

"Somebody shot Mr. Kingi!" Fender exclaims. He slaps his pen down on the table so suddenly that he makes me jump. "We have two different versions of the shooting. And I guarantee you that both cannot be correct. While I have no doubt your husband is a volatile man, the forensic evidence remains clear. The shot was fired from Mr. Manning's rifle. They would have to get Mr. Manning into the chopper, then take his gun and shoot Mr Kingi with it."

"That is what happened, more or less," I tell them.

"Okay. Let's look at the alternative. Which is a lot less elaborate explanation. I put it to you that you were in a state of shock at the time your husband and his rescue team pulled you out of the hut. You simply assumed Mr. Manning was in the helicopter with you." He placed his palms on the table and leaned forward. "You are telling us you heard gunfire coming from inside the chopper.

And Mr. Manning was in the chopper—but—he was unconscious."

"Yes, I—"

He raises his hand to stop me from interrupting him. "Let's leave aside the question of Mr. Manning's location for the moment. Let's deal with the loud bangs you say you heard that you are sure were the gunshots. Okay?"

I want to scream. But I tell myself these men are stubborn bulls that must blow and bluster until they've run themselves to exhaustion.

"I say those two loud bangs came from the chopper," Fender says. His voice is polite as he fixes me with the unblinking gaze of a snake about to strike. "After all the engine is behind you… Have you considered that?" He picks up his pen and taps the end of it against his teeth as he waits for my answer.

"I did think those sounds were from the engine. That it had some mechanical fault. That was before I found Paul lying in the hut with gunshot wounds! Wait! Are you talking about the noise a helicopter engine makes when it backfires?"

Fender waves the end of his pen at me. "Yep, a backfire. Exactly."

"How would you know what that noise sounded like?" I ask him.

Fender leans forward in his chair. "Excuse me?"

"How would you know if a helicopter engine was backfiring?"

"How would I know?" He asks, repeating my question. He frowns and glances up at his partner.

"It happens all the time," McClary suggests with a shrug.

I fold my arms and stare back at them. "No, it doesn't."

Fender stabs his pen into the air. "A chopper engine can backfire. I've heard them, and it sounds like a shotgun discharging."

He glances at McClary as if for confirmation.

"That can happen with a learner pilot behind the controls," I tell them.

Fender blinks. "Oh, and you're an expert on choppers, are you?"

"I'm no expert, but I do have over sixty hours flying time in a helicopter."

McClary scratches his scalp with the end of his pen. He pulls out the chair in front of him and sits down. "You're a chopper pilot?"

"I'm licensed to fly a helicopter in Japan. I did my basic training in the US—after I quit college."

"Someone has a rich daddy," McClary mutters.

"At one time," I reply.

"You said it couldn't have been a backfire," Fender prompts, but I see the hesitation in his face already.

I give a nod. "Yes, a turbo engine on a helicopter backfires—if you don't operate the collector properly."

He opens his hands. "So what exactly is a—what'd you call it?"

"A collector is like a throttle. You find it beside the pilot's seat." I pull on an imaginary lever beside my chair to show them the action. "If too much air goes over the compressor blades, they can go out of sync, and they stall. You get a loud noise that sounds like a shotgun. It's not uncommon when the pilot is inexperienced." I glance at McClary, who's writing once more in quick, jerky motions. I long to see Bill's face.

"I could see the guy flying the helicopter was no amateur," I tell them. "He really knew what he was doing! You can check with the Japanese police that I have a license to fly," I add quickly.

McClary looks up from his notepad. "Oh, we will be doing that."

The fat detective turns to his partner. "The pilot was a local, wasn't he?"

"Yeah," McClary replies, and he flicks through his notes and pulls a page from a plastic sleeve. "From this Mr. Tua Naho has a military background. It says here he was in the NZDF. In the late nineties, he was under contract with a mining company operating in Bougainville. Let's see…" He flicks back a page. "Recently—he worked in New Guinea as a chopper pilot. That was for a security company. Going from the brief here, he's a crack chopper pilot and in high demand. Flies for—"

"Alright, I get the picture," Fender says, waving McClary to move on.

McClary runs his eyes quickly over the page again.

"Ah, his family lives down the coast not too far from here."

"So, he's a merc then?" Fender asks.

He glances across at McClary when he doesn't get a reply.

The detective stares at me like he's having an epiphany of a sort. "Yeah, I guess you could call him that," McClary says.

"I would," Fender says. "And what about the other one?" Fender asks McClary, carefully avoiding my gaze.

McClary reads from his notes again. "We haven't yet got much information about Rick McDonald. He's also ex-military. We know he and Naho were in the same Army unit, and they did at least one tour together in Afghanistan. They got out of the Army around the same time, and both worked for the private security company in New Guinea. I wouldn't doubt they worked security for a mining operation. The local government was facing terrorist actions by rebel groups at the time. McDonald's background has a few noticeable gaps we are trying to fill. Here and there he appears to fall off the radar"

"What is a merc?" I ask.

Fender busies himself sorting through pages in his clipboard. "Merc is short for mercenary," he replies without looking up at me. "Soldiers of fortune. That's what we used to call them. They fight for the side that pays the most."

He holds the block of papers upright and squares the block, then he slides it under the heavy metal spring and releases the clip with a thump. The two men glance at each other, and as if on cue, stand at the same time.

"Thank you for your help, Mrs. Shimano," Fender tells me, but he hasn't finished. "For the time being, while this investigation continues, you must not leave the town boundaries without first reporting to the police. If you think of any more information or have any questions, please call us. You can ask for me."

"You want to interview me again?" I ask in surprise.

"You will be at the address you have given, right?" Fender asks.

I nod my head in reply.

"Oh, and I believe your husband is waiting for you outside," he says.

At the end of the corridor, there's a small window set in a door. Through the glass, I glimpse Nori's face on the other side. I step back into the interview room.

"I want to see Bill!" I tell them.

"Mr. Manning is in custody," Fender tells me.

"Why can't I still see him?"

"He's locked up in Auckland," McClary says.

"When then?" I persist.

"We'll check that for you," Fender tells me.

There is nothing left for me to do but to walk out the door and face Nori.

47

S o they interviewed you too?" Nori asks.

"Of course they did!" I say. "I was a witness."

"I could tell them I made a mistake about who it was I saw fire the gun," he tells me.

"If you start changing your story, they won't believe anything you say," I reply with a cold laugh. "So what really happened, Nori?"

He pokes the end of a cigarette between his lips and rummages about in his pocket for the lighter.

A young Maori constable at a desk behind the reinforced glass partition raps on the partition window until he has Nori's attention. "Sir, the sign above your head clearly states this is a no smoking area. Do you see it?" He jerks a finger in the direction of the white plastic notice screwed into the wall above the desk.

"*Ah, sumimasen*," Nori says with a polite nod of his head and takes the cigarette out of his mouth.

We move to sit on a vinyl-covered bench next to a traditional tapestry that hangs inside a glass case. Two tattooed youths dressed for rebellion in tattered jeans, red T-shirts, and worn leather jackets beat us to the seat. They sit, one at either end of the bench without so much as a glance in our direction. As if we were not standing directly in front of them.

"I will be very happy when I get back home," Nori mutters.

On the street outside the police station, I persist with my questions until he relents. I see the look of relief on his face when he finally talks.

Rick had seen the gun lying in the grass in front of Bill when they flew over the hut. He told Nori he was going to use it to shoot Paul's horse. The gun and the bullet would provide forensic evidence pointing to Bill's role in the shooting. Rick said he would drop the gun close to the clearing. Somewhere the cops would find it.

Nori told me he never liked the idea there would be shooting. It didn't matter what he thought, because Rick went ahead with his plan, anyway. Once Bill and I were inside the helicopter and they were in the air Rick asked Tua to bring the chopper close so there would be no mistakes. He fired twice at Paul from the open door. The horse was later found to be uninjured.

"I was shocked," Nori says, lowering his voice. As if anyone would understand what he was saying. "I didn't want to believe Rick-san shot him on purpose. I did see him wiping his fingerprints from the weapon and pressing Bill-san's hand to the gunstock."

Nori shook his head at his memory of the events of that day and gazed across the street. "Rick-san was cool and calm. He was like a machine." He turned to me. "I only wanted to hire a pilot, but Tua-san told me he and Rick-san came as a team."

"Where are they now?"

"They were sharing a hotel room in Rotorua," he says.

Then Nori reveals the true depth of his delusional state.

"You know Ya-chan, the Japanese media would like to see us reunited. The publicity would be good for both our careers."

"And what will they think when I tell them you framed an innocent man?" I tell him.

He flicks a smoking butt into the gutter, his eyes darting from me to the door of the police station. His thoughts are but one hundred cats in a burning house. He has no control over them. "It looks bad, doesn't it?" He glances at me, nods his head and sighs.

48

In a café crowded with sunburned tourists and excited children, a young waitress hurries to clear cups and plates from a table. She sweeps the tabletop with a damp gray cloth, spreading crumbs and spilled coffee across the surface. Looking up with a start when we sit down.

"Why don't you go to the police and tell them it was Rick-san?" I ask him.

"If they arrest Rick-san, they will arrest me too!" He blurts out the words like a small boy who reacts defensively when asked to show responsibility.

"They are going to arrest you soon enough. Once they interview Paul-san, Tama-san and Noel-san are going to tell the truth. The police will match up the stories. Guess who they are going to believe then, Nori!"

"Those two didn't see anything. They were well out of the area when we arrived in the chopper."

"Don't you know? They picked Bill out of the

riverbed where you dropped him. They saw the shooting."

I watch with a sense of satisfaction as the color drains from his face.

"They saw the shooting?"

"And they picked Bill out of the riverbed," I repeat for good measure.

"I didn't know," he mutters, and he lights a cigarette. "I will tell the police they are blackmailing me," he says finally. "I will tell them they are trying to extort more money from me." His face is gaunt as he stubs out his half-smoked butt. "If you agree that we go home together —I will make a statement to the police telling them that Rick fired the shot."

"They will charge you for giving a false statement," I reply. I can barely hide my scorn.

Nori pulls his ringing mobile from his pocket and stares blankly at the display. "It's the police," he says as he reads the text.

I see the flicker of fear in his eyes. His hand drops to the table as he rubs his forehead, and I pick it up and read aloud. I glance up at him.

"Detective McClary wants you to tell me I must return to the police station. He says it's an urgent matter."

"Mrs. Shimano, we best go to the interview room," Detective McClary tells me.

"You called me on my phone," Nori says, waving his *keitai* at the detective. "She is my wife. I go too."

McClary doesn't argue with him. At the end of the corridor, the detective opens the door to the interview room, and when we go in, he quietly closes the door behind him. "Please, take a seat."

McClary looks at me with an odd expression. I brace myself for the worst. I know now they are going to charge Bill with kidnapping and attempted murder. I realize I may not get to see him outside of a prison again, and my heart sinks.

He clears his throat. I don't know what it is with hands, but I always notice what people are doing with them. Eyes and hands are pretty much how I read people, and I can see that McClary is preparing himself. He's stilling the turmoil he feels inside. He opens a small notebook and runs his eyes down the page as if to check he has his speech correct.

There's a millisecond when he looks up to blink at me, and I know with absolute certainty before he can get out a single word of his rehearsed lines.

"Mrs. Shimano, I'm afraid I have bad news for you. Ah, for you both. Mr. Paul Kingi passed away three hours ago at Rotorua Central Hospital."

He sucks in his breath and deepens his voice. "Given what you have told us, I thought it best you hear this directly from me…"

"What about Bill?" I ask as my world stops spinning.

"Mr. Manning faces serious charges. I can't tell you more at this stage."

His words gather about my feet, sticky and heavy like wet winter leaves. I get up from the table and walk out the door into the empty corridor. There has been a mistake. I turn back to the detective who gazes after me, and I hear myself speaking as if from a great distance. "They said Paul-san's condition is stable."

The detective's face is drawn and gray. He opens his notebook again. "It seems... In the case of a shooting... We are often faced with postoperative complications. It appears the projectile striking Mr. Kingi traveled diagonally through his body—causing significant damage. A full report..."

I tightly close my eyes and turn away. I hear McClary telling Nori that if we go back to the interview room, he will bring back two cups of hot tea into us. I feel myself shaking.

49

I want to write a song about time and space. Human beings like to think of these two dimensions as separate. It isn't easy to think of time and space as being one and the same, and yet we do perceive our passage through time as a movement through space. This is one way we can conceive of them being the same.

It is as if we think of ourselves as carried like butterflies by currents that are out of our control. With our limited range of senses, we conclude we are imprisoned by time. So it is that we find ourselves asking the same question over and over again. Where does a particular even begin? Where does it end? We believe we are not able to change a thing and set about marking the stages. Our life then becomes a series of little beginnings and little ends that affect only ourselves. This is why we see our existence as speck-like, endlessly sentenced to a meaningless journey through time and space. So we believe.

It is only a belief.

I won't reduce myself to an inconsequential speck. I am not dust *blowing in the wind. Surely, such a belief denies the footprint each of us leaves behind in the world? Surely, we should not think of any lives as mere existence? Not when we love and hate and dream and change things around us. Ultimately the world changes us, and then we make changes to our world all over again. As we live our lives together, we can change almost anything. If we are united, we can make big changes. We decide together where to begin and when to end. But I can't put all this into a song. Who would buy it?*

Nori hands me the keys to the rented Toyota Land Cruiser, telling me he's too shaken to drive. I say there's a local place I want him to see. I hope it will help bring Nori to his senses. Like me, he is not allowed to return to Japan until the inquiry into Paul's death is completed. So, he will go with me. What else is there for him to do?

It isn't difficult to find the spot. The road to Makara Point simply follows the coastline after all.

I pull off the road onto the grassy shoulder at the top of the cliff. It feels like no time has passed since the day they dived for *koura*.

I turn off the engine when we are behind a station wagon parked beside a battered-looking van. We sit in the cab and watch the storm clouds mass over the steel gray ocean.

Inside the station wagon, four teenagers are drinking from cans. Wetsuits are hanging over the open doors, and surfboards are tied to the roof rack. They turn to watch our arrival with only a vague interest before they return to their conversation.

Two girls climb out of the back of the car with barely a glance in our direction. They walk over to the van. The young guys pull their wetsuits off the doors and throw them onto the backseat. The doors of both vehicles slam closed. The van's exhaust pipe puffs white smoke that is sent scudding over the grass by a gust of wind.

One of the girls leans out her window to tease the driver with a joke and a gesture. The hoots and howls of the boys are lost in the clatter of tired engines revving. The van turns out onto the road, the car following close behind, and the two vehicles disappear around the corner in the direction of the town.

Nori stares across at the dark sheet of approaching rain. "Why this place? It's desolate."

"It's peaceful," I tell him.

I gaze through the glass at the trail that zigzags down to the stony shelf.

"You liked Paul-san?" He asks.

"Yes," I tell him. "He's a gentle, funny man."

I can't think of him as belonging only to my past. I prefer to imagine him in the here-and-now. I can still hear his voice as he walks behind me down to the sea to the rock they will use to dive off. At the dinner table, folding slabs of butter between white bread. Astride his horse, telling jokes and chastising me for not finding them funny.

Bill stares at the rickety old fence. "Did he have children?"

"He has a wife. Her name is Carol-san."

He falls silent.

"They wanted to make the orchard work. He bought Carol a Toyota truck." I laugh. I remember how Paul defended his decision to us. "I think that he really bought it for himself."

"Everyone is a little selfish," Nori says quietly.

"Yes, that's true."

He looks down at his hands resting on his thighs palms up, the way old men sit in the heat of summer and gazes out his side window. "There's nothing I can do to change things, is there?"

Is he finally coming to grips with reality? I hope so.

The thunder rolling over the bay is loud enough to drown out the boom of the sea slamming against the cliff. We can both feel the electricity in the air. The storm is not far away.

Before I realize he has his hand on the release, he opens the door and steps outside. I reach him as he stands by the fence. He folds his jacket into a neat square and lays it on the grass.

I pick it up like a dutiful wife for him to put back on. I hold the jacket out to him, flat in the palms of my hands, so I don't lose the folds.

He turns away.

"Nori, what are you doing?"

He straightens the cuffs of his shirt and tugs on the

arms of his shirt. It is as if he was checking his appearance in front of a mirror.

I reach out or him. "Come back to the car."

"You have the long fingers of a violinist," he says, gazing at my hand resting on his. He lifts his face to catch the drops carried in the breeze and closes his eyes. "I forgot how good rain can feel…"

"You are not well," I tell him. "Come back with me."

I am beating down a strong urge to drag him to the car, but I've no chance of performing the feat alone. To even try as much might be enough to cause him to take action. The wind is getting stronger, and I reach out for the fence post to steady myself as a gust, and a cloud of rain hits us.

He turns into the squall and stares out over the gray ocean. When he looks back at me, I see the emptiness that was in his black eyes moments ago is replaced by resignation.

"Go back to the car, please," he tells me. "Go back to town."

Now I see what he has in mind. It was there before I bought him to this place but I have given him the perfect backdrop. That wasn't what I thought he would feel from this place. A rising sense of panic grips me. "You can't bring Paul back by jumping off a cliff," I tell him. "That's ridiculous!"

A shiver runs through him. He runs his hands down the front of his shirt his body buffeted by the gusts of wind. "Will you come back to Tokyo with me?" He calls out and he waits for my answer. When he doesn't get one, his lips tighten in a sardonic smile. "I didn't think so."

"Let's go back, Nori—please!"

"You are best to let me go," he says, and he laughs, but there is no joy in it. "That is what you wrote in the note you left me in our apartment."

I step closer. "How will this help mend anything?" He grimaces.

"Does your father still grow rice?" He asks. His eyes are as dark as the storm clouds overhead, and yet they are clearer than I remember seeing them before. I see in his face that the moment has passed and he is seeing me anew. Am I what he expected?

"Father's rice fields are ruined. The soil is poisoned."

He nods his head slowly. "It is going to take a lot of effort to restore what was lost. He must try harder."

"Yes," I reply.

"Without farmers, there is no Japan," he says. I can tell he is beginning to feel a little embarrassed, and I know he's struggling to control his emotions.

"That is true," I say.

He takes his jacket out of my hands and slips it over the wet shirt. "I could never make a good rice farmer."

I watch him walk to the car, and only when I see him get inside and shut the door do I allow myself to relax a little

When we turn onto the road that will take us off the peak, he looks at me. "I thought I was ready to do that," he says. "I guess I'm not, after all."

On the outskirts of the town, he tells me to take him to the police station, then he tells me he has thought of a *haiku*. I ask to hear it.

Spring in a mirror
    I see you are me
    In search of a heart.

arol's sister hands me the house phone.

"Yayoi, I've been calling you!" Shizue tells me with a mix of impatience and relief.

"I'm sorry." I feel embarrassed. She will know almost everything that's happened now.

"Ya-chan!" She screeches. "I heard your husband was arrested?"

"Yes, I took him to the police station myself."

"Why didn't you tell me?"

"I'm sorry. I haven't been thinking clearly." I explain my story and that things are no longer so good between Carol and me. I mention that the police have told me I cannot leave the town for a while. I tell her how much I want to see Bill again.

She tells me that Koga is blaming her for the lack of information, but I am not to worry, because she knows how to handle him. She says J-Big is telling the media almost nothing. Yet the leaks are coming out. There are even whispers that Nori Shimano has been arrested in a foreign country. The story has been breaking across the news channels in Japan for the past twenty-four hours.

I tell her I dread what it will be like when I return and I remind her how much I dislike the paparazzi.

She tells me again not to worry, that she will arrange a quiet re-entry. She will keep my location in New Zealand a secret.

In the days leading up to the funeral, Carol's sister moves into the extra bedroom in the house. Carol gives me little opportunity to talk. The two sisters are constantly together. Friends from town visit.

When the police release Paul's body to his family, a *tangihanga* is held on the *marae*. Aunty Margaret asks me how things are with Carol when we meet again at the *tangi*. I try to pretend that everything is okay between the two of us, but the old lady sees right through me. She suggests I stay at her house. I immediately accept her offer, and I tell Carol's sister, she replies that she thinks it's a good idea.

I offer money to the old couple for my board and breakfast, but they refuse to take it. Aunty Margaret is adamant I am with Billy, and that's the end of it.

Uncle Hemi and Aunty Margaret say many in the tribe want to make an official complaint to the authorities for forcing the *tangi* to be delayed. A three-day ceremony to honor the dead must wait for all the official processes required by the state. The old man says it's right to make the complaint, but in the end, he doesn't push for it. I can tell he's upset, but he refuses to make any more of it.

It seems like most of the town shows up for the *tangi*. Later, outside the *marae*, I talk to Noel. He says Tua and Rick disappeared and good riddance. Only he says it with more feeling. I ask about Tama who is nowhere to be seen during the three days of mourning. Noel tells me Tama has some loose ends to chase down. When that was done and sorted Tama will pay his respects to the family. I heard a little later that Tua handed himself over to the police.

The day after the family buries Paul, the police visit the farmhouse to interview me. Aunty Margaret serves cups of tea and biscuits while I wait for them to ask me questions about Nori. They want to confirm I went into the mountains of my own free will. Aunty Margaret pokes her head into the room to tell them this was definitely the case. They tell her that she is not to interrupt a police interview, and she tells them that since it's her house, she can do as she pleases. She stays within earshot as they finish the rest of their questions, but she doesn't say another word. They seem to be satisfied with my answers.

Uncle Hemi has cleaned up his old car for me to use. The car is an antique that's twice my age. It is round, green, and very British. Although it has no air-condi-

tioner, I am grateful to have the use of it. The first thing I
after Uncle Hemi hands me the keys is to drive to the
beach and park outside the Life Savers Club House.

The sky is a piercing blue the cab already feels like an
oven. I plan to walk as much of the beach as I can. I'm
not sure why I chose to visit the ocean. I decide that I am
here to test my courage. I gulp down the last of the spring
water I have brought with me, drop the keys in my
shoulder bag, open the door. It's barely any cooler
outside.

When I walk in the sand the first thing I see is the
young mothers playing with their children. Kids and
moms together building castle towers and digging moats
with plastic buckets and spades. An old man sits on a
folding camp stool, watching over several fishing rods
spiked into the sand. Occasionally he gets to his feet and
checks the rods, running the lines through his hands to
feel for a nibble. He's happy enough simply to sit and
wait. The fish may not bite today, but there is always
tomorrow.

Out in the surf, three adolescent girls hold each
other's hands as they jump and scream, waves splashing
up to their shoulders, the foam enveloping their legs, and
threatening to pull them out on the return. They don't
notice how cunning the sea is as it moves them little by
little away from the spot they left their towels and shoes
on the sand.

The dunes run into the distance like a line of ancient
burial mounds. As I walk on, the young mothers and their

toddlers, the teenagers, and the fishermen all disappear behind me. Their voices drowned out by the noise of the waves and the screams of hungry seagulls.

I find on an old splintered stump to sit on and rest my head in my hands, I close my eyes. It is another test. I want to find out how long it will be before the sound of waves rolling in overwhelms me and drives me back to the car.

I did not mind sleeping on the beach when I was with Bill. I felt safe then. Or perhaps I was just too tired to care if the sea took us while we slept.

I don't have to wait long before they all come back to me. My family. My childhood friends. My neighbors. They run through the pages of the library of photos. An album I keep locked in my head. All those pale memories. Not yet faded away. The smiles, the laughter, and the tears. I have never been able to let them go.

51

The evening sky is a luminescent blue cut through with pink when the little jet taxies off the runway and turns onto the strip of tarmac opposite the terminal building. The last Eagle Airways for the day has landed five minutes after its scheduled arrival time. When he walks through the gate, I am so excited I barely notice how drawn he looks. When I release his thin frame from my hug, I notice his eyes. They are staring, and yet they do not stare at anything.

"You must be hungry," I tell him. "We can stop somewhere to eat before we go home."

"I wouldn't mind if we head straight back to the farm," he tells me.

"Sure," I reply.

I take his hand and pull him through the crowd. He doesn't speak as we make our way across the parking lot. Before we get to the car, his hand has slips out of mine.

. . .

He stares through his side window at the white volcanic plume rising from the island on the horizon, the smoke hanging in a long veil across the bay. He turns to me when we exit the last hill range before the farm.

"There's a picnic stop around the next corner," he tells me. "If you don't mind, I wouldn't mind if we pulled in for a little while? I want to get out and walk for a bit."

It's the most he's said to me since we left the airport. I turn the little car into the rest area. Alongside us, there's a wooden bench table. On the warped boards lies a collection of crushed beer cans in a pile. He gets out of the car without bothering to close the door.

I watch him in the rearview mirror until he vanishes over a rise in the road, then I get out to lean against the side of the old car. It is not a cold evening, but I notice the heat of the engine, and it feels comforting. I lean against the side of the hood with nothing to do but to wait for him.

The long broad fronds of the gray-green flax bushes that shelter the rest area are rattling in an evening breeze. The empty tin cans on the tabletop roll back and forward, clinking together in empty toasts.

I watch a large indigo bird running on long bright red legs along the verge of the bitumen. It gives a loud beep-beep before it dives into the marsh grass. Not far behind run four gangly legged chicks chasing ungainly after their mother.

I am swept by the headlamps of a car coming over the rise and turning the bend. The vehicle passes by with a rumble and a clatter leaving behind the smell of oily smoke. I look around again when I hear the crunch of gravel.

He walks up without a word and leans his back against the wheel guard next to me.

"Are you okay?" I ask.

"Mm, I just needed to walk."

There's a distance between us that I thought had melted away on the beach the night before he was arrested. I want to comfort him, but how can I do that? "You want to talk?

He shakes his head, but he talks anyway. "I saw you out of the plane window when we landed," he says.

It's almost dark and I don't turn to look at him. I don't want him to turn away from me. Then, I realized just from the tone of his voice, that he sounds as though he's smiling. I find his hand and squeeze it. "I've waited a long time to see you again," I tell him.

"Yeah—I've missed you too," he tells me. He leans his head on mine.

I turn to him and kiss away salty tears.

Uncle Hemi embraces him. Then so does the old woman. She hugs him for a long time.

Even though he tells them he would rather sleep than eat, Uncle Hemi insists he at least enjoys a cup of tea with them while they have their meal. "We will bore you so much, you'll fall asleep in your chair," Aunty Margaret tells Bill. The old couple chatter through the homecoming meal of sweet crab meat, roast pork, sweet potatoes, pumpkin, and cabbage.

Later, I lie on my bed unable to sleep. I hear pieces of conversation drifting down the hall. They are broken sentences. Expressions of remorse, regret, and forgiveness. I fall to sleep only to wake sometime later to the old man's sobs and the voice of the old lady as she consoles him.

In the morning, I sit up in my bed and squint into the sunlight that escapes between the drapes. I run my hands over the raised box pattern on the bedcover, the texture reminds me of a woolen blanket my mother would throw over a chair when the weather turned colder. Although the bedcover is worn and old, the texture feels good.

Bill's head appears around the door.

"*Ohayo gozaimasu,*" I call out in greeting.

"Hey, sleepyhead!" He replies. "How about a quick breakfast before we head off? If that's okay with you?"

I nod my head and smile, but he doesn't come in.

"There's plenty of hot water if you want a shower," he calls out as he walks down the hall.

"You can come in here if you like," I tell him. But he's gone, and I wonder what I am to him?

I hear him calling outside my window, then the sound

of dogs running up the steps, their claws scraping the wooden boards as they slide to a stop in front of him. I can hear their tails beating the deck of the porch.

Aunty Margaret yells at Bill from the kitchen window, telling him to get the animals off her porch.

I shower and change into my clothes. I come out of the bathroom to a quiet house. Uncle Hemi is outside doing his chores, and Aunty Margaret has already left for Rotorua with a long list of supplies to buy.

I find Bill sitting at the kitchen table eating toast. He pushes a plate in front of me. He tells me I had better eat because I will need the energy. He says we are going to be walking across the fields to a place he wants to show me. It's a secret place, he says, where he and Paul sent much of their time together when they visited the farmhouse as children.

52

The ocean is a sparkling blue, all the way to the horizon. It stretches beyond the curve of the hill, and past the last gate that we pull closed behind us. I can smell rotting seaweed as we draw closer to the noise of the ocean splashing against the rocky shore.

"Do they own all of this land?" I ask him.

"In a way," he says. "They share the farm with the rest of the *hapu*. Uncles and aunts, brothers and sisters, nieces, and nephews—all the cousins."

"So Uncle Hemi is a caretaker?"

"They manage the farm. The property, along with costs and the profits all belong to the extended family."

"Do a lot of people in the town have a share in farms like this one?"

He looks at me as if I am crazy. "A lot of people in the town don't own squat—maybe they own a car."

We come to a steep decline that runs to the edge of a

rocky shelf projecting into the sea. Further along, I see how the foreshore meets a cliff that climbs a few hundred feet above the sea. Beyond the fence line at the top lies green pastures.

"You still there?" He asks with a grin, glancing over his shoulder at me.

"Of course. This is a piece of cake," I tell him.

"Paul and I spent a lot of our holidays out here together with our cousins," he says over his shoulder as we clamber down the bank. "I remember family get-togethers. There was always plenty of seafood like crabs, *kina*, mussels, and whatever fish we caught off the rocks."

On the ground, I see bright blue crabs scuttling over the sharp ridges of the rock, scattering before me with pincers raised above their carapace, ready to fight for their lives. They splash into the rock pools and sink beneath the clear surface, finding sanctuary in the seaweed on the cracked, stony bottom. Others scuttle under long, thick, shiny, brown straps of kelp drying in the sun. The entire ledge of rock I stand on is bejeweled with micro-worlds. Tiny pools are decorated with myriads of bright red, pink, and orange tendrils of sea anemones, tiny fish, and the small blue crabs.

I walk on after him and realize he's no longer in front of me. I pick my way down the loose scree expecting to find him around a corner staring at the dark blue swell lapping the rocky shelf. He has completely vanished. I turn to see where he might have gone. There is no fork in the path. There is nowhere to hide unless he dived into the sea.

"A boy playing games," I mutter, hoping he hears me.

Kuso! They're all the same. I should know that by now. I consider whether I shouldn't walk back to the farm-house. The cliff ahead of me falls directly into the sea. I stop and listen to the sloshing, slow, deep, and resonant coming from the rock. On the other side of the cliff, there has to be a sea cave.

A disembodied voice shouts, and I see him waving to me. The light blue of his short-sleeved rugby shirt tattered over a tanned arm. "Hey!"

I trudge back to the pillar of stone I had walked by. I see a deep, wide, dark split in the rock. I had walked right past without noticing it, hidden by the stone pinnacle.

He steps back inside the gap, and I peer into the blackness and see that it's a narrow opening arching high above. It reminds me of images I have seen of European gothic stone masonry.

"It's okay," he says his voice echoing in the chamber. "Come on in."

"Are there any bats," I tell him.

"I have never seen any here."

"Okay," I say, but I'm not convinced.

"Keep to your right," he tells me as he backs into the tunnel. "You're doing fine. Stretch your left hand out and touch the rock. You don't want to bang your head."

"Where are we going?" I ask.

"Wait and see," he says, already walking several paces ahead of me. "Never mind. Stay where you are, I'll coming back to you."

I feel his warm breath on my cheek.

"It takes a while for your eyes to adjust," he tells me.

I can see his outline, vague at first, but as my eyes get used to the gloom, I realize I can see a faint glow of pale light behind him.

"This way. Watch your feet! The cave floor is lumpy, and it's just a bit crabby too."

I feel something tiny and sharp running over my toes, and I shriek and jump aside, stepping on an object that crunches with a wet sound.

He chuckles. "You have to give them a better chance to get out of the way," he says. "Keep walking toward my voice."

I feel his warm hand slipping into mine, and I allow him to lead me ahead. Something rattles over my feet and I yelp.

"Shh! We need to be very quiet," he whispers.

"Things are moving on the ground," I hiss at him.

"Never mind the crabs," he says, his hand on my shoulder. "Stay close and watch your head."

I duck out of his reach. Dark, enclosed, and unfamiliar spaces like this are another thing hate! "I can't see any crabs around my fee, but I do see some light," I tell him.

"Look up," he whispers.

Above our heads are thousands of blue stars flickering, fading, then brightening again.

"Glow worms!" I exclaim. "Oh, they're so beautiful!"

"Aren't they great!" He exclaims.

The galaxies dim as we continue on, drawing closer to the sound of water dripping. I can see the glow of daylight ahead, and as we draw closer, we hear the hollow sloshing of waves. The dark cavern no longer seems mysterious and exciting. It is beginning to feel threatening, and I slow, no longer sure of myself or Bill.

He tugs at my hand.

The narrow passageway widens into a sunlit cavern with a wall of rock at one end, and at the other, the cave mouth opening to the outside world. Just outside the entrance to the cave sits a tiny island that glistens in the bright morning sun. It is only a few strokes by rowboat from where we stand. In the center of the island, an ancient pohutukawa tree stands triumphant at the highest point of the rock, although it isn't much taller than Bill. He tells me the tangled roots form a lattice that must run deep into the cracks in the craggy surface of the black rock. The tendrils drill to suck out the soup that's formed out of dead plant and animal matter, and that means the tree is well anchored. It is a beautiful thing. Even the waxy surface of dark leaves shine like polished gems in the bright morning sun.

"It will red flowers in a few weeks," he says, sitting down cross-legged at the entrance.

"Nature's own *bonsai* tree," I laugh. "It's beautiful.

This is what you wanted to show me."

"Yes," he says with a shy smile.

I sit down beside him and run my hand over the tiled surface of the cave floor.

"Cool, huh?" He grins proudly. "They are made of cork. They've been laid as far back as the end of the cave. Your feet don't hurt, because you are not walking on the sharp rock."

"Who laid them?"

"The *hapu* I guess. Maybe Uncle Hemi did. I don't know." He reaches into his backpack and produces two bottles of water and a couple of pears he stole from the kitchen bowl. We sit and eat and look at the tree on the tiny island.

He leans over and licks the juice from my chin. I push him, but he's waiting for me to do that, and he grabs my arms. We wrestle like children, and finally, he is on top of me, pressing me against the tiles.

I run my finger over his face and down his neck. "You're too heavy," giggle and I poke him in the chest. "You are going to squash me."

He kisses me on the lips slow and tender, and I embrace him, but soon I lift my head to peer over the edge of the seaward entrance.

There's a swell coming in. I can hear it.

From the side of my eye, I see the great, green translucent jelly splash over the steps cut into the rock a long time ago. It is a mooring made for a rowboat to tie up. The steps are to allow people to step on or off without having to clamber and slip. The slop of water against stone resonates off the cavern walls.

He chuckles, nibbling my nose, distracting me. I concentrate on him again, baring my teeth at him, snapping my jaws and growling. He runs his hands down my chest and pulls at my shirt. I place my ear against his chest, pretending to listen to the beat of his heart, and turn my face to kiss him and I bite his nipple.

"Hey!" He's whispers and he cups my face in his hands.

I shift under him and as I slide my hands up under his shirt, and down over the muscles of his stomach I feel him tremble. I work the tips of my fingers to the edge of his jeans and unfasten them. Then I freeze.

There is something in this chamber with us.

The booming sound comes from deep below the shelf, and I can hear it growing louder. "No!" I tell him and I try to lift him off me.

"What?" He protests, bewildered by my reaction. "We're safe in here!"

"You have to let me up. Now, please!"

I squeeze out from under him. Pushing myself upright on the palms of my hands to see for myself. But what is I am looking for? I have no idea. My damp hair whips across his face as I snap my head to and fro, trying to remember where the water level was when we first came into the cavern.

He rolls off my legs. "What is it?"

"The tide's coming in," I say.

He stares at me, not comprehending what is happening. "No... I mean, yes. But, we're almost ten feet above the water!"

Of course, he has no idea about the succubus. It doesn't care for a particular prey, it can be man or woman, young or old, healthy or infirm, one or one hundred thousand. It likes to count them in multiples. It's always hungry, and it has an ice-cold grip of death. It will wash in, and when it washes out it takes everything back to its lair in the deep, only to spit out whatever the remains.

"Let's get out of here," I tell him.

How do I make him understand!

"But, we're okay in here," he protests.

"We—I have to get out of this place. Can't you see?"

I crouch beside him as I try to calm myself. I pull up my hair to retie it high on my head. I can feel my hands shaking, and I know that he thinks I have gone mad.

"Okay then," he says unhappily. He gets to his feet and tosses the water bottles into the backpack.

I no longer notice the creatures that scramble to get out of the way. I hurry to the break in the wall where daylight cuts around the obelisk of stone outside the tunnel entrance. I feel only blind panic and a need to get out of the cavern and to step into warm sunshine as soon as possible.

I walk ahead of him up the hill, and I keep walking, deeper and deeper into the field of green until, at last, I can no longer hear the sound of the sea.

53

"Tell me what happened back there?"

I slow my pace and let him catch up with me. "I'm sorry," I reply.

"You panicked."

"I was afraid."

"Of what? Of me?"

"No. I felt like we were trapped in there."

"Well, I admit I wouldn't want to be in the cave in a storm. But, on a day like this—even with the tide turning. Jeez. We had plenty of time, Yayoi. I thought you might be having a seizure!"

We sit down in the middle of the field.

"I know you are disappointed," I say. "I'm sorry."

"Quit saying sorry. You say it all the time."

I expect him to get up and walk off, but he doesn't. Instead, he sits and puts his arm around me.

"Can we just sit here a while?" I ask.

"Sure," he replies.

I need him to know what happened. I need to tell the story I've locked away for years.

"Father and Grandmother never liked to talk about what happened on the day of the tsunami. Then, one day I asked Father, and he did tell me. Only that one day and never again. He said that day turned his world upside down."

I've buried the past so deep inside, and for so long. It's like a cancer that's eating me up.

"My home is in Miyagi prefecture, in the Tohoku region. It's a regular farming village, only about twenty minutes in a car from Saitama City. My family has grown rice there since forever. On the day of the earthquake, Father spent the morning fixing farm machinery. In another four weeks, the cherry blossoms would be out. That's when the farmers would begin planting.

"Grandmother wanted to walk by the rice fields. So after lunch, she and my father left Mother in the house and joined two neighbors for a stroll in the sun. The earthquake hit when they were in the fields. It was such a big jolt they had to sit on the ground. They heard the warning sirens sounding on the town office building, not far from their village. An emergency announcement called on them to run to the highest point they could reach without delay. For my village, that was a hill with a Shinto shrine at the top. It was about one mile from my father's fields.

"They should have known then and there to run, but

no one could know just how bad it was going to be. Grandmother thought it was a big quake but she said a tsunami had never reached as far as the farm in her life-time. It was only when they saw the sparkling line on the horizon and watched it shimmer like the heat haze in summer they really became concerned. Instead of running, they were mesmerized by the sight. They stood in the fields watching it grow larger.

"There was a busy road only four rice fields away from them, and cars were traveling down it at speed. Grandmother had never seen traffic on the road behave that way before. In reality, they were fleeing from the city.

"A neighbor driving his little white farm truck down a track passed by without a wave or any sign of recognition. But he realized in time and quickly braked some two hundred yards from them. He jumped out of the cab and yelled for them to get on the back of his tray."

I rip at the ground, pulling handfuls of grass from the dirt and casting them to the wind. Every green spear tip was someone I knew back then. Each of them a part of my life a long time ago. Now they are a memory I can't let go.

"Father told Grandmother to get up on the tray of the truck. Then he started running toward the farmhouse to bundle Mother into the car and make an escape. At that point, the shimmering line was a great silver eel thrashing in rice-flour. He fixed his eyes on the house and ran as fast as he could, but it seemed to him he was running through molasses. The house was too far away for him to make it in time.

"The writhing monster was already turning black. After racing through the city blocks, it had reached the rich soil of the farmland. Father realized he wasn't going to make it to the house and be able to get Mother out in time. He looked back at Grandmother and the small group behind him. He tried to wave them away, but they were gesturing for him to come back. Then he saw Grandmother standing beside the vehicle. She had not climbed on the back. He knew she wouldn't get on the truck until he returned, so he turned back.

"They made it to the hill just as the black wave bore down on them. The noise it made was like the *shinkansen* sprung from its tracks. It was tumbling and rolling toward them. Grandmother said the wave was so high that the crest could have easily washed over the roof of our two-story farmhouse.

"When they reached the bottom of the hill, they saw many trucks and cars from the village parked at the stone steps that led up to the shrine. Grandmother doesn't remember when getting off the truck. She only recalls clawing her way up the slope. The people already gathered at the top screamed to those still climbing the slope to move faster.

"They helped her climb the final few feet to the top, and when she turned to look back, she said she saw the wave tossing pieces of her village against the hillside. There were cars too, floating in the surge as the water was retreating to the sea. She saw white faces of people pressed against the windows, as their vehicles swirled and knocked into each like dodgem cars at a fairground.

"On that day, Japan learned that ordinary people have the courage and determination to start over again. We can reshape our destiny so long as we work as one, with a single purpose in mind. People like Father and Grandmother—the whole village really—showed me what it means to have strength."

An offshore breeze is coming over the rise, bending the grass as it sweeps wide, down into the dip, and up the other side.

"I saw some footage on TV, but I had no idea what it was like," he says.

"I know the dark side of the sea and what it can do," I tell him.

I open my fist and I watch as the blades of grass in my hand blow away.

"You are lucky to be so talented and popular, because you can use all of it to help others," he tells me.

"I was lucky. It isn't like I did it all by myself. My parents were already well known."

"I think people become famous because they are special in some way," he says.

Bill's a stone head. I don't want him thinking like this about me.

"It was the help of others, encouraging me and nour-ishing whatever talent I had that got me there. Anyway, all my hits came after the tsunami, and without the contract with J-Big, I could never have helped Father to return to his farm."

"It's too bad you need to stick with the company if it makes you so unhappy," he says.

"You want to know what I think is bad? Japanese having to live in shipping containers in their own country. Metal boxes with doors and windows cut into the sides. Our government calls them temporary shelters. They may as well be permanent! People have been living in them for years."

"There must be money to help out local farmers?"

"Public money was supposed to rebuild tsunami-damaged housing, and all of that, but the government had other priorities," I reply. "They used a lot of those funds to build up the whaling fleet, to build the Tokyo tower, and to train military pilots.

"There are Japanese companies building greenhouses on poisoned land to grow vegetables for supermarkets across the country. They get cheap labor from locals who no longer have work because of the disaster. People desperate enough to accept pitiful wages. It's bullshit! I should write angry songs about stuff like that!

"In my prefecture, there's lots of damaged farmland. Rice fields covered in oil and other shit. Chunks of concrete are scattered everywhere the tsunami went. The local government tells us it's too expensive to clear the rubbish away."

I get to my feet.

"Things are gone, but people remain, and doing nothing means accepting defeat."

It's time and I'm sure he knows.

"Bill-san, you know I'm going back, right?"

The breeze ruffles his hair across his forehead.

I reach out for his hand and run the edge of my nails across his palm. I want his hand to close tight around mine. But he turns away.

"I'm sorry I brought such great sadness to you and Carol-san," I tell him.

He opens his mouth to say something and closed it again. He smiles and shrugs. He doesn't know what to do, but he can't tell me that.

I put my arms around him and rest my head against his chest. This time I won't let him pull away from me.

"We shared a few fun times too, didn't we?" I say with my head on his chest.

I hear his heart beating, and I give him a shake. "We did, didn't we, Bill-san?"

"I thought we were done with calling me Bill-san."

"I could call you worse," I tell him.

54

I know it's crazy, but I really don't know where we go to from here, and for once, I don't mind. He tugs at the corner of my jacket.

"It's a bit warm for this, isn't it?"

"It's my habit," I reply. It seems I only visit graveyards on cold days.

Mother visited our ancestor's monuments behind our farmhouse every year in the first week of spring to clean the site and to say thank you to them. It was cold. As a small child, there I was, bundled up in my coat and muffler, watching Mother pulling weeds and sweeping the grit away. While she polished the marble until the surface shone brightly, I traced with my tiny fingers the *kanji* characters of my relatives' names etched into the stone.

She placed freshly cut chrysanthemums into a stone vase and burned incense. I watched her light the incense sticks and the blue spirals of smoke that climbed the sides of the obelisk to vanish into what was usually a clear blue late-winter sky.

She told me to honor the ancestors by telling them all the good things I have done during the year, and especially to tell them my plan for the coming year. Listening to what a child had to say would hardly be of interest to people I had never met, but later I recognized the point of her lesson was to be aware of the continuum, and one day I would become an ancestor too.

The cemetery where Paul is buried lies in the hollow between two hills. There are a few trees around the perimeter to cut the edge off the sea breeze. It is a pretty and quiet place. Exactly what a cemetery should be. He gazes at the mound with its blanket of fake green grass and the little white cross marker that fills the spot until the gravestone replaces it.

"Tell me what we're supposed to do," he says.

"We must talk to Paul with respect because now he's a god."

"Oh, come on," he laughs.

"That is what they say in Japan," I explain. "It's old thinking," I add quickly.

"Hey, Paul. You'd like that, wouldn't you? You'd say that was the way girls saw you—I mean before you met Carol."

"We forgot to bring a jar for the flowers," I tell him.

He places the flowers on the mound. "I don't think he minds," Bill says then he flourishes a bottle of rum from his backpack. "Since I also have this for him." He twists the top off the bottle and sits down cross-legged beside the pretend grass. He fills a tumbler, raises it in a toast, hen swallows the lot in one gulp.

"Argh," he says, screwing up his face, and passing me the empty glass. "Go on. Have a drink. You can't refuse a deity. You said it yourself."

Without waiting for my answer, he splashes rum into the tumbler.

The liquor burns my throat and sends me into a fit of coughing. He takes the glass from my hands and fills it again. "Bill!"

He ignores me and pulls back a section of the sheet of garish green grass to splash rum onto the fresh earth.

"I'm sorry I missed the *hangi*, bro. I heard you had a good one. I heard the old man spoke well about you. It's a pity the silly bugger didn't do that more often a little earlier when you were still with us, eh?" He snaps his head back and drains the liquor. Gasping and grimacing, he shakes his head, and refills the glass, continuing all the while to talk with a phantom. "I never got to join your birthday parties when I was in Auckland, did I? Then I go and miss your funeral."

He screws the base of the tumbler into the soft soil, slopping rum over the rim. He watches it soak into the ground. "You're not wasting a drop, are you? Straight down. That's the way." He brings the bottle to his lips and swallows.

"Take it easy!" I tell him.

He shakes a lock of hair from his eyes and turns to me. "This place is awfully empty; don't you think?"

I try to snatch the bottle from his hands, but he's amazingly fast for a half-drunk man and waves a finger at me in mock admonishment. "The three of us together again," he says to Paul. "This is good, don't you think?"

"Yes," I answered.

"You're getting behind," he tells me and hands me the glass.

"I'm driving," I say and I give it back to him.

He turns back to Paul and tells him that Carol is keeping things together. Then he gives me the glass and tells me it is my turn to talk to Paul. Several rows of headstones from us, a woman and a small child are making their way to the parking lot.

For some reason, I am thinking about how I can be a much better friend to Shizue. I promise Paul I will write to Carol, and that I will toast the two of them every New Years Day. I don't expect a reply, but I ask him what he thinks about Bill and me as a couple.

"Did you mention us?" Bill asks.

"Yes, I did," I tell him.

By the time we get to our feet, the light has almost disappeared. I watch him stumble. He chuckles and sits down again. "You want me to stay awhile longer, don't you bro."

"Come on, Bill," I say. "Time to go."

"Wait," he says and sets the bottle at the top of the mound. "He wants me to stay… a little bit longer." His voice is hoarse, and he is slurring his words.

"It's okay," I tell him. "There's no need to rush." I start walking back to the car.

"Stay here," he calls out softly to me.

A crescent moon has begun it's slow ascent as I start again down the path.

"Yayoi," he calls again, and I turn to see him tottering after me. He reaches for my hand and I draw him close to my side. "I'm shit-faced drunk, aren't I?" He asks.

"A little," I tell him. "Not too much."

"How do you know?"

"I can feel the difference."

"How do you do that?" He slurs.

I put my arm around his shoulder and give him a little shake. "I can see you."

"See me in the dark, huh?"

"I especially see you in the dark?"

Tires crunch gravel as the woman drives her car out the gate and onto the main road, her headlights sweeping the hill.

"Do you really fly a helicopter?"

"Come to Japan, and I will show you."

"Let me think about that," he replies. "I didn't tell you, but I don't much like flying. Especially not in a chopper."

I rest my head on his shoulder. "Don't worry. I don't think I will be able to afford to do any flying for a long while. There's time for you to psyche yourself into going up with me as your pilot."

I tell him I have a new collection of songs. I tell him too that it's going to be exciting, and I can't wait to get started. There will be some things I need to do. Loose ends that need tying up. I am ready for it.

When we arrive at his car, he pulls out his keys and places them in my hand.

"So, what do you want to do?" I ask him, and I turn to face him. I know that he's smiling just from the tilt of his head. Before he can think of an answer, I dig my hands deep into his jacket pockets and pull him close, and he slips his arms around me.

"Well, I have this idea," he mumbles.

I know that whatever he suggests, I will give a bright little laugh, no matter what fanciful thing he tells me. After all, he's trying to say goodbye without saying the word. Yes, in the end, he will do whatever he wants, and I have to do what I must.

"Well—don't you want to know?" He asks, brushing his lips against mine.

"Ah… Sure. Tell me."

He whispers his thoughts in my ear, and I listen.

I know it's crazy, but I really don't know where we go from here, and for once, I don't mind at all.

GLOSSARY

The dialog contains colloquial language sourced from languages other than English. All the following words and phrases are Japanese or Maori, or New Zealand English.

Japanese

Ah sou ka: This is a shortened form of *ah sou desu ka*. The meaning is similar to the expression 'ah, now I see'.

Bachi: The picks used to play the *shamisen* are shaped like a putty knife. They are traditionally made from tortoiseshell as well as wood.

Bonsai: A traditional art involving the cultivation of miniature trees generally grown in ceramic or stone containers.

Chonmage: A traditional samurai topknot since at least the Meiji period. Over the past few decades, the style has become associated with sumo wrestlers as well as artists and artisans.

Dozo: 'Please'. A shortened form of *dozo yoroshiku onegaishimasu*. A casual expression used between people already on friendly terms or when in a relaxed situation.

Gaijin: 'Foreigner'. The literal meaning is 'outside person'.

Gomen: 'Sorry'. The casual form of *gomenasai*.

Inkan: A small red stamp personalized for each owner pressed onto the bottom of a form being finalized in the same way as a signature. It contains *kanji* representing family and first name. A relic of a long tradition that persists in modern Japan.

Ike: When used as an imperative it means 'go' or 'come on'.

Hai: An acknowledgment often expected in reply and akin in meaning to 'I hear you'. It is common for non-Japanese to mistake the term as one of agreement.

J-Pop: An abbreviation for Japanese popular music. It has its roots in traditional forms of music blended with western pop, most particularly the 1960s. It became mainstream in the 1990s and has gained popularity across much of Asia.

Kabuki: A highly stylized and traditional form of theater in which the performers wear elaborate costumes and masks.

Kakkoii: 'Cool', 'handsome', or 'stylish'.

Kanji: Chinese characters making up one of the four scripts used in Japanese writing to write the names of people, places, and things. The characters retain a Chinese as well as Japanese meaning.

Kanpai: 'Cheers'. As with making a toast.

Keitai: A cell phone. It is a shortened form of *keitai denwa*, meaning a portable phone.

Kiku: 'Too strong'. An expression used when drinking alcohol.

Kotatsu: A traditional low table generally found located on a *tatami* floor.

Kuso: 'Shit' or 'crap'. A vulgarity used as an expletive in Japanese similar in both meaning and use with the English equivalent.

Moushiwake arimasen: A highly formal apology usually issued to a superior. It conveys a much stronger feeling of 'sorry' than does either *sumimasen* or *gomenasai*.

Ne: A tag word at the end of a sentence by a speaker seeking agreement. It appears in both Japanese and Maori with similar form and function.

Oyasumi: 'Good night'. The casual form of *oyasumi nasai*.

Sake: Traditional Japanese rice wine.

Sensei: An older and, or, 'learned one' and, therefore, teacher. Anyone who shows mastery in a profession or art. Society requires due respect be shown to someone holding this status.

Shamisen: A traditional three-stringed instrument played by striking the strings with a tortoiseshell *bachi* in a percussive slapping style.

Shinkansen: The name given to Japan's high-speed railway service. Most often referred to in English as the 'bullet train'.

Shochu: Traditional Japanese distilled liquor made from rice, barley, or sweet potatoes.

Sumimasen: 'Excuse me' or 'sorry'. The word functions both as a polite request and an apology.

Sumo: Traditional wrestling characteristically featuring very fat but physically powerful men. Considered in Japan to be the national sport.

Sumo rikishi: A sumo wrestler.

Tatami: Traditional rice straw mats. Most newly built Japanese houses and apartments still have at least one *tatami* room.

Yakuza: The collective name used for the traditional organized crime syndicates of Japan.

Yokatta: It's great.

Maori (and Maori English)

By hokey: An expression of surprise or intensification.

Haiku: A traditional Japanese no-rhyming poem with 17 syllables, written in a 5,7,5 pattern, and usually containing a reference to a season.

Haere mai kite kai: 'Come on, let's eat.'

Hapu: A number of families constituting a sub-tribe. A number of *hapu* related to one another constitute a tribe.

Kai: 'Food'.

Kapai: 'Good'.

Kia ora: A traditional greeting.

Kina: Sea urchins, otherwise known as sea eggs. Harvested by Maori and Japanese alike for their sweet roe.

Koura: Red crayfish, or rock lobster.

Marae: A traditional meeting place and considered sacred. A modern *marae* is purpose-built for communal meetings.

Ne: A tag word at the end of a sentence by the speaker who seeks agreement from the other conversationalist. The word and its use are similar in both Japanese and Maori languages.

Tamariki: Children,

Tangihanga or *Tangi*: A traditional funeral wake held on a *marae*.

New Zealand English

Bach: A holiday home (or considered as a weekend home), or a shack beside a large body of water. A bach is often located near a large body of water. A bach can also be referred to as a crib, depending on the regional dialect.

DOC: The Department of Conservation is a central government organization in New Zealand government protecting the country's natural and recreational heritage. It manages all national parks, forests, and wilderness areas.

THANK YOU FOR READING

Join my growing community of readers, and receive updates on Books 3, 4, and 5 of Atoma's adventures. Coming soon!

Sign up for my newsletter

www.gerardoneillbooks.com

Have Your Say

If you have enjoyed this book then let other readers know by posting a review on Amazon or Goodreads.

You can also find me here:

- Email: gerardoneillbooks@gmail.com
- www.facebook.com/gerardoneill.books
- www.twitter.com/GONeillBooks

ABOUT THE AUTHOR

GERARD O'NEILL was born and raised in New Zealand, and now lives across the great ditch in Sydney, Australia. He writes science thrillers, but more recently has dived into science fiction for the teens and young adult audience.

Gerard is the author of four novels.

Jubilee Year (The Erelong Trilogy, Book I)
May Day (The Erelong Trilogy, Book II)
Atoma and the Blockchain: YA Science Fiction (Book I, Atoma Series)
The Girl With Two Names

Atoma Series, Book II will be out soon!
The long promised *Book III* of *The Erelong Trilogy* is scheduled to be published late 2021 - early 2022.

www.ingramcontent.com/pod-product-compliance
Lightning Source LLC
Chambersburg PA
CBHW051129030726
47504CB00004B/783